Dead Dogs and Englishmen
A *Kirkus Reviews* Best Book of 2011!

"Buzzelli will have you packing your bags for a move to northern Michigan."

— *Kirkus Reviews* (starred review)

"Emily is a detective for our times: She can't afford health care, but she can make flour out of cat tails and work three jobs at once."

— *Christian Science Monitor*

Dead Sleeping Shaman

"Buzzelli's well-crafted third Emily Kincaid . . . [features] sharp prose and spirited characterizations."

— *Publishers Weekly*

"Readers will find the same strong sense of place and great characters that are hallmarks of Sarah Graves and Philip Craig."

— *Library Journal*

"The appeal of this third in the series comes both from Emily — a likable character forging a new life after her divorce — and the evocatively described, nicely detailed small-town setting."

— *Booklist*

Dead Floating Lovers

"Every woman who's ever struggled with saying no, fitting in, and balancing independence against loneliness will adore first-timer Emily. . . ."

—*Kirkus Reviews*

DEAD
LITTLE
DOLLY

Elizabeth Kane Buzzelli

Beyond the Page Books
are published by
Beyond the Page Publishing
www.beyondthepagepub.com

Copyright © 2013 by Elizabeth Kane Buzzelli.
Cover design and illustration by Dar Albert, Wicked Smart Designs

ISBN: 978-1-937349-67-7 (ebook)
ISBN: 978-1-937349-68-4 (trade paperback)

As always: Tony, for his patience and
all those trips to Norwood.
Don Bellinger of the Kalkaska Museum,
for the introduction to Grace Gilbert,
a truly amazing woman.
John Mullin, my intrepid Webmaster.
Josh Mullin, a true computer genius.
Oh, and Eli Benson,
because he's such a beautiful child.
And for Mary Deriemacker,
who insisted that Harry and Delia wed.

The sun was thick and warm on Deputy Dolly Wakowski's back, and on her neck, and on the top of her head. She pulled off her blue uniform hat and set it on the damp cemetery earth beside where she knelt.

A quiet May Sunday afternoon. Quieter, because there was no one else in the old Leetsville, Michigan, cemetery. No one there, among the tombstones, but Deputy Dolly, of the two-man Leetsville Police Department, who bowed her head over the bearded lady's grave then laid a bouquet of wilting white daisies atop the mossy headstone:

GRACE HUMBERT
1873 – 1926

"Another year, Grace," Dolly bent to whisper as she patted Grace Humbert's grave, fingers brushing over the prickly sprouts of new weeds and grasses.

"Happy Mother's Day. It's me, Dolly."

The day was all washed-fresh light. The shine of new spring green spread over the sunken graves of Civil War soldiers and around old headstones standing crookedly, slump-shouldered, names of the poor wiped away by harsh Michigan winters.

Tiny yellow dandelions — bright little toys — speckled the clustered graves of babies dead in a long-ago epidemic. Toward the back of the cemetery, proud family plots, surrounded by rusted and crooked iron railings, bloomed with new weeds.

Dolly's uniform pants were damp at both knees, but that

was as it should be. It was proper that once a year she came here and knelt to talk to Grace Humbert, the famous bearded lady of a long-ago Barnum & Bailey Circus.

She'd heard about Grace when she first came to Leetsville from southern Michigan, thirteen years before. Grace Humbert, memorialized in the museum down the road, in Kalkaska, but forgotten by everyone else except as an oddity a local newspaper or magazine would revisit every ten years of so: a woman who didn't fit anywhere, not with her flowing beard and mustache, not with eyes direct and slightly amused, never part of the world around her, but never cowed by that world, her look steady and challenging, her back straight in satiny gowns draped across an ample bosom.

"Forty-seven Famous Freaks," a 1903 photo hanging on the crowded old depot wall had screamed at Dolly, and there was Grace, a dark image in the third row, smiling, happy to be among her kinfolk of sword swallowers and tiny people and tall people and leopard-skinned people and pinheaded people. Different. An outsider.

Like Dolly Wakowski.

Dolly turned a squinting frown at robins in the leafing maples. Too loud, all that mating stuff, for a cemetery. Birds chirping playfully in a graveyard didn't obey Dolly's "seemly" rule. There should be quiet and reverence when a pretend-daughter knelt beside a pretend-mother's grave, honoring her because there was nobody else for Dolly Wakowski to honor. And nobody else came to honor Grace. That was a fact— nobody, and that meant Grace Humbert needed Dolly as much as she needed Grace.

Dolly moved from her damp right knee to her left. She

looked around before bending to whisper, "Found my grandmother this last year. Cate Thomas, she's called. Livin' with me now. And guess what . . ." She waited, as if somehow she'd get an answer. Her small, homely face puckered into a smile. "I got a baby." She nodded a few times. "Name's Baby Jane. I call her that so she can pick her own name when the time comes. You know, get the name she wants. Not like me. Stuck all my life with a name like 'Delores,' foisted on me when I couldn't sit up and say "No" to that woman who never wanted me anyway."

She turned to look over her shoulder toward the scout car she'd pulled up under the high cast-iron cemetery gate where four-month-old Baby Jane slept in her car seat. The windows were down so Dolly could hear if she woke up. Nothing to fear. Not in a town where most of the crime was of the teenager variety—weed smoked in EATS restaurant bathroom, mailbox battings, fights, windows shot out of cars—things like that. Oh, and a few murders, ever since Emily Kincaid, her friend and journalist and mystery writer, came to the area. A murder here. A murder there. But nobody would hurt a baby.

"I'm not sayin' where Jane came from. You understand, don't you, Grace? I mean, no virgin birth or anything. I got her legitimately. Well, dumb luck." She looked around, frowning hard in case somebody thought it was funny sneaking up on Deputy Dolly while she was alone, praying in a graveyard.

She cleared her throat. "Still, my genes and all, Grace. And, to tell the truth, I never expected having a family of my own would feel this good. Always thought it would be nice, back in those foster homes when I was dreaming about a mother and a father. And even back when I was married to Chet Wakowski, for that short time he hung around, and I thought about having a baby — but I never expected something like this."

Dolly looked over her shoulder again. Really, it was too bad there was nobody else there on this perfect Mother's Day. The sun was warm liquid on her face; sky blue as all the vast lakes and running streams around Michigan; high white, painted-on clouds barely moved overhead. It made her even prouder — coming to honor Grace, the way she did. She knew her duty.

Grace's story still made Dolly shake her head. Like, if there was something different about you the world never let you forget it. Like being born with fine red hair all over your body was a sin. Or being a woman and having a full beard and mustache. Or having no mother, no father, so that you were awkward and never knew what to say to people and kids laughed at you and called you names because you wore clothes those foster parents picked up at Goodwill to save money from what the state paid them to take care of you.

Or having a mother who didn't want you and left the country to join a religious cult in France and didn't give a damn if you lived or died or stayed with people who took you in to make you clean their houses or turned their backs when their men did things to a little girl no little girl should ever have to put up with and then punished that little girl when she screamed and ranted and told the social worker stories that made that worker's hair stand up on her head.

If she'd learned anything from Grace Humbert that she could pass on to Baby Jane it was to keep going, no matter what. It was to never care what people thought about you. It was to know who you were and keep on your own path. If she could give all of that to Baby Jane, that would be a lot.

Dolly Wakowski shifted from one knee to the other, sorry that her uniform pants were getting wet, but not quite ready to leave Grace. She checked over her shoulder. No sound from the squad car. There was time. Jane was a sound sleeper.

It was going to be a good day. When Baby Jane woke up they'd go and pick up Cate Thomas at home. Then they'd get over to EATS for an early supper. Eugenia was running her Mother's Day special, in honor of Grace Humbert: two Coney dogs for a dollar.

"Like circus dogs," Eugenia would tell people and flounce off when they said that wasn't much of a special and anyway hot dogs were for ballparks. Every year Dolly made sure she rounded up enough people to make it worth Eugenia's effort, having a circus special.

Dolly thought about calling Emily Kincaid to come into town for lunch. Do Emily good to get out of that writing studio of hers and sit down and talk to real people.

The wind picked up in the old trees. And then a different sound. Something. Maybe a motor—far off. Nothing from her scout car. Not Jane crying. Jane's cry was very small, but it packed big punches in Dolly's guts. And made her breasts ache if Cate was babysitting and she called home and heard her baby crying. It was better to bring Jane with her on the job. Better to drive her around and be visiting felons and talking to a kid at the high school in big trouble for vandalism, and have the kid reach into the sling Dolly wore across her chest, where a little blond head stuck out, and talk to the smiling baby instead of Dolly. Emily said babies helped soothe the savage breast or beast, or something like that, and she was right. People—even bad folks—melted around Baby Jane.

Time to go. She reached over and straightened the daisies being blown toward the edge of the stone by a soft breeze coming from the west, off Lake Michigan. Next time, she told herself, I'm bringing a pickle jar to hold 'em. She'd told herself the same thing for the last few years but she never remembered.

Dolly stood slowly, sorry that her time with Grace was over for this year. Next year Jane would be walking around the stones, probably getting into trouble, poking pudgy fingers into old carved letters and pulling up dandelions in the grass. Next year, Dolly promised again, as she settled her hat on her head, she would bring a pickle jar filled with water so the flowers lasted longer. Next year, being a mother herself, maybe she'd know how to do the things other women knew to do without being told. Maybe it would all just come on her now that she had a pretend-mother, a real grandmother, and her own sweet baby.

She bent forward to brush the grass and dirt from the knees of her uniform pants when she heard the next sound — a motor revving, and then the screech of brakes. She reared up, hand flying instinctively to the handle of the holstered .38 on her hip. She began to run toward the road, heavy boots holding her back, as a large black SUV, coming from the west, veered off the road, directly into the side of Dolly's parked squad car with a stomach-sinking crunch of metal.

Dolly pounded up the cemetery path toward where her car was pushed and twisted so it strained against the metal gate, heaving the gate up out of the ground. The gate hovered over the car a minute, and then dipped dangerously, bending toward the broken squad car beneath.

"Jane!" Dolly screamed as she ran.

The dark SUV slammed into reverse, backed down the side of the road, then, with wheels spinning, throwing grass and dirt, pulled onto the road and sped off.

"Seven KXU," Dolly whispered to herself as she ran—all she'd made of the license number.

"Seven KXU."

"Seven KXU . . ."

She muttered and muttered as she pulled the twisted back door of the car open then reached in to where her baby had been sleeping in her car seat. The seat was thrown sideways. Tipped so she couldn't see Baby Jane.

Dolly pulled hard at the dislodged seat, rocking it back into place until Baby Jane's small blond head swung up, arms and legs and body hanging between the twisted straps.

The baby's eyes were closed. She made no sound. The little body hung at a wrong angle. Limp. The silence was a huge fist catching Dolly in her stomach and tearing straight up into her heart.

ONE

I missed the call from Lucky Barnard, Leetsville's sheriff and Deputy Dolly Wakowski's boss, because I was out in the woods taking in spring and not thinking about Mother's Day. My mother, Joan Kincaid, had died of a brain tumor when I was twelve. I could barely remember her voice or touch and that filled me with the kind of misery I didn't want to go near on a sunny Sunday in May.

All I thought about was how great it felt to walk free in the bright northern woods after picking my way carefully — for months — over ice and through deep snow. I chased my clumsy dog, Sorrow, up an old logging road, and sensed him laughing just the way I was laughing as I stopped to pick another yellow violet, then a bloated lady's slipper, and then knelt in last year's damp leaves only to find myself at the center of a fairy ring of morel mushrooms.

I wondered if you could make a wish at the center of a ring of mushrooms, then decided to make one anyway, and wished for my mystery novel to sell, now that I had an agent. And I wished for money so I wouldn't be scared when bills came in. And I wished my ex-husband, Jackson Rinaldi, wasn't coming up to see me. "Soon, Emily," he'd promised. "With wonderful fresh pastas and a flat of pansies for your garden." Which almost made me want to see him — but not really.

There was no need to wish for loons because I heard them out on Willow Lake, singing those wonderfully odd songs they sang, songs that echoed through the trees and over the beaver dam and all the way up to Willow Lake Road.

Wishing for something I knew I'd already gotten was a sure way of making my other wishes come true. Or, at least, in my magical, mystical, sometimes miserable way of figuring out what life was all about, this was the way I got everything I hoped for.

And not a damned bug anywhere. That could have been a wish, too. No bites on my neck while digging in my garden. No vampire mosquitoes. No stinging horse flies. No nits, gnats, or no-see-ums. Not yet.

Spring was a gentle time of the year in northern Michigan, unless a sweeping-clean storm came through and toppled huge trees, broke weak branches overhead and gave last year's leaves one more chance to blow around searching for that peaceful place where the wind stopped and everything came to rest.

I picked the mushrooms and put them into the mesh bag I carried (so the spores could drop and produce next year's crop). I would stuff the delicate mushrooms for dinner, and find some leeks and even a few tiny milkweed pods to boil in three waters and fry in butter.

After six years up in northwestern lower Michigan, at a place between the third and baby finger of Michigan's mitten, in a small, golden house on tiny Willow Lake, I was finally over the Snow White dream I'd brought up with me. The dream where bluebirds sat, singing, on my shoulder. The dream where the flowers in my garden bloomed freely in the Kalkaskian sands and where I would live a simple life without dear Jackson Rinaldi, a University of Michigan professor of English who copulated with every willing coed he could urge into his bed or the front seat of his Porsche, and who once claimed the frilly panties I found in his glove compartment were only rags he used to wipe off his headlights, and who pretended the crying girl who called to tell me what a bastard I was married to was a psycho he'd kicked out of a seminar on "The Wife of Bath."

"With good reason, Emily. Good reason." He'd sighed and batted his dark pretty eyes at me.

I'd dropped his name, Rinaldi, and went back to Kincaid, but I couldn't seem to drop him. Jackson kept showing up. And since I'd once been in love with him and he was still a part of my history and, from time to time—when he became the man I'd married: funny and charming, and courting me the way he once had courted me—well, this new kind of loneliness made me a sucker for his wheedling: *"I've got to see you, Emily."*

As I walked, I thought up another wish. To support myself by selling the mystery novels I wrote. Nothing had happened yet but I had an agent and a book out to editors and, as always, hope was springing eternal, though my money was running very low and the jobs I got, writing for a Traverse City newspaper and northern magazines and a few editing jobs, didn't pay a whole lot.

I hooked my bag of mushrooms to the belt of my raveling jeans and kept on my Johnny Appleseed way through the woods. Sorrow ran ahead, stopping to sniff at a chipmunk hole and then at a larger hole even I knew had to be a skunk's den. I yelled him away from that one since I wasn't ready to start spring with a tomato juice bath.

Even with all the sunshine, I walked through tendrils of cold. Cold that made me shiver in my red cotton sweater. Cold that could be present even on the warmest days. A kind of warning to trust nothing—not completely. Winter could come back at any minute. One year we had snow on Memorial Day.

I wished I'd brought a hat out with me. I'd had my blond-streaked hair cut very short at the newly rebuilt Gertie's Shoppe de Beauty in Leetsville and my head was cold. I told myself I looked just the way I wanted to look: a woman free of makeup and bad-hair days and worries over clothes or putting on a few pounds or any expectations of who I was and how I looked—beyond my own.

I shivered. Despite the sun and color, there could be strange things in the woods. Even on a May afternoon. Things you could feel but not really know. It was the spring version of an uneasy fear that swept the woods before hunting season. Or in summer—tension when a thunderstorm rumbled overhead.

Sorrow, ahead of me on the road, stopped racing in circles to snuffle and paw at the earth. He tore at something, pulled it free, and carried it back to me as fast as he could fly. He dropped his prize at my feet. The ravaged pelt of a dead raccoon. Killed by winter or a predator. It took a while to get him to forget that particular prize.

We headed into a thicket of thorns. Beyond was Willow Lake Road and easier walking but I got hung up in the bushes while Sorrow bounded up the slope. I pulled at my sweater and yelled at Sorrow to wait for me. The clunk-head couldn't remember about cars and being careful on streets. Damn, I whispered to myself. Everything came with a catch. You couldn't just be stupidly happy. Always one of life's rotten picker bushes around to horn in and ruin things.

I yelled at him again as I pulled strings of red cotton yarn from my sweater. I groused and climbed the hill to the road where Sorrow waited dutifully, giving me a judgmental eye roll as he lifted his leg and peed on the mailbox post—communicating something about me to neighboring dogs. When he finished, he looked at the box and barked, then turned to see if I was smart enough to get it.

Something in the box.

I pulled the mailbox door open the rest of the way to find a yellowed piece of paper, folded, with EMILY written on the front fold in big block letters. A note from my neighbor, Harry Mockerman, handyman and woodsman, and once even a log skidder during the last of the northern logging operations. Harry lived across Willow Lake Road from me, down a burr-infested driveway, in a tiny crooked house surrounded by trees. The first time I saw Harry's house I couldn't help but think of forest homes in fairy tales. Places where bear families and little men who worked in diamond mines lived.

EMILY KINCAID GOT TO SEE YOU RIGHT AWAY DON'T SAY NOTHING TO NOBODY ABOUT THIS JUST COME ON OVER SOON AS YOU CAN

I sighed—there went my perfect day.

I set off across Willow Lake Road and up Harry's overgrown driveway.

Harry's watchdogs, in a chain-link-encircled kennel back near the house, barked and howled before I got halfway up the drive. Sorrow heard, sat, and gave me an eye roll, his way of letting me know he was too particular to spend time among a pack of howling spaniels and shepherds he'd heard baying through the woods when Harry went out hunting. I guessed he'd be waiting there when I came back down the drive. He always was.

Harry's crooked little house was the very house he'd been born in seventy-two years before. He'd lived in the woods his whole life, roaming free, unrestricted by things like hunting licenses and fishing licenses and car licenses. When his freezer was empty he filled it with deer meat and raccoon meat and meat he found out on the road after a bad night of speeding pickups left carnage behind them. If the coho were running he was out in the water, and he was known to pull the biggest fish from the fastest-flowing rivers and disappear the quickest when the game warden stuck his head out from among the trees.

The back end of the slapped-together vehicle standing in front of the house, half pickup and half old black Chevy, was totally license-free. My friend Deputy Dolly swore she'd catch Harry driving one day and get him off the road for good. But what Harry knew, and Dolly Wakowski didn't, or ignored, was the vast network of logging roads still running through the woods behind his house. Roads that got Harry anywhere he needed to go—even into Leetsville, where he could park among the trees and walk to Eugenia Fuller's EATS restaurant for a Sunday breakfast with old friends, or to Chet's Garage, or to the hardware store, the Save-A-Lot, to Jake Anderson's Skunk Saloon, or even over to the feed store for dog food.

"Come on in, Emily. I got something to talk about here," Harry greeted me, his grizzled chin working, thick eyebrows going up and down, bony body bent forward as he pushed the crooked screen door open.

He'd set two coffee mugs on the white metal table in the kitchen, where he motioned for me to sit. He brought the coffeepot over from the stove and pushed a milk carton toward me.

On the old porcelain stove, a pot of stew simmered, the loosely balanced cover bouncing with steam. The smell was of slow-cooking meat and potatoes and morels—and maybe some boiled purslane thrown in at the end for good measure. A good smell. I liked getting a jar of Harry's soup or stew, sometimes left beneath my mailbox with my name on it and other times set on my side porch. The taste of Harry's cooking was pungent. At first it seemed a little too wild for me but I was used to it by this time, and not as particular as I once was. I even looked forward now to the next Ball jar tucked just inside my screen door when I got back from doing an interview for Bill Corcoran's newspaper, the *Northern Statesman,* or was out hunting for a place to hide a body in my next book. Anything beats cooking for myself.

Harry's house was always neat—in the way a man keeps a house neat. Nothing much to get in his way. Everything practical and useful and easy to live with: no little rugs on the floor; no pretty dish towels hanging from the oven handle. Only a few plain white dishes, two more mugs, and two shapely Coca-Cola glasses set up on an open wooden shelf. The bare wood walls were painted white over old wallpaper, the seams running floor to ceiling every few feet under the paint.

Harry stirred his stew then came back to the table. He cleared his throat and chewed his bottom lip. Finally, he sat down across from me and cleared his throat again. "You know me and Delia Swanson always planned on marrying one day," he said, stating a fact everyone in the North country had known for years.

I nodded.

He nodded back at me. "And you know we just been waiting for her mother to . . . well . . . pass on. Ever since she took unkindly to me back when I was a kid . . ."

I nodded again. "And was mad a few years ago when you wanted Delia to run away with you."

"There's that," he agreed.

"And when you stole Delia off to come live here for that week, bringing on her mother's first heart attack at the thought of Delia being . . . well . . . deflowered."

"Delia was eighty. Now, let me talk, will you?" He wiggled his eyebrows at me. "So, you heard the old lady finally died last week."

"I was at the funeral, Harry."

"One hundred and one. Thought she'd outlive us all. Think that was her plan. Providence fooled her." He nodded fast now. "We're planning on gettin' married just as soon as we can."

"Have you asked Delia? I mean officially?"

"I will. That's where you come in . . ."

"I'm not asking Delia Swanson to marry you."

He sniffed and frowned. "What I want you to do is help me plan this weddin'. Want to do it up brown for my future wife. A big celebration with food. Maybe even a honeymoon except I'm not goin' no farther than up to the bridge. Mackinaw City. That's as far as I'm goin' and even that means I gotta find somebody to take us 'cause I can't take that car of mine out on the I-75. Then, too, I need somebody to feed my dogs and watch the house."

"For what?"

He frowned. "What'd you mean: 'for what'?"

"I mean, watch your house for what? Who's coming near it

with your dogs barking and jumping at the fence the way they do?"

"Still . . ."

"Maybe I could feed the dogs," I offered. "But only if I can throw the food at them. I'm not going in there."

Harry nodded. "Work that part out. Got something else I need your help with. What I was thinking was you could maybe do the ceremony. You got a college education."

"If you mean marry you, I'm not a licensed minister."

"That don't matter. Jake, in town, told me you can get your license on that Internet. You get that, we can have the ceremony right here."

"Where? Here? In this house?"

"That's what I was thinkin'. Have it here, in the house. Have some tables set up outside for the celebration afterward."

"How many are you planning to invite?"

He shrugged. "Don't know. Leetsville—I suppose. Most of those folks."

"And you want it in this house that holds about four people —max."

He gave me a thinking look. "Maybe have the whole shebang outside then."

"What about the dogs? Your kennels don't exactly smell terrific sometimes. And they'll be barking right through everything . . ."

Harry slapped a hand on the table. "Then you tell me. How can we do this and make it nice for Delia? This is her first marriage, you know. Well, mine, too, for that matter."

"I do know. Delia is a sweet woman and just maybe she deserves a little more than what you're planning so far."

"Okay, like what?"

I thought awhile. "Let me look into it. How about the Church of the Contented Flock in town? Bet Pastor Runcival will marry you two. And after that—a reception at EATS. Eugenia will come up with something nice."

He shook his head. "You're not lookin' at a millionaire here, Emily. An' I got a freezer full of meat out in the shed I was gonna use."

"I know . . ." I thought awhile longer. "Let me see what I can do, okay? You go ahead and propose. We'll have something . . . well, nice. But not in this house."

"Could do it down to Delia's. The place is hers now, with her mother gone."

"That's an idea. You moving down there? It's a bigger house."

He shook his head. "I don't have to move, I figure. She can stay there and I can stay here and we'll visit when the mood grabs us . . ."

"You have a date in mind?"

He puffed his old lips out. "I was thinkin' the second of June. That's a Saturday. Week after Memorial weekend. Think that's okay?"

"Sounds good."

He nodded. "No sense waiting."

I had to agree with him there. Neither one of them was getting any younger. I said I'd do what I could do and he was to get to that proposal as fast as possible.

• • •

I trotted down my long, sloping drive, whistling back Sorrow, who'd spied one of the crows nesting in an old oak by the lake and chased him even as the canny bird taunted and teased. Then he found one more tree to mark, one more hole to snuffle, and one more squirrel trail to follow while I waited at my side door.

Inside the house, the phone rang. I heard it through the screen door but there was no rush to answer. I wasn't expecting a call so it couldn't be anybody I really wanted to talk to. Sunday — so not my new agent about a huge sale and eternal fame and fortune.

Not — I certainly hoped — Jackson Rinaldi.

Couldn't be Bill Corcoran with a story for me. He wouldn't be at the newspaper on Sunday unless there was some emergency.

Maybe Dolly. Some new scheme to land me a full-time job on Bill's newspaper and solve all my financial woes. Or some new problem in Leetsville requiring coverage in the *Northern Statesman*. Maybe another murder.

Nobody I really wanted to talk to.

I could just let it ring . . .

I didn't.

It was Lucky Barnard. Calling for the third time, he said, his voice rumbling deeper than usual. "Terrible news, Emily. Dolly's been in a hit-and-run. We took Baby Jane to Kalkaska Emergency. You better get over there."

TWO

The hospital smelled of nothing when I ran in through the ER doors. Nothing. Not antiseptic, not cleaning compounds . . . maybe dead air. That's all I could think, though I didn't want to. Dead air. God help me—why words like that when all I wanted was to know that Jane, the little brown-eyed baby who'd just learned to smile, was okay?

Dolly paced the brown carpeting, her uniform rumpled and stained at the knees. She looked up with the kind of eyes you don't ever want to see on a friend. Something burning her up inside, a terrible fire that could consume her entirely if all of this went wrong. Her small face was blotched, her lank, almost colorless hair lifeless. Her hands were pushed down into the pockets of her cop pants, formed into fists, little knots at either hip.

I didn't notice all the others from town: neighbors and friends; Cate Thomas, Dolly's grandmother. Not right then. I watched Dolly. She stopped still and pulled one of her small hands from a pocket and held it out to me the way I've never seen Dolly do before.

"Is she okay?" I asked.

She nodded then took a deep breath. "She's upstairs with the doctor. They're taking X-rays."

"Of what?" I asked then wished I hadn't.

"Her head, the doctor said. Because she passed out the way she did. Probably hit it on the car seat or . . ."

"Anything broken?"

She shook her head hard. "They don't think so. Still . . ." She lifted her slumping shoulders then dropped them. She stiffened because a doctor came through the double doors, looked around, but walked to an elderly couple seated in a corner by themselves. The news wasn't good. The old man glared at the doctor. The old woman put a hand over her mouth and cried soundlessly.

"How'd they all hear so fast?" I said quietly and nodded toward where the women from Leetsville sat, along with Cate in one of her more colorful Gypsy outfits. Cate had come to town close to a year ago and claimed Dolly as her long-lost granddaughter after Eugenia, owner of EATS, did Dolly's genealogical chart and brought Dolly news of a grandmother she'd never known.

Cate, a talker, was talking now, nervously bending toward the townswomen, head down, face flushed, her monologue seeming to fall on closed ears. Eugenia didn't look happy and kept her head turned away from Cate and toward the other women. Gloria, a waitress at EATS, stared across the room, at nothing. Flora Coy, an elderly woman with a happy house filled with canaries, sat straight in her hard chair ignoring Cate, head going one way and then the other, then dead ahead. I could say she was a little canary-like, but I won't.

Dolly, watching Cate closely, shrugged as she answered my question. "Like they always do. Police scanners. Called each other. Eugenia and Gloria picked up Cate on the way."

I nodded to Cate and everyone else as Cate reached out and tugged at Dolly's holster. "You know, Dolly." Her voice was low and shaky. "I've been telling everyone here how I found your mother's address, over there in France—in that commune. And they think I'm right, that Audrey Delores needs to know about Jane."

Eugenia swiveled her sturdy body in her chair and shook her head. Gloria blinked. Flora Coy, Deidre Holmes, Sally Chance, and the others frowned at Cate then up at Dolly. Angela Williams smacked her lips a few times but said nothing.

"And you think this is the right time to tell me that? Here?" Dolly asked. "About a woman I don't care the first thing about?"

"You just stop and think," Cate went on, her voice low but straining to be heard, her made-up face frowning into wrinkles. "Might make a difference. Might bring her back to this country from France. Wouldn't that be wonderful? If my own sweet little Dolly comes home? And you'll be needing help with Jane. I mean, look now, you can't take her with you anymore . . ."

"Why not?"

"Why? What just happened here? Hurt, and in the line of duty. You keep taking her out in that patrol car of yours and the state will step in. You just wait and see. I don't mind watching her once in a while but I told you when I first came here . . . can't go back to watching babies . . ."

"And I'd leave her with *my mother*? With a woman who walked out on her own child thirty-three years ago? Last person in the world *I* want to see. Never made a single move to find me, or help me."

"You don't know that for sure. And how much better, a mother of your own, than going over to that cemetery on Mother's Day, taking flowers to that . . . that bearded lady."

"My baby don't need anybody but me." Dolly dug the toe of her shoe at the floor. "Way too late for that."

Cate clucked. "You're just being mean, Dolly. It's not good

for your soul, you know." She dabbed at her eyes with a very used tissue, lifted a shoulder in her flowered top, and leaned closer toward Dolly, her eyes going from one to the other of us. "I told you before, my little girl couldn't help what—"

"Cate, stop it," Dolly demanded through clenched lips. "I never had a mother. I don't need one now. Far as I'm concerned I'm not named after anybody on this whole wide earth and if I was I would've gone to court to get rid of that name of a person who treated me like a piece of garbage just fit for throwing away." Dolly waved the thought of a mother, any mother, away and, with the clank of her dangling handcuffs and the squeak of her damp boots, stomped off, leaving Cate behind her, shaking her head and clucking her tongue just as Jake Anderson and the guys from the Skunk Saloon ambled in and took seats among the women, asking after the baby.

"Awful," Eugenia leaned around Gloria, whispering toward me, her tall pile of too-blond hair stuck through with four teetering tortoiseshell combs. "I'm prayin' as hard as I can pray for little Jane."

Flora Coy seconded the praying while Cate kept talking to the backs of women who ignored her.

Every time the doors to the ER opened, Dolly turned expectant eyes on the nurse who came through, then whispered numbers to herself: *Seven KXU.*

Too nervous to sit, I got up and joined Dolly's pacing. "I'll get the story in the paper . . ." I promised.

"Yeah." Dolly turned red eyes on me. "Gotta get that bastard. It's already out to all departments in Michigan: Seven KXU—that's all I got of the license plate. Can't believe I didn't catch it. I'm trained . . ."

"Where were you?" I pulled a reporter's notebook and pen from my shoulder bag.

"At the cemetery. Left her in the car—what was going to happen?" Dolly sniffed and rubbed hard at her nose.

"What were you doing at the cemetery?"

Dolly reared back and made a face at me. "It's Mother's Day. Where else would I be?"

"Oh, Grace Humbert. But that's a quiet road. Not like 131 or M72. How could somebody hit you? You leave the car sticking out too far?"

Dolly seemed to welcome getting pissed off at me. Being mad was normal for Dolly and our friendship shouldered a lot of that—on both sides. Being scared to death and feeling useless as we were feeling now wasn't normal to either one of us.

"What kind of driver do you think I am?" she growled. "Of course not. Had it pulled right up under the gate. SUV swerved deliberately, hit the patrol car, then backed up and took off."

"Somebody spooked by a deer or something?"

"Yeah, that was it." Sarcasm dripped. "Spooked by a deer, hit me right in the side then backed up and took off because of that deer."

Dolly stopped talking as another nurse came into the room, looked around, turned, and went back through the double doors.

"Who'd want to hit your car?" I asked.

"I can think of a lot of 'em. You know, like those Trombley boys. Jack's still in jail and that other one's mad 'cause I broke up all their fun, shooting windows out at the school."

I looked up from my notes. "Did you see the guy behind the

wheel?"

Dolly rolled her eyes at me. "You think, if I saw him, if I knew who he was, that Lucky wouldn't be after him right now? I didn't see nothin'. Not a shadow. Not a person. Just the ass end of that car peeling off toward 131, then north, and that was the last of him."

"What kind of car?"

"Black SUV. Ford Escape. 2006." She shook her head again and again. "I'll find it. Don't you worry. I'm gonna . . ."

"How was Jane when you found her?"

Dolly frowned, then clipped her words when she answered. "Not makin' a sound. Had to get her here right away. Chief brought us in."

I nodded, stomach sinking. I already loved that little round-eyed kid who stared at everybody as if we were from Mars. A little kid who shot her eyes left and right when you talked to her, like she was checking out the territory, see what you were bringing with you.

"Concussion?" I asked.

Dolly shrugged. "We'll know when they get through. I just . . . I'm just . . ."

I put my arm around Dolly and hugged, though Dolly, unused to being touched, hunched her back. One thing Dolly couldn't take was people being too nice, but I hugged again anyway.

I left Dolly and the group of sorrowing women to go find a quiet corner where I could call Bill Corcoran, at home. Of course he wanted the story, Bill told me, and took down the information over the phone since I wasn't anywhere near a computer and my iPhone was having trouble getting a signal.

He said he wanted to focus on that partial license number and the car. "2006 Black Ford Escape," he repeated. "Be in the morning paper. And give Dolly my best, Emily. I'd hate to think —you know—if anything happened to that baby. I never saw a new mother as happy as Dolly. Awful thought . . ." He stopped for a minute. "You think I should come out there, to the hospital? I'll bet you're as upset as Dolly is. Maybe I could help . . ."

"Nobody can do anything right now, Bill. All we can think about is Jane . . ."

"You stick with your friend until they catch whoever did this. You'll be paid to cover the story. It's going to be a big one. And, Emily, if there's anything . . . well . . . call me when you know how the baby's doing."

I hung up and went back to pacing beside Dolly.

When Deputy Omar Winston, of the Gaylord State Police, walked into the waiting room, Dolly caught her breath.

"Darn," was all she said and shoved her hands deep into her pants pockets.

The stiff little man—buzzed head covered with blond fuzz, pale eyebrows, pale eyes, pale skin, his uniform as pristine as Dolly's was a mess—wasn't who Dolly wanted to see right then.

Deputy Winston stopped just inside the door. He looked around, found Dolly and me, and then, with robotic movement —arms stiff at his side, hat tucked, military-style, under his arm —made his way across the room and stopped in front of us, asking formally if he could speak to her in private.

Dolly opened her mouth to answer just as a doctor came through the doors and called out, "Delores Wakowski."

THREE

"Hairline skull fracture." The tall, woman doctor—blue beaded necklace on a yellow blouse showing under her white coat—smiled at Dolly and the rest of us as we stumbled over to hear the news. Omar Winston, at Dolly's side, stood at stiff attention.

Dolly's hand flew to her mouth. "So what's that . . .?"

"Not usually a problem in a baby," the doctor said. "A four-month-old has a very pliable skull. She will heal fine. We see no swelling, at least not so far. She opened her eyes and smiled at us in the X-ray room."

"Smiled?" Dolly gave the doctor a wide-eyed, uncertain look. "Baby Jane doesn't smile at just anybody, you know."

The doctor laughed. "Smiled at me, Mrs. . . . . Ms. Wakowski. Bright little girl. With all her troubles, she knew I was helping her."

"Bright little girl," Dolly echoed then turned to us. "Jane smiled at the doctor. She's gonna be okay."

We murmured and nodded, agreeing—bright little girl—then passed the news back and forth again and again. Omar Winston, behind us now, grinned from ear to ear.

They were going to keep Jane overnight, the doctor told Dolly, then had to reassure her all over again that it was only for observation. "You can stay here at the hospital. Not in the room with her, but in the waiting room upstairs. That'll be fine. A nurse will get you a blanket."

Dolly hurried to see Jane while we waited downstairs. None of us seemed to be able to leave just yet, not until we heard the news directly from Dolly.

"No real damage," Dolly said when she came down. "The hairline thing is all. Babies get them all the time. Fall off beds. Stuff like that. Doctor said it happens. Jane'll be fine." She nodded again and again, assuring us and Omar, one after the other, as she reassured herself.

"I'm bringing her home in the morning," she said. "You can all come to the house tomorrow and see for yourselves. But if you're gonna bring casseroles, remember it's just me and Cate eating. So don't overdo it."

Satisfied for the moment, we picked up purses and bags and prepared to leave while Cate protested she should stay, too. "I'm her great-grandmother, after all, you know."

Dolly took her by the arm and steered her toward the outside doors. "I don't want to stay up all night talking, Cate. That's what you'd do. You go on home. I'll call. The chief'll pick us up in the morning."

I followed the others, leaving Omar standing alone behind us. Dolly grabbed my arm, pulling me back beside her.

"Wait a minute, okay? I gotta eat and I want to talk but I'm not leavin' here until he goes." She bobbed her head toward Omar Winston, standing obdurately nearby.

Taking Dolly's attention for his moment to speak, Omar stepped up, snapped his heels together, and said, "I'd like to see the baby for myself."

He tucked his chin down into his blue tie and gave Dolly a stern look that missed being stern because there was so much of the lonely cherub about him.

"So? Go. Nobody's stopping you. And you can come tomorrow, too. Over to my house. If you want to."

Omar made for the double doors into the hospital.

Dolly gave him a last look, turned to me, and rolled her eyes. "Let's get out of here," she said. "Trout Town. I gotta eat and I'm gonna need your help. Lucky's out there already, running a few people down, but I gotta get goin'. This is about me, you know. Somebody don't like me. I gotta get 'em. They hurt my baby and that means this is personal."

• • •

We settled, me and Dolly, into a back booth at the Trout Town Cafe, a favorite among Kalkaska locals. The waitress, a thin middle-aged woman in jeans and T-shirt touting the Trout Festival, hurried over. "Heard what happened out there at the cemetery, Deputy. Your baby okay?"

Dolly assured the concerned woman Jane was doing fine. She had it down pat now. "Hairline fracture. Happens to a lot of babies. They get over it . . ." Still with relief in her voice and a kind of sacred belief in her eyes. She said the same thing again, with even more conviction, when an older couple stopped by the table to express their concern. Finally we ordered and I dug into my Cobb salad, Dolly into her plate of ribs.

"You know," Dolly said without looking up at me. "That Omar can be a real pain in the ass. He told me he'd like to watch Jane every once in a while. Like I'd let him. He said it isn't good to keep taking her out in the scout car with me." She blew her lips out. "You think he knows anything about taking care of a baby? Think any of 'em do? Him and Cate . . ."

I said nothing. I picked at a piece of avocado then put it

slowly into my mouth and chewed while I wondered if I had the nerve to bring up what was on my mind. Then I chewed some more and decided that Dolly never worried when asking embarrassing questions about Jackson, nor ever stopped herself from giving me gratuitous advice on how to dump the man she called a "cheating creep." So I got over any reluctance I had about interfering in her life and came out with it.

"Omar is Jane's father, isn't he?" I said while fighting the urge to tuck my head down between my shoulders and huddle back in the booth, out of Dolly's arm shot.

Her pale eyes flared wide at me. She thought hard, searching for a comeback. Finally she shook her head. "Jane don't need a father. She's got me and I'll always be there for her. All a girl needs is one good person to depend on."

"That's not fair . . ."

"What do you know about 'fair'? You had a good family. Mother. Father. Well, at least a father. What'd I have? A bunch of people paid to treat me like crap."

"But . . ."

"Don't tell me 'but.' I know what I know. A person doesn't need a mother *and* a father. She don't need a grandmother. Baby Jane's got me and I'll protect her as long as I'm on the face of this earth."

Her face was red. She pushed her plate away, too mad at me to finish the ribs.

"And I'll tell you another thing, Emily." She leaned across the table, pointing a finger hard at me. "I don't miss never having that Audrey Delores woman around. Not anymore. Since Cate told me she gave me up and went to that religious cult thing, you think I ever want to see her? You think I got any feelings for a mother who could turn her back on her baby for some religion? Ever? Maybe help destroy her own flesh and blood? How did she know I'd turn out so good?" She shook her head hard and signaled the waitress to bring more coffee. "I never want to see that woman. Don't know what I'd say to her. And here Cate tells me she's gonna write her, over there in France. 'Oh, my poor little doll baby,'" Dolly mocked. "I told her do what you want but don't mention me or Jane ever. Don't need a person like that in my baby's life. Nowhere near her. I don't know what's wrong with Cate. Going on this rant right now." She stopped to nod at two women working their way up between tables to the front counter. They waved and asked about Jane.

"She's okay. Hairline fracture is all," Dolly called back then turned to me. "What I'm thinking is that she heard from Audrey Delores and she wants to come back to this country and has nowhere else to go. Kind of means they're both trying to use me and I'm telling you, Emily, it's not going to happen, no matter what."

We sat for a while, both thinking our own dark thoughts.

"And not Omar either," she went on. "He's not worming his way into my baby's life. He's no daddy to Jane. He's nothin'. I don't care what the rest of you people make up in your head. Only me. That's what Baby Jane's got. And I'm gonna be enough."

"Fine. Your business. Still, what'll you do with her now? Who's going to watch her? You can't keep taking her with you to work. And Cate's not up to it. At least not full-time. Or says she isn't."

Dolly blew at her hot coffee and thought awhile. "Cate's

gonna have to help out or . . ."

"I'll do what I can," I offered, reluctantly, not used to babies unless they were puppies.

Dolly made a face. "You don't know a damn thing about babies and you got that crazy dog. He lands on Jane and she'll be flat as a pancake. Nope, Cate'll do it or I'll find somebody who can. I'll just come home more when I'm working. Maybe only a few days anyway and she'll be back out on patrol with me."

It hit me, how I'd just been rejected as a possible caretaker for Jane. I was incensed at being dismissed as if I didn't have brains enough to watch a four-month-old. I sat in the booth, thinking and getting madder: Of course I could take care of a little kid if I really wanted to. What was there to it? Babies slept most of the time. The rest was sticking a bottle and some jarred food into them. What else? Burping. Changing clothes. Wiping spit-up off your shoulder . . . changing shitty diapers . . . washing shitty diapers and stained Onesies and lots of sheets, and walking with them and bouncing them when they didn't stop crying and rocking them and giving them baths in the sink . . .

Sorrow was easier, I figured, and got over being angry. Let Dolly think whatever she wanted to think of my motherly skills.

"Maybe," I said, pulling the two sides of my brain back together. "Between everybody. I mean, Eugenia said you could bring her to the restaurant. All those women there—they'd do a great job watching her. Even the guys at the Skunk said she'd be welcomed, didn't they?"

"Yeah, Jake and the others. I guess they mean well but . . ."

She covered her mouth and laughed.

I got it—the idea of Jane sitting atop the bar at the Skunk while the guys told her old dirty jokes.

"Yeah, well, we'll see when the time comes," Dolly said.

"Anyway, you can't ask me because Bill wants me to stay close to you. He's paying me to keep on the story. Find out what's going on. You heard anything from Lucky? Got anything on the car?"

Dolly shook her head. "In the first place, I wasn't going to ask you anyway. In the second place, everybody, all the departments across Michigan, they're doing what they can about the SUV. They'll get 'im. Even with a partial number. What I need for you to do is go over to the station tomorrow morning and pick up my files. Lucky's getting everything together for you. Says he'll leave the stack on his desk, case he's not there when you go. You come on over to the house afterward and we'll go through them—see who might have it in for me. Gotta be somewhere in there. Something I didn't think of already."

"What're we looking for exactly?"

"People with a grudge, I guess. Somebody mad 'cause I put 'em in jail. Somebody's brother, maybe. I gotta couple of court appearances ahead of me. I want to take a long look at those. Then—if Cate'll give in and keep Baby Jane just until we're sure she's okay—we'll go talk to as many as we need to. This was no accident but I don't think they knew Jane was in the car —only a crazy person would try to hurt a baby."

I agreed.

"Chief said that car had to be coming at top speed, dug deep ditches in the dirt after the guy put on his brakes. He backed up and dug more deep ditches. Ground's still wet. Laid rubber on the pavement gettin' outta there. Chief thinks there's gotta be damage to the front of his SUV. Couldn't've done what he did to my car—bending it almost in half—and not have plenty wrong with his."

The waitress brought me a pot of hot water with a new tea bag. She filled Dolly's coffee cup, then cleared our plates as a young girl came over, bent down, and hugged Dolly. "Heard your baby's all right. I'm so glad." The kid was off before Dolly answered but Dolly smiled at the retreating back.

"Anyway, they're pulling everything with the numbers I gave them. With the make and model, they'll narrow it down fast, see if somebody up here's got a car like that. Still, he could have hidden that Ford anywhere by now. Could be at the bottom of one of the lakes. Except, it's not an old car and not too many would be willing to sink something worth a few dollars."

Dolly wiped barbecue sauce from her chin with her napkin. "You got the story going in tomorrow's paper, right?"

I crammed in the last of my lettuce. "Bill's taking care of it. Just got to stop by the cemetery on the way home. Take a couple of photos."

Dolly waited while I dug my share of the bill from my purse, counted out the change plus two dollars for the tip, and got up.

"Right now, what I really need is those files," Dolly said. "And you keepin' newspaper pressure on."

Back at the hospital, I dropped Dolly off then watched the sad little figure in her wrinkled uniform, with what looked like a toy gun on her hip, make her way back inside. Deputy Dolly

Wakowski, Leetsville's tough guy, upholder of the law, never looked as small and alone as she did then, with the hospital doors sucking shut behind her.

FOUR

When I got home there was a note taped to my door. Harry Mockerman, wanting to know what I'd got planned for him so far. *So far?* Did the man live in a vacuum? Didn't he know what was going on? Dolly? Jane?

Inside my house, with an overexcited Sorrow dripping pee on the floor as he leaped in the air around me, I noticed the message light blinking. Two messages. The first was a call from Jackson Rinaldi telling me, in his smarmiest voice, that he had a terrible case of spring fever, missed me miserably, and wondered about a visit. "Soon, dear. Very soon. I seem to be in need of your tender ministrations . . . oh hell, Emily. Call me."

The second call was from Bill. "Calling about Baby Jane, Emily," his deep and hesitant voice said. "Heard she was going to be fine but I wanted to tell you again—anything you or Dolly need from me. Just ask. And, Emily, keep the stories coming. Every detail. Everybody here in Traverse is up in arms about Jane getting hurt like that." He took a deep breath. "And anyway, what I figure is that we can do our part to keep the pressure on whoever did this. I'd like something—anything— every day. But you know that . . . I guess you're not there. No need to call me back tonight but let's talk tomorrow . . . uh . . . Emily."

I moved Jackson and Bill to a file cabinet way at the back of my mind and took Sorrow down to the lake

It was one of those evenings—the kind that brought me north in the first place. A mauve and pale orange sunset with dark blue at the edges. I could enjoy it now that Baby Jane was going to be all right and Dolly had her mind turned to catching the hit-and-run driver, and I'd done my part, with my photos sent from my cell phone and my story for tomorrow written.

I could let the sunset take my breath away, let it make me feel small and aware that the universe was too big for me to really think about. As I stood at the reedy shore of Willow Lake, I concentrated on shadows of swimming loons and then their breathless cries as they took off over the water. I concentrated on places where bass leaped and set off circle after widening circle. I breathed in northern air and dusk with ice at its edges though it was almost summer, then closed my eyes, fingers of cold on my skin, and thought about women and their babies and what kind of strength it took to bear them and love them and maybe lose one. And I thought about my fierce friend with this new fear in her eyes.

I went back up to the house and settled in a chair on the deck to watch the last sliver of sun disappear. I wrapped myself in a big blue sweater and poured a glass from the half bottle of Pinot Grigio I'd brought out with me, salve to calm emotions Baby Jane and Jackson had stirred. Maybe it was that infamous internal clock I heard ticking in my head. No baby in sight. And Jackson's familiar voice had stirred other feelings. Hey, it could be fun planning a baby and then roping Jackson into a little roll in the hay for old times' sake. And then being pregnant and huge and unable to bend over to hug Sorrow, and throwing up, and stretching my skin so little shiny silverfish raced across my belly.

I shelved that idea.

Later, when it was true dark and a universe of stars shone overhead and even the baggy sweater wasn't warm enough, I went back inside to sit at my desk and make notes for the new novel I hoped to work on soon—something about a little lake not far from my house. The lake was drying up. The last time I was out there all kinds of things had surfaced around the edges. With a mystery writer's brain, I was asking myself what else could be down there and, of course, I'd come up with a grinning skull.

I didn't call Jackson because I didn't respond that quickly to his needs anymore. Ever so slowly, I was weaning myself from the leg-hold trap love can be. Ticking clock silenced, I assigned him a new place in line, far behind more important things.

I nodded off, sitting up, and woke after one a.m. to stumble back to my bed, where Sorrow had laid himself crosswise, snoring worse than Jackson ever snored, and protesting with shocked grunts when I pushed him to the floor.

I grabbed a cup of tea the next morning, fed Sorrow, patted his head, and promised I wouldn't be late. I patted him again until he understood and rolled his eyes so the whites showed. I closed him out on the screened porch knowing full well, if he felt like it, no matter what I did he'd soar through the screening and terrorize the loons.

At the Leetsville police station, I pulled in and parked next to Chief Lucky Barnard's old car. Inside, Lucky was at his desk in an office down a side hall, beyond Dolly's broom closet with her tiny desk and chair shoved in a corner, and a single file cabinet. There was a baby's rattle left on top of her desk, causing the smallest tug of pity inside me.

Lucky looked up, then slapped a tall stack of files he'd set at one corner of his desk. "Got Dolly and Jane first thing this morning. Should've brought the files but I wasn't thinking.

Found a couple more when I got back here anyway. No way of knowing which one went off like that and tried to do in Dolly's car."

"And Baby Jane," I reminded him, taking a chair and slouching, tired already. A lot to get done in the day ahead.

Lucky was quiet a moment then leaned forward, his muscular arms braced on the desktop. His lined face was worried. "I got something to tell you . . ." He hesitated. "Don't want this in the paper though. And you can't tell Dolly just yet. She's got so much on her mind right now. But I got a call from Jack's Towing. He's the one picked up the squad car from the cemetery."

Lucky hesitated. "Just called a minute ago . . ."

I waited, hoping he'd get to whatever point he was making.

"There was a note stuck up under the windshield wiper. Had to be put on the car sometime last night. He found it this morning."

"A note? You mean like 'Sorry for the damage' or 'Didn't mean to do it'?"

Lucky shook his head, his face gravely serious. "It just said, 'Thou Shalt Not Steal.'"

"Steal? What?"

Lucky sniffed and glanced down at his rough hands. "Can't say. Dolly's the straightest shooter I ever met in my life. She never stole a thing from anybody."

"This has got to be a terrible mistake."

He narrowed his eyes at me. "Mistake? You hit a marked police car by mistake?"

"Did the note say anything about Baby Jane?"

"That was all. I'm going out there now. Jack didn't touch the note so I'm picking it up and taking it to the state police lab. Maybe we'll get fingerprints. If it's one of these guys she put in jail, the prints will be on file and we can get him."

I set my hands on the wooden chair arms and got up, hesitating. "You know I'll have to put this in my story. I can't . . . Lucky . . . you can't ask me not to report something so important. Somebody might come forward. You know how people are up here—they'll protect each other, but only so far. This is way over the line . . ."

"Well, if that's how you're gonna play it I won't be able to tell you things from here on in. I only said something because you're Dolly's friend."

"And as her friend, I'm telling her about the note. She can't investigate without knowing everything. You can't protect her, Lucky. You ought to know that by now."

Lucky pulled in a deep breath. "Okay, you tell her and I'll call as soon as I get back from the lab in Grayling. And tell her I'm going out to talk to the Harpy boys and to see Will Friendship. They've been heard blowing their mouths off about Dolly over at the Skunk. If you guys can get out, go see those I put on top of the pile, then let me know. I got a feeling this will break fast. The whole town's mad as hell. Going after an adult, if you've got a beef with somebody—well, that's one thing. But you don't hurt babies while you're doin' it."

I went back out to my Jeep. Dolly was home. I had those files she wanted. Still, she'd be distracted by visitors for a while and I was hungry. I headed over to EATS for tea and toast— since I'd had no time for breakfast. And for a talk with Eugenia about a wedding party.

FIVE

Because it was ten thirty, halfway between breakfast and lunch, EATS was almost empty. The early farmers and men and women on their way to work at the Dollar Store or the hospital were gone. Even the old guys group—with their own reserved tables—were out of there. Eugenia saw me, wiped her hands on the towel she had draped around her waist, and came away from the menu bulletin board she'd been working on. She sat down across from me in the booth, and asked first about Baby Jane and then about Deputy Dolly.

"You know, Emily"—Eugenia dipped that head of towering and sliding blond hair—"we all grouse about Dolly. And to tell the truth, she deserves it a lot of the time. But we don't wish her bad luck. None of us do. Not even those guys who come in cussin' her out 'cause she gave them a ticket for five miles over. That's why I just don't think it's anybody from around here."

I shrugged. "Lucky's out talking to people . . ."

"He's not going to find 'im in Leetsville. We're not that kind. Nobody's that bad—I don't care how many fights some of us get into or how much somebody steals at the market. There's nothing really bad in anybody around here. Just people tryin' to make it in a tough, tough world. Sure nobody who'd hurt a baby."

"You've had your share of murders . . ."

Eugenia waved a hand, blowing off the suggestion. "Not by us. They're outsiders—one way or the other. Not us."

I brought up the wedding, which seemed to be no surprise to Eugenia.

"'Bout time," she sniffed. "Those two rutting around out there."

I told her what Harry had in mind and that he didn't have a lot of money.

"Can't be on June second. My niece, down in Cadillac, is getting married. I'm going to that. Tell him the third's better. That'll be a Sunday."

She thought awhile. "He want it catered someplace, or have it here?" Eugenia frowned. I could see she was running party menus through her head.

"Maybe at Delia's house."

"He wants me to bring the food out there?"

I nodded.

"What's he got in mind?"

"Well, he says he's got a freezer full of meat you could use . . ."

Eugenia threw back her head, tendrils of wild hair shivering around her face. She snorted. "You expect me to cook up meat with tire tread on it?"

"No, no . . ."

Eugenia slapped her hands on the table, bouncing my teacup. "Let me think about this. I'll come up with something. How many, would you say?"

I shrugged.

"Probably the whole town," she said. "Let's make it a picnic. Got lots of hot dogs left over from yesterday. Froze 'em. So, that's what we'll do. A big blowout picnic. And soon. You tell him not to wait around the way he's been doin'. . ."

Eugenia got up and went back to the bulletin board she'd been working on—striking off Sloppy Joes and inserting meat loaf. Gloria hurried over with another pot of hot water and dipped her head close to me to whisper, "Check out Donald Throes and his brother, Ralph. I heard them say they were going to fix that deputy, oh, maybe a couple of months ago. Sitting in here. Breakfast: fried eggs and white toast. You tell Dolly, okay?"

SIX

I nosed my Jeep in among the other cars parked in front of Dolly's plain white house. I hurried up the front steps to stand outside the screened door and knock. A large terra-cotta pot on the top step still held a single washed-out plastic Poinsettia. Dolly's stab at Christmas decorating back in December.

"Dolly!" I gave up knocking and called, hoping to be heard over the rumble of voices coming from the house.

Dolly came to the inside door and waved me in. "Come on. Ya gotta see Jane. She looks great. Everybody's making over her. Kid's gonna be spoiled." Dolly smiled as broad a smile as I had ever seen on that little face. I followed in behind her, into a living room filled with talking and laughing townspeople.

Flora Coy, with her thick glasses and frizzed white hair, sat on Dolly's shabby plaid couch holding a wide-eyed Baby Jane in her arms, the baby's head snapped back and forth, watching and listening like a wise little owl. The thing with Baby Jane was that it wasn't just that she was a pretty baby — with one of those pursed pink mouths and plump cheeks and bright little brown eyes — but she looked at you as if she knew you in a way you'd never know yourself, straight through to where nobody ever looked anymore. You couldn't help but fall in love with Baby Jane. Maybe part of it was the aura of love Dolly cast around her. Hard not to see Jane through Dolly's eyes. And hard not to wish the both of them the happiest lives people could ever have.

Cate Thomas sat beside Gloria, reaching over to straighten the large bow stuck on Jane's almost bald head, then pushing back the epaulets on Jane's tiny cop suit, a present from the men at the Michigan State Police Post in Gaylord. Cate's lined face was drawn and pale. I imagined this was as tough on her as it had been on Dolly. I bent to beam down at Baby Jane, who looked up hard, thrashed her arms and legs, and made a cooing noise toward me. I would have picked her up but there was still something that scared me about holding a baby—any baby. It was like they had hooks attached that could grab on to a woman's skin and then you couldn't get loose afterward.

I nodded to Julie, the pretty blond from the post office, then the women from the beauty shop and the Dollar Store, all standing at one end of the living room. Chet, from the garage, stood under the high windows at the far side of the room along with men from the Feed and Seed and a couple of farmers. Churchwomen passed trays of homemade cookies and pieces of pie to the people standing around in little conversational knots.

I couldn't help but wonder if any of the town's businesses were open that Monday morning.

"Omar called. He's comin' over," Dolly, standing beside me, leaned close to whisper.

I shot her a look and whispered back, "He has a right to . . ."

"Don't tell me about 'right.'" She poked me hard in the ribs, frowned one of her particularly fierce frowns, and directed me into the kitchen, where I dropped the stack of files I carried down to the edge of the white painted wooden table covered with plates of cookies I was soon forced, by the smiling bakers, to sample.

"I've got something I've got to tell you." I leaned in close to Dolly when I could.

Dolly's head snapped up. "They get 'im? The guy who hit my car?"

"No. But Lucky told me something . . ." I looked around the room. Two women near the sink were filling plates with fudge. "He thought maybe I should be the one . . ."

Dolly moved her shoulders back and forth, uncomfortable, then took a chair beside me so we could huddle.

"Over at Jack's towing . . . sometime during the night." I glanced at the women but they were talking and paying no attention to us. "Somebody put a note on your patrol car."

Dolly sniffed. "What? It really was an accident? Insurance information? That it? Doesn't seem right. I don't care what they're sayin' now."

I shook my head at her. "All the note said was: 'Thou Shalt Not Steal.'"

Dolly reared back and looked hard at me. "What's that supposed to mean: 'steal'?"

I shrugged.

"Who'd I steal from? You think that was meant for me? Me — steal?"

I shrugged again then shook my head at a piece of coconut cake stuck under my nose.

"What kinda thing is that?" She sat back, perplexed. "'Thou Shalt Not Steal.' Sounds like some religious nut. Or maybe they got the wrong car . . ."

I made a face at her. "You think they were after some other Leetsville patrol car?"

She shrugged. "Could've been the chief. Maybe they thought I was him."

"'Thou Shalt Not Steal.' You ever know the chief to be

anything but on the up and up?"

She made a face, thought awhile, then shook her head. "Okay. So it's me and somebody's mad about something I did. Let's get at the files and then get the hell out there and find this creep."

I told her Lucky went out to see the Harpy boys, over toward Gaylord.

"Yeah, those Harpys. They said it right to my face—that I'd be sorry. They have a tendency to drink and smoke weed and then go out looking for trouble. They found it, coming into Leetsville, over to the Skunk. Tried to wreck the place. Swore they were going to get me—but that was the liquor talking. Everybody says that. We'll see what Lucky finds out. Now, let's get going. I'd say the Throes first. Out 131 toward Boyne Falls."

SEVEN

The divided stack of files lay in Dolly's lap. She went through them one by one as I drove because she didn't have a car until Lucky Barnard made some arrangements to get her one.

She read each file carefully and then tried to put them into some kind of order, though they slipped, one by one, to the Jeep's floor and she had to struggle to pick them up and by that time was spitting mad at me, the car, and anything else she could think of to be mad at.

"Don't know what's wrong with Cate. All of a sudden it's such a big deal for her to watch Jane. Like she's afraid something's going to happen to her. Doesn't make sense. Just for today, is what I told her. After this I'll get somebody or take her to EATS. And on top of that, now she's pushing that woman in France at me, like I'd ever want to hear from her." She shook her head. "I don't get it. So determined to write to her. Like she's got this right to know I've got a baby. Like that would turn her around and she'd be the perfect grandmother and fly right back from that commune, or whatever she's connected up with over there, and we'd all be so very happy together."

She grunted. "Never going to happen. I told her, you want to go over there and see her, that's fine with me. She's your daughter, after all, and I understand now about having a daughter. But that person in France is no mother to me. She gave me away and nothing's going to change that."

"You ever think maybe she had a reason for giving you

47

away?"

She gave me a dark look. "Like I was too ugly?"

"Don't be a jerk. Like she couldn't take care of you. Maybe she didn't have any money. Maybe she didn't have a place to live. What's Cate ever said about her?"

She shook her head. "Nothing. I asked her questions and she said all she knew was that Audrey Delores—middle name same as mine—signed papers giving up her rights to me and took off for France."

"And where was Cate? Why didn't your grandmother take you?"

"Says she didn't even know Audrey was pregnant. She ran away from home when she was nineteen. Cate didn't know anything about me until Eugenia started that genealogy business of hers and was looking for my relatives. She's the one who found Cate and brought her up here as a surprise." She made a sour face but changed it pretty quick. "Not that I'm not grateful. First person I ever belonged to—Cate. I'm glad to have her in my life, but I wished she'd stop this stuff about being afraid to watch Baby Jane."

"She'll get over it. Probably the accident scared her. You know, she realized what a responsibility a baby is."

"Yeah, I hope so. 'Til she gets over it I'll take Jane to EATS when I got to work. Eugenia don't mind. Lots of women there to keep an eye on her. And women coming in all the time. Like one great big family. I don't think Jane's gonna be any the worse for being out with friends and neighbors all day long."

I headed north on 131, through Mancelona. My cell rang a few times. Jackson Rinaldi. I ignored the calls and then shut off my phone. Whatever Jackson wanted badly enough to call me three times in a row was certain to be something I didn't want to hear. I had enough with one difficult person on my hands.

After a while, Dolly grumbled, "My baby," and shook her head. "Jane ever do anything to anybody? She's four months old, for crap's sake. Four months old! Even I didn't get people going after me 'til I was almost seven."

She bent over the top file, thumbing through a long rap sheet. "So these Throes guys said they were gonna 'fix' me, eh? That puts them at the top of my list. Ralph was blazing mad when I caught on to his acre of marijuana out beyond their place near Dead Man's Hill. Donald got himself in the middle when I arrested Ralph and he served a little time, too. I did what I could for him but those guys don't look at it that way. I don't know what they're complaining about. Both out of jail. I'm telling you, Emily, if these idiots are the ones who thought it was funny to wreck my patrol car, they'll be doing the max this time. I swear it. Attempted murder. No easy prison camp. Up to Marquette."

I knew the Throes brothers. More than once they'd figured into stories of local break-ins and a couple for bar fights. There was only one thing that made me think maybe the Throes couldn't have possibly been involved. These two men, in their early forties, would never take the chance of wrecking a perfectly good 2006 Ford Escape. As far as I knew, neither one ever had a car younger than a 1988 Mercury Grand Marquis so, even stolen, that 2006 Ford was worth a lot to them. But not with a smashed-up front and everybody looking for just that kind of vehicle. The Throes brothers were maybe short in the morals department, but they weren't stupid and, if I remembered right, they weren't that bad as criminals went.

I turned left at Whiskey Road, just past Dead Man's Hill. We bounced along a two-track into the woods and then down a worse two-track with high weeds already growing down the middle. The clearing around their small trailer bloomed with the rusted bodies of old Fords, a few tires melting into the earth but planted with pansies, and a square plot of earth freshly turned to plant a garden. At one end of the garden a row of daffodils bloomed.

Odd. Somehow daffodils and pansies didn't sit in my mouth with the Throes name.

The trailer sat back behind a chicken coop, a couple of unpainted barns, and one bulging shed with two-by-fours nailed across the front to hold the doors shut.

Donald and Ralph Throes. When they were sober, I liked them. Backwoods born and bred. The kind of guys who weren't comfortable around women, unless it was a woman they met in a bar who was twice as drunk as they were. When I talked to them, the time the *Statesman* asked me to follow a story on a woman missing from the Pot Licker Tavern in Alba, they called me "ma'am" and nodded at almost everything I asked, except knowing where the woman got to and then "Swearing to God, me and Ralph, here, don't know nothing about it."

It turned out they were right. The woman woke up down in Detroit, in the front seat of a traveling salesman's car, and called her husband to tell him she was sorry and wanted to come back home.

So I had nothing against the Throes and decided I'd stay neutral until we had more evidence: like a black SUV with a ruined front peeking out from that nailed shut shed, which I was determined to take a look at while Dolly talked to the men.

EIGHT

Ralph was planting seeds along a furrow at the far side of the spaded garden. The man looked a lot older than forty, but often these backwoods men aged early. Too much hard work. Too much disappointment. Sometimes it was just too much drinking and smoking and thinking.

Ralph put a hand up to cover his eyes against the sun then picked up a hoe from the ground beside him and leaned on it, waiting to see what this yellow Jeep was bringing into his property.

Dolly got out and gave Ralph a perfunctory wave. "It's me, Ralph. Deputy Dolly. Just want to talk to you."

As Ralph set his hoe down and walked along the garden row toward us, the trailer door opened and the younger brother, Donald, leaned out, keeping one hand on the door handle and one hand on the doorframe, dumbstruck at the sight of company.

When both men took in who'd come to see then the response was swift and surprising.

Ralph picked up speed as Donald swung off their small porch. Both headed straight for Dolly.

Ralph got over to her first. He put his arms out wide and folded them around a stiffened Dolly, hugging her close to his skinny chest. "Heard about what happened." He looked down sadly into Dolly's startled face. "Me and Donald here said right away, what kind of scum-sucking jerk would do that to a baby? Geez, Dolly, no matter how drunk me and Donald get from time to time, we'd never do something like that to your baby."

Donald, younger by about five years but otherwise almost a carbon copy of Ralph, was right behind his brother. "Heard and we jist wanted to tell ya we're happy she's gonna be okay. Why, I seen Baby Jane over there to EATS that one time and told Ralph here I never seen a prettier baby. That's what everybody for miles around here's been saying. No baby prettier, Dolly. Sure hope you get the guy who did that to your car."

Ralph put his hand out to shake mine. "Know you, too. Yer Emily Kincaid, that writer. Heard you was trying to sell some book you wrote. Should get it up there on that Internet. Heard books on there sellin' like hotcakes. Me and Donald was talking jist the other day about writing one about our life and seeing to getting it put up on there."

I kept my mouth shut as Dolly toed the ground then kicked a rusted beer can a good fifteen feet. "That's kind of why I'm out here, boys," she said. "Not about a book. I heard you were saying something about getting even with me for putting you both in jail."

Ralph's eyebrows shot up. Donald's mouth dropped open.

"Us? Geez, Dolly, we'd never do anything to hurt yer baby," Ralph said.

Dolly toed the ground again, keeping her head down so she didn't have to look at the stricken faces. "That's not what somebody heard you saying."

"You mean that 'We're gonna fix Deputy Dolly' stuff Donald was spouting at EATS a few weeks back?" Ralph waved a hand as if wiping it all away. "He didn't mean anything at all, did you, Donald?"

Donald snapped his mouth shut and shook his head vehemently. "Listen, Dolly, there were guys in there laughing at us 'cause we just got outta jail and so I said that to shut 'em up. Like if I can take care of you I can take care of them easy enough."

He shook his head hard. His eyes got red around the edges. I thought the man might be about to cry. "You know that stuff don't mean anything. Let's go in the house. I'd like to make you a cup of coffee and talk this out. Man to man, so to speak."

Dolly took more than one deep breath. She seemed about to get mad at Donald then changed her mind and nodded. To my surprise we followed the boys into their trailer for what I imagined was some kind of peace talk.

I wasn't eager to sit down with the Throes boys in that trailer. I'd been in many backwoods places where people just didn't notice how they lived until they had no room to sleep anymore and either sealed up the place and moved away or put up a tent in the yard until winter came and forced them to pull at least some of their stash out to leave for the coming winter's snow to squash flat.

This trailer wasn't like that. I'd never seen a neater place. If you stacked my haphazard housecleaning up against the Throes, I'd come out the loser.

The place was small but immaculate. The little living room had a pullout sofa covered with a crocheted throw. Magazines were neatly stacked in a wooden bin. A coffee table held a collection of carved wooden figures I had to ask about.

"Mine," Donald said proudly. "Learned to carve like that when I was a kid. After our mom and dad took off and left us the way they did, I didn't say a word for about three years. Just carved my animals. Ralph thought it took too much time, but look at what I've got to show for it now."

The air inside this home was sweet. A Mason jar crammed full of daffodils sat on a kitchen counter free of dishes or anything much beyond an old cracked set of yellow canisters.

Dolly and I looked at each other as we took seats on the sofa, careful not to disturb the precisely draped orange throw.

"Donald makes a great cup of coffee." Ralph smiled a kind of painful smile. "If you like coffee, that is."

Obviously these men weren't used to company. Especially not the company of women. I figured they wanted to talk to Dolly more than me and I wanted to take a look at that shed. While Dolly waited for the old metal coffeepot to perk, I made an excuse—had to make a phone call—and went back outside.

I stood in the cluttered yard, so different from their home, and thought long and hard about people not being what I expected. There were no stereotypes in the north. Every time I told myself I had them all pegged, I'd be proven wrong again.

A slight wind came up out of the south, warming the air around me. Might be hot enough to swim in Willow Lake by Memorial Day. I cheered myself with the thought of my lake and the loons, then depressed myself with the thought that I was more alone than Ralph and Donald, and not as neat.

I looked off at the bulging shed and figured I'd better take a look, though if these two guys were the ones who went after Dolly's car they were better actors than Tom Hanks and Anthony Hopkins put together.

It was a slow amble over to the rickety shed with shingles torn off the roof, exposing gaping holes, which I imagined skunks and raccoons and other assorted animals made good use of. I checked the sky again—pretending I had nothing special on my mind. Then turned to make sure the door to the trailer stayed shut.

The boards were crossed and nailed over the shed doors but not doing too good a job as the doors bulged outward. I put my eye to the gap, leaning hard with a hand to either side of me. There was some light, coming from the holes in the roof. I half expected the eye of something or other to look back at me. Instead there seemed to be a mattress pushing from the other side. And not much else to see.

There could be a black SUV hidden in there, behind the mattress, or just a lot of other old junk the boys had accumulated over the years. Maybe Ralph was the hoarder, while Donald kept things neat — even to boarding up Ralph's collections.

I pushed my eye harder — squinting one way and then the other, seeing if the slumping mattress inside gave a view of something else beyond it.

"Lookin' for something?" Donald's voice behind me made me almost jump out of my Nikes.

I stumbled back. I knew my face was red, along with my eyes — pushed up against the shed the way they'd been.

"Why . . . eh . . . I was just seeing what you had in there that the doors had to be boarded up the way they are."

He shook his head. "Ralph." He snickered. "Got more stuff than one person ought to have. Says he's keeping it but I say you can't live in a mess like that. I boarded the shed shut and he's still threatening to take the boards off except he knows that junk of his'll come flying out and about kill him."

He sniffed and eyed me closely. "You interested in antiques? Got quite a selection in there, if you are. I could pull the boards off. Take a while. Need help. And we'd have to run when I get it down to the last nails . . ."

I assured him I had no interest in "antiques."

"Lots of good stuff. Old Coca-Cola signs. Seen those. A pinball machine. Got an old Ford truck. Think he's even got the trunks our great-grandparents brought with them from England. I'm tellin' you, Ralph saves everything. Me, I'm a thrower. I don't like mess, that's why I clean up after Ralph and hide it all away."

He stopped to point to the other two old barns. "See those barns?" he asked.

I nodded, still embarrassed at having been caught snooping.

"All full. Just didn't have to nail them shut like this one. Don't know where we'll go with it all from here on in. Maybe just make a bonfire. Let it go at that."

Ralph and Dolly came out of the trailer, talking as they stepped down from the cinder-block porch.

Dolly waved. "You missed coffee," she said. "We got a lot of places to get to, Emily. Better get going, if you're through talking to Donald there."

The Throes told us to come calling whenever we were in the neighborhood and we were out of there and back on the road.

Dolly slumped in the front seat, the stack of file folders back on her lap.

"You think I should have asked him to take the boards off that shed?" I said after a while. "That SUV could've been in there. That's what I went out to check on."

She nodded. "Doubt it," she said. "Most they probably got in there is a new stash of marijuana. I don't want to be arresting them again over that stuff."

"You busted Ralph three times already."

"Yeah, I know, and I've been thinking. Those are real nice men. They care a lot about Baby Jane. I could tell."

She glanced over at me. Her scowl went deep. "I heard the story about their parents taking off on them when I first came to Leetsville. But I never heard Donald didn't talk for three years after that. All I ever knew was they got a note saying their mom and dad would be in touch and to take care of things around the house 'til they got back. Only they never came back. Not a word. You ask me, those boys are still waiting. Keeping the place up the way they were told to. Sad to think about it. I sure wish I hadn't sent them both to jail like that."

"Doing your job."

"I know. I know. Still, sometimes people should come first. I mean, if you understand what they've been through. I mean, if you've been through the same kind of thing . . . well . . . seems there's got to be a way to fix things better."

NINE

Cate called my cell phone, which was a good thing because Dolly was driving and getting madder by the minute over that "Thou Shalt Not Steal" business rolling around in her head. She'd been repeating the phrase again and again as if there might be something hidden in the words—if she could just get them in the right order.

"Can't call *her*," Cate said to me, her voice clipped and angry. "She won't listen. I don't want to take care of this baby by myself. Poor child needs her mother. You gotta tell Dolly to get home here, or take Baby Jane someplace else. With that hairline thing on her head, I just don't want to be responsible. Wouldn't you think . . . ?"

"Calm down, Cate," I said, which made Dolly lean over and grab first my arm and then the phone, right out of my hand.

"Jane all right?" Dolly demanded and then listened, sputtering as Cate talked on. As she got madder, she slowed. "Okay. Okay. Stop talking. I'll call Eugenia, see if she can send one of the girls over to get her. Or maybe stay awhile and help . . .

"Yeah, sure," she continued, looking more and more unhappy. "I don't see what you're so worried . . .

"I said I'd call right now. Be just a few minutes."

She punched the end call button fast, then rolled her eyes.

"I don't get her. She didn't have this problem at first. Said she loved watching Baby Jane. Now, all of a sudden . . ."

I shrugged. "Baby's just out of the hospital, Dolly. I'd be scared to watch her myself—with that hairline fracture. I mean, if you don't know kids that well . . ."

She dialed another number. One eye on the road—which made me nervous, though we were still on the two-track and hadn't passed a car going in or out. I watched her fumble with the phone and couldn't help thinking about my Jeep getting wrapped around one of the gnarled old trees along the roadside.

She talked to Eugenia at EATS, seeing to it someone would go over and help Cate or bring Baby Jane to the restaurant, where everybody in the place would be making over her, making her laugh, and just showing what good people thought of babies in general.

"Eugenia's going herself," she said when she was off the phone. "I told her how Cate's acting and she's gonna talk to her; see if she can find out what's wrong all of a sudden."

She stopped before turning out on to 131. "Where are we going next?"

"I've got to get this follow-up into the paper soon. If we're going to Traverse City I'd like to get the story turned in."

"While I wait in the car? With all I've got to do? You said you wanted to ride along, not the other way around." She put the car in park. "Give me those files. I was thinking of one . . ."

"Tommy Worfman," she said, pulling a folder from the bottom of the pile. "Ran a meth lab way back in the woods. Started a fire back there. Surprised as hell when I followed the fire truck out and walked right in and got him. But I think he's still up in prison—Marquette."

"So? What about friends of his? Somebody getting revenge for his buddy?"

She nodded. "Could be. Gotta think about that. How bad

they want to get me. And his mother, Claudine Worfman, hates me like a plague of grasshoppers. Be kind of good to get her stirred up. If she thinks I'm blaming any of this on Tommy or his trashy friends, she'll get the word out to finish the job."

"Wow, well connected, huh?"

"She should be the one in jail. I don't think Tommy even knew what he was cooking out there in that lab she set up for him. Some mothers, you know, they got acid in that amniotic fluid stuff."

"Seems a long shot. Couldn't be him if he's in jail."

"Yeah, well, you don't know police business much, do you?"

I bit my tongue and went back to the "who, what, where, when, and how" of the story I wrote as she drove off.

"Claudine lives over by Rapid City," Dolly said after a while. "That's where we're going. After that I want to see Ramon Valderez. Mean s.o.b. Beats his wife. He told me once he was going to get me when I didn't expect it. He's not in prison right now. Wouldn't put anything past him. When they're mean, they're just mean."

"And then around to Traverse so I can turn this in to Bill." I waved my reporter's notebook in the air.

"I said I'm not sitting, waiting for you. I got too much to do."

"Make phone calls while I'm in with Bill. Don't you have to check in with Lucky? See if they found the car yet? And maybe what he found out at the Harpys', or from Will Friendship." I hesitated, thinking. "And by the way, lady. This happens to be my car. It goes where I go."

"That's not our deal. Told you I'd share the gas. Lucky'll

reimburse us. And about calling him, if he had anything, he'd call me. Still, I guess I'd better check in. But I'm not going to Traverse. You drop me off at the station first. Or wherever Jane is."

"All that extra driving," I complained but got nothing more. "I won't be long at the paper."

I was ignored. Dolly was thinking.

"Can't always leave Jane at the restaurant. Who knows what kind of germs she could pick up there?"

She stomped on the gas. I wondered if she was missing her siren, which Dolly used like a calling card, announcing her arrival wherever she went.

"After Claudine," she said later. "You drive. I'll call Lucky. Said he was going to call body shops, too, but I don't think that's gonna happen—that the car turns up at one of those. So many guys back in the woods'll do body work a lot cheaper than the regular places. And keep it quiet."

The house was little, almost lost under towering old oaks and behind thick sumac bushes. The open fields surrounding the house had been cut back long ago to a far ring of woods. Now the fields were covered with the low green fuzz of spring growth. No farming going on anymore. One of many hardscrabble farms started by people who kept coming to northern Michigan to plant corn and rows of soybean in sand and finally gave up when the soil and the farmer were exhausted and broke.

Claudine Worfman sat on the front porch of her house. She rocked as she watched us pull in and park in her drive that was nothing more than a bare earth track over humps of dead tree roots.

I saw the woman and poked Dolly.

"That's her," Dolly said and smiled a wicked smile. "I'm not going to be making her day, I'd say."

She got out. I followed, staying behind her. I wanted to watch and listen to Dolly handle this big woman in a ruffled sundress, hair permed to within an inch of its life and held back by a green headband. Kind of a Medusa look to Claudine Worfman.

"Miz Worfman," Dolly said, approaching the bottom of the steps.

"Deputy." Claudine kept rocking.

"Could I speak to you a minute?"

"What if I say 'Hell no'?"

"Then I'll ask my questions anyway."

"What if I go in the house and get a big broom to sweep you outta here?"

Dolly thought a minute, took off her hat and scratched at the back of her head. "Then I'm gonna have to take that big broom away from you and arrest you for assault."

"On my own front porch?" The woman twisted back and forth in her chair but kept right on rocking. "You mean I can't defend my property from troublemakers?"

"I'm not here to make any trouble, Miz Worfman. Just got a couple of questions for you."

She rocked hard. And waited.

"Somebody ran into my car yesterday. It was parked. Done deliberately. I mean, they left the road to smash into it."

"You want to take a look at my car? It's in the garage, over there." She pointed around to a one-car garage back beyond the house. "1988 Buick. Got a few dents but not what you're looking for."

Dolly shook her head. "No, I didn't think it was you . . ."

"Not that I wouldn't like to see that happen." The woman smiled a wicked smile.

"My baby was in it."

Claudine nodded, her face expressionless. She said nothing.

"She's okay. Thanks for asking," Dolly added facetiously.

"Why would I care about your baby? You care about mine? Sitting up there at Marquette?"

"Mine wasn't cooking meth and almost blowing up a neighborhood."

"That was a little fire. Nobody in danger."

"Well," Dolly went on as I stood there, not introduced and having no desire to be. "The reason I'm here is to ask you about Tommy's friends. I remember some of them, after the trial, bragging they were going to get even for him . . ."

"I don't know nothing about that. Seems more your problem than mine."

Dolly turned slowly, as if to walk away. "Sometimes my problems get to be other people's problems, too. Like now. If I heard you were the one egged those boys on to do something . . ."

"Well." Claudine Worfman stood and stretched her wide and tall body. She flipped a slipping ruffled sleeve back up her arm. "You ever hear such a thing, you come right back here and we'll talk about it. Until then, if you don't mind, I got a cake with a file in it to bake for my poor child."

T E N

We skipped Ramon Valderez and headed straight back to Leetsville after Dolly took a call that there was a standoff with an armed man in the pharmacy. I stayed in town until that was over then headed toward Traverse City.

What I needed was an iPad. Something to keep in the car with me so I could write my stories and not always be looking for a computer. For now, I was going in to see Bill and use a newspaper computer.

Bill Corcoran was a good editor. Particular. He went over every word of every piece of copy and I loved seeing that he'd made few changes in mine. A matter of pride, that I got things right, and I hadn't had a lot to be proud of lately, with money getting low and not too many prospects for gleaning cash anywhere—except that agent who had my mystery out to a couple of publishers right then and kept giving me hope for a "quick" sale.

Only now she'd had the book for six months and I didn't know anymore what "quick" meant.

It seemed writing wasn't going to be a fast track to anywhere. Too many writers. Too many cheap choices on Amazon. No way to break in. My agent told me not to worry about that but I couldn't help it. Life has a way of demanding seriousness when all I wanted to do was daydream about me accepting my Pulitzer with grace and dignity—or at least that's what the *New York Times* would say. *Grace* and *Dignity*. Two of my favorite words. Unattainable virtues no newspaper would use to describe me.

I pulled in next to the ivy-covered brick offices of the *Statesman* and gathered my notes. I was there later than I'd hoped but now I was bringing Bill two stories: an update on Dolly's hit-and-run along with the armed guy at the drugstore. Lots of photos of him coming out with his hands in the air.

I read my scribbling—not sure about writing the "Thou Shalt Not Steal" note into the story or not. Lucky didn't like it, but Dolly didn't say one way or the other. She seemed willing to put everything out there, anything to get the man who hurt Jane. If ever there was a vengeful mother on the warpath, Dolly was it and I wasn't far behind. No matter what I said about babies, I was already attached to Baby Jane.

Maybe it was from the first moment I saw that little flattened head and scrunched-up face in the hospital after Dolly delivered her and I worried about Dolly's reaction to delivering a Martian. Maybe it was because the little head rounded out and she dropped the lobster color and turned beautiful. Maybe it was because when she saw me now she smiled a gummy smile that broke my heart. The kid was truly beautiful. Considering her parents, this was what I now thought to be the miracle of birth—that a kid could overcome some pretty unremarkable genes.

I'd stopped in at the police station but Lucky Barnard didn't have a whole lot of new information to give me, though he said he thought both Harpy brothers were out of contention.

"The Harpy brothers are staying firmly on the straight and narrow," he said, leaning back in his chair, yawning. "George Harpy got religion. He said to make sure I let you and Dolly know about that. Willie went to trade school. He's got a good job. Both the guys were sorry to hear about what happened.

George is praying for Jane. Said to tell Dolly everything'll be okay."

"Weren't they the ones got drunk and tried to tear out the clock in the park?"

"Yeah, but they seem sincere. Saw a Bible on the kitchen table."

"You check to see if there was a pistol in it?" I couldn't help asking.

"Now hold on there a minute, Emily. Don't go judging people like that. These boys trying to make something of themselves and I say go for it. Give 'em the benefit of the doubt."

I stood with my head down, properly chastised for a few seconds before Lucky stuck a manila envelope out toward me. "Give this to Dolly," he said. "Should've thought about her first. Ariadne Wilcox. Child endangerment. Think you and Dolly should get out there. That boyfriend of hers got eighteen months for burning her baby. Dolly testified at the trial that got both Ariadne's babies taken away from her."

"Aren't we looking for a guy? I thought that's what Dolly said. I mean, the car that ran into her."

"That's what I'm saying. The guy's a monster. Didn't get half enough time. Worth looking at. That man popped off everywhere, what Dolly did to his 'family.' That could fit with the 'Thou Shalt Not Steal' business. Guy like that, brain like that, could think he had a right to do whatever he wanted to do to little girls he fed and sort of clothed."

I looked down at the file envelope in my hands. "Ariadne," I said almost to myself. "King Minos's daughter. Kind of like a spider. A weaver of webs."

"Yeah, well," Lucky, no student of mythology, said and took a minute to get his face under control. "This one's a spider all right. She's the one left her hopped-up boyfriend alone with her little girls. Just as evil as he is, you ask me."

I didn't want to think about evil like that and didn't ask any more questions.

After a while, Lucky went on. "About that Will Friendship. Tell Dolly he's off probation. Nobody's seen him in more than three months."

"Anything on the prints from the note?"

He shook his head. "Nothing so far."

When I got into the newspaper Bill Corcoran sat behind his desk, mussed head of thick brown hair dipped down over an article he was editing, muttering to himself as he worked. I hated to interrupt, but if you didn't interrupt Bill he'd never look up.

As it was, I startled him, the middle finger of his left hand flying to hold his horn-rimmed glasses in place, or push them up on his head. He always took a minute or two to focus, then he'd place you, then break out a wide, warm smile that never failed to make my day.

"So, Emily." He leaned back in his creaking chair. "How's your friend doing? Baby okay?"

"Fine. Hairline fracture. It's all here in my story."

"I'm happy for her. Hope she doesn't take that baby out with her anymore."

I shrugged then shook my fistful of notes at him. "I need to use one of your computers."

That arranged quickly, I occupied an empty office and got to work.

I put in the "Thou Shalt Not Steal" bit after all. If the lead on the article featured that—and I was sure it would—a lot of people would be drawn to the story and not pass right over it. What I figured was that Dolly and Lucky needed all the help they could get right them and I was a conduit to the public. Somebody always knew something that could help.

As I was leaving, Bill called me back into his office to say the newspaper was throwing a picnic for the employees, plus stringers like me. He assured me it would be fun. He'd let me know the date. Fun wasn't what I was interested in right then but I promised I'd make it if I could, and for that I got a funny look, as if maybe he'd asked me for a date and I'd missed it completely.

After I stopped at the library to pick up a book on caring for babies and was on my way home, I told myself to stop reading things into looks and offers. A picnic was a picnic was a picnic and nothing else. By the time I pulled down my drive, I'd gotten over worrying about Bill's feelings and decided the look I got from Bill was because I forgotten to say I'd bring the potato salad.

ELEVEN

A couple days later, with not much happening in Dolly's case and me milking old facts for a daily story, I came home to a note tacked to my screen door:

GOT THE WEDDING PLANNED YET?

Under the single question were numbers. One through three had lines drawn through them. Four stood alone. That meant Harry had been over four times for an answer while I was gone. If I hadn't returned when I did, who knows how many times he'd be visiting in that vehicle of his or walking up his drive and down mine to see me.

I'd have to call Eugenia for a menu and a price.

So many complications. I wanted to sigh and pack it all in.

When I walked in the door Sorrow came bounding across the living room to greet me — which shouldn't have happened since I'd closed him out on the screened porch, but there he was and there was the porch door wide open. My amazing Houdini of a dog.

And then he piddled his happiness on my hall rug, which called for a bucket, and a scrub brush, and a rag, and me down on my knees, swearing and scrubbing as Sorrow stupidly stuck his nose in my ear.

But who can get mad at anybody so happy to see you? I sat back and scratched his ears and patted his black shaggy head and talked baby talk to him because I figured I was always going to be one of those women who maybe should have had a baby but got a dog instead.

At least it wasn't a dozen cats.

Yet.

I poured myself a full glass of Pinot Grigio and ambled down to the lake to sit and watch the loons dive then make bets with myself as to where they would surface. A fun game for the end of an uneventful day.

For a while I tried to think about nothing but Sorrow barking at the beaver and the beaver slapping the water hard with his tail, neither one of them settling anything with their aggression. And that led me to think of Middle East wars where one side slapped a tail and then the other and they all grumbled for a hundred years until one slapped a tail again.

And that led me back to Dolly, who was slapping her tail in every direction she could think to slap in.

So wearying, seeing Dolly Wakowski turned inward, and churned up and mad and thoughtful but maybe not thinking at her best. This wasn't the Dolly I used to know, before Baby Jane. All I could think about as I set my empty glass at the edge of the dock was what a strange metamorphosis motherhood brought on some women. Like, all of a sudden they stopped thinking about themselves completely and there's this new person with needs; a being depending on them for life. Dolly would die before letting anything happen to Jane. Not only die, but first launch her body like a missile to protect that tiny, kind of boring, person. I liked the kid all right. But give my life for her? I'd have to think about that one.

I sat down beside my empty glass and stuck my bare feet into the water, creating circles moving off into the growing darkness. It was getting cold, though the day had been a warm one. After a time of stillness, tiny fish came over to take a look at my skinny feet until I wiggled a toe. Another great game.

I wasn't thinking about much of anything so there was room for other worries to slip in and Jackson came to mind. I had to call him. He wasn't one to be ignored for long. One day there would be a barrage of calls, or he might come zipping down my drive in a hail of gravel, angry with me for making him worry.

All of that got me up off the dock with a shiver, a wave to the angry beaver and the dispersing loons, and then back into the house to face the dreaded answering machine.

I hit the play button and hoped against hope it wasn't somebody wanting to sell me a cemetery plot, which on more than one occasion had ruined a perfectly good day.

"Emily, this is Madeleine Clark . . ."

My heart sped up. It was my agent. Agents only called when there was something important to say. Rejections came by mail or email. This was a phone call . . .

"We have an offer. Please call as soon as possible. I would like to discuss this with you . . . eh . . . well . . . Call me. I'm staying late."

No time for the second call. I dialed Madeleine Clark's number and held my breath until she came on the line.

"Emily! Isn't this exciting? Our first deal together."

"Yes," I choked out. "Exciting."

"It's from Crestleg Publishers. Your editor's name is Faith Cardoni. She had to go out of town but will be in touch as soon as we've got the contract signed. She has a few changes she'd like you to consider . . ."

So much at once: I had an editor with a name. I had a publishing house that wanted to bring out my novel. And . . . oh, oh . . . the editor wanted changes.

"They're new to mystery publishing, but looking solid, I'd say. Very, very solid. I think this will be a good career move for you . . ."

How could I help but think: *Any career move would be good for me!*

"It isn't a lot of money . . ."

Here came reality.

"Standard royalties. A ten-thousand-dollar advance. Half on acceptance and half on publication. Advances are lower these days, you understand."

I nodded, realized she couldn't see me, and croaked out, "Sure. Sounds fine."

The rest was how good she thought the book was and that she hoped I'd get right to work on the next one and a final congratulations, a promise to get the contract to me as soon as she got it, and then good-bye.

I danced in circles around the house with Sorrow leaping beside me, wanting to be a part of whatever this grand celebration might be.

There was a knock at the door and I happily answered to find Harry standing on my tiny porch, his heavy eyebrows drawn together.

"Come in! Come in!" I opened the door wide. "Oh, Harry, I just heard from my literary agent. My book is sold!"

I could hardly stop myself from leaping up and down again, then reaching out to take his gnarled hands in mine and do a jig.

Harry leaned back and eyed me coldly. "This is my fifth time over to see you."

Feeling a sudden rush of ice over my skin, I stopped still

and blinked at him. "I was in town."

"Yeah, figured. But, you know, I asked Delia to marry me and she said yes and now all that's holding up the works is you."

"Yes, but . . ." I was going to try again to make somebody happy for me. "It's hard to think right now. This is such good news! I've been working . . . so . . ."

"You mean me and Delia. Yeah, I think so, too. Good news. Be great for both of us. Figure I could stay at her house during the winter. You know my house gets cold."

I gave up. "I'll call Eugenia. She was talking about a picnic, maybe hot dogs and things like that. Over at Delia's house."

"Can't be there. Delia says she'd feel like she was rubbing her mother's nose in it. You know, getting married so soon after the woman died."

"Can't be at your house. Those dogs . . ."

"I know. Thought about here. You got plenty of room."

"Not for the whole town." Appalled wasn't a strong enough word for what I felt.

He shrugged and started for the door. "This'll do fine. I'm paying for the food. And you tell Eugenia hot dogs are okay, but I got that freezer full of meat."

"I told her," I said, then added, meanly, "She said she wasn't cooking meat with tire tread on it."

He was still sputtering when he stepped out to the porch and I shut the door behind him.

That left me one phone message to check.

I figured I was running fifty-fifty when I heard Jackson's voice and wished I'd taken a hammer to the machine before answering. All I wanted was maybe ten minutes to celebrate.

And somebody to celebrate with.

I got Jackson Rinaldi.

"Terrible, Emily. Just terrible. My book: *On the Way to Canterbury: The Days and Hours of Chaucer's Pilgrims*, has been panned in the *New York Times*. Can you imagine? I mean, a scathing review by a cretin from Yale who knows nothing, absolutely nothing about Chaucer or his pilgrims. I'm devastated, nonetheless. I have to come see you this weekend. I'm pleading. I promise not to bring anyone with me. It will be me, alone, along with my sad and bleeding ego. Please call me back immediately. We have to talk. You know how long I've worked. This is the book to end all books on Chaucer, but there's such jealousy in academia. Such pettiness. Listen to this . . . he calls the book 'unreticulated, without coherent structure.' Can you imagine? 'Unreticulated!' Doesn't that mean without lines or something? He's a fool. A total fool. If I could get my hands on him . . . Oh, Lord . . . I don't know where to turn. You have to let me come up there and stay a few days. There's no one else . . . and you know I still love you best . . . Well, call me. Immediately."

I felt my joy turn to nails in my bloodstream and rip their rusty way into my heart. I thought I heard happiness hit the floor behind me with a loud thunk. Jackson. Miserable. It would be cruel of me to tell him my good news. It would be cruel to tell him he couldn't run to my cabin to hide.

And my news, if I dared tell him, would be, *"Nice. Popular literature, after all."*

Maybe it was the mothering thing going on inside of me, or just the habit of Jackson. I called him back and thankfully got his machine to "tsk, tsk" into and tell him I'd be happy to have him come tomorrow night and leave on Sunday morning, limiting the visit to one long Saturday, which, in itself, was a step forward for me—the limiting, not the mothering bit.

I hung up and thought about my good news and his bad news. I gave a sudden snicker, a fist pump, and then a single click of my heels as I jumped in the air, along with Sorrow, my very best friend.

Loved me best, huh. Out of how big a field, Jackson?

Come on, Jackson. Come see me.

I decided to save my news until he was there in person.

TWELVE

"You gotta come get me," Dolly said over the phone. "Lucky just got word they found the car. The black SUV. He's out there now, in Elk Rapids. So that means you gotta take me. No car."

I was in my little studio behind my house thinking happy thoughts about eventual solvency and starting a new book, which would surely carry me to the heights of literary stardom. I wasn't thinking about Dolly, which was a kind of "shame on me" since Dolly's problem was bigger than my sorry economics any day.

"You at home?" I was already out of my chair and leaning over the phone.

"Where else would I be?"

"I'll get right into town."

"Bring your camera. Or your telephone. Whatever you use. You'll want pictures for the paper. And, Emily, it was reported stolen last Saturday night, right there in Elk Rapids, the chief says. You're never gonna believe what else Lucky told me."

"What?"

"They found it parked right back on main street where it disappeared from. If it weren't for the busted-up front, Lucky says you'd never think it was moved at all."

"Left on the street?"

"Right there downtown."

"Nobody saw who parked it there?"

"Nope. Had to be sometime during the night. Elk Rapids doesn't exactly swing at two, three o'clock in the morning."

"So, as if it was returned to the owner?"

"Yeah. Like, whoever did this only borrowed the car."

"As if they didn't steal it."

"Seems like that. Strange."

We both thought a long time, until Dolly said, "Anyway, bring your camera. The front's all banged in. You'll want a picture of that. We're gonna talk to everybody in town, if we have to. That car was noticeable."

"What about Jane?"

"I gotta call Gloria. She said she'd come over anytime and watch her. Cate's still acting scared of . . . I don't get it but I can't budge her and I don't want to force anybody to watch my baby." I heard a catch in her throat. "Geez, Emily. What was I thinking? Getting pregnant like that."

What do you say to somebody this miserable just because she got what she always wanted? I said nothing but, "I'll drive right in. And look, if we have to, we'll take Jane along. I can watch her while you see about the car."

The phone went dead.

This time I didn't bother to lock Sorrow out on the porch since it didn't do any good. He'd been showing me he was a grown-up dog, at least some of the time. I figured he could be trusted not to tear sofa cushions to bits or pee on my oriental carpet that I'd brought with much difficulty from Ann Arbor and treasured—by me as the one good remnant of my marriage, and by Sorrow as a handy bathroom, which he was getting over, except for that occasional happy drizzle.

As I drove I wished I'd read that child-care book I'd picked up at the library instead of working on the new novel.

At Dolly's house Cate was wringing her hands and in tears

about being too afraid to watch little Baby Jane, who swung in a baby swing at the center of the living room, smiling, and not looking like a thing to be feared at all.

Dolly kept shushing Cate, telling her it was all right, she understood. "No problem." She stuck Jane's feet into a pair of hand-knit bootees and her arms in a hand-knit sweater over pink pajamas with *I love Mommy* on the front, which I had bought as a new-baby present.

"We'll drop her off with Eugenia until Gloria gets back into town," Dolly said.

Cate, in obvious distress, said again, "I just can't do it. The baby's got a problem. That hairline fracture. I'm so afraid . . ." Her dark eyes, lost in a mass of tiny wrinkles, were huge. "Later. Later. When she's better. Then I won't worry . . ."

Dolly grabbed Jane out of her swing to dandle on her hip. I grabbed the car seat on the way out the door, and we were off.

At EATS, Dolly set the car seat, with Jane in it, on top of a counter. Immediately Leetsvillians gathered around her, cooing and laughing and enjoying every smile Jane gave them.

Eugenia hung over the car seat, mugging at Jane, her tower of tight curls nodding overhead like a puff of dangerous meringue.

Lucky kept calling, telling Dolly to get there as soon as possible. They had the place cordoned off, she told me. "Techs on the way. Lot of damage to the front of the car. Whoever did this was lucky they could drive off like that." She gave me an excited look. "I'll bet anything we'll get 'im now."

Eugenia grabbed my arm as I headed toward the door. "Tell Harry I'll do it for eight dollars a head. Okay? You tell him and not a penny less than that. Just got to give me a date and how many."

"You know they're not sending out invitations with RSVPs."

She shrugged. "Then I'll start a sign-up sheet in here. That'll take care of it."

I said I'd pass the word to Harry. "He wants to have it at my house," I added and couldn't help making a face.

Eugenia shrugged. "I don't care where I cook hot dogs. We'll get you chairs and tables from one of the churches. I'll do the rest. Tell 'im potato salad and macaroni salad, cucumbers in sour cream, chips and dip, beans and franks, and two sheet cakes. One chocolate and one white. No drinks. He's got to supply those."

Sounded fine to me.

The drive over to Elk Rapids, almost on Lake Michigan, took half an hour. Dolly spent most of her time on the phone with Lucky, but in between phone calls I told her my good news.

"I got a call from my agent. She sold my book."

Dolly frowned over at me. "Just one book?"

"Sold my manuscript to a publisher."

She thought awhile and then her face broke into the first real smile I'd seen since long before the accident. "Wow! That's great news. You gonna be rich?"

I shook my head. "Just a way to get in. Take a lot more books before I even get noticed. Got to get good reviews. Got to sell 'em."

"You can do it," she said and nodded hard. "I'm really happy for you, Emily."

After a thoughtful few minutes, Dolly said, "You know

what, Emily? Now that I think about it, this lets the Throes boys off the hook. You know, finding the car like this. I was ready to get out there and make 'em open up that garage. I was almost sure it was them, after all. But that pair would never give the car back. Not the Throes boys I know. They don't fool me with that flower patch of theirs. Still planting marijuana out there somewhere."

We drove down the main street of the little resort town. I pulled in and parked in front of a tiny restaurant, between an insurance agency and a gift shop. The stolen car and some of the sidewalk was ringed with yellow police tape. A small crowd of locals and early tourists were gathered behind the tape, watching the techs in white suits and gloves check out the inside and outside of the vehicle. Police cars from four different jurisdictions were parked down the center of the closed-off main street.

Before climbing out of the Jeep, Dolly leaned across to remind me, "You don't put me in any of those books of yours, right? We talked about that already."

I didn't say anything back. I was too happy and pleased that I had a friend who actually got it, how happy I was. I didn't want to mess up the moment with an argument.

Jack, from Jack's Towing, waited on the other side of the street, leaning back on his white truck. He would take the car to Grayling, where the forensic techs would go over it. I joined him to wait for Dolly.

She walked back to where Jack and I stood. She leaned in close. "Just what I said before, the car's in exactly the same place where it was stolen. That driver took a big chance bringing it here. Like I said, we'll be talking to everybody in town. Anybody who was around during the night. Anybody who thinks they saw the damaged car in the area."

Her tone said she was speaking on the record so I grabbed my reporter's notebook from my purse and caught up with her.

"Check out the license plate." She pointed to the back of the car. I made out the first part: seven KXU. "That's the car all right."

"Did they find anything in it?"

"They're still collecting fingerprints. Some blood on one of those broken headlights, like the driver got out and ran a finger over the glass. Dumb. Still, it gives us something."

When I had everything she could give me I pulled out my iPhone and got photos of the front and all the damage: headlights smashed in, grille almost nonexistent, and hood bent at an odd angle. I talked to Lucky and got a little more background: the Elk Rapids police coming on the car at 3:10 a.m. and calling him at home.

"At first none of us believed it was the same vehicle," he said then shook his head. "Who brings a car back where they stole it?"

"I was thinking . . . you know . . . about that 'Thou Shalt Not Steal' note," I said.

He gave me a funny look.

First he leaned back on his heels. Then he gave me another look and nodded. "Could be. This is truly weird, what's going on. Brings back the car—but it's a mess. Is that what this guy sees as returning a borrowed vehicle?"

I shrugged then went to sit in my car and wait, in case I needed to take Dolly back to town. A couple of cops I didn't know walked over and asked what I was doing there, but when

I said "reporter" they seemed satisfied, though I decided to drive on down the street, to the park near the shore of Lake Michigan.

The lake had the kind of calm I wasn't feeling inside me, but welcomed. Bits of sunlight bounced off the edges of soft breaking waves. Nobody was around. I had the lake to myself and toed my sneaker into the sand. I thought about reappearing black cars and babies with injured heads and wondered what rent in the universe occurred that let this insanity rain down.

I took my shoes off and walked into the lake. This early in the year, the water was still cold, my toes wrinkling against it. I bent to stick a finger in the water. More cold. And powerful: all that blue water as far as I could see. This thing with Dolly and Jane made life seem so fragile suddenly, as if I only kidded myself that I had a lot to do with my years on earth and eating yogurt instead of ice cream was going to keep me around forever.

I went back to my car and called Bill Corcoran to bring him up to date on what was happening.

"Give me what you've got, Emily," he said. "I'll fill in the backstory. You have photos for me?"

"I'll send them right over." I hung up, emailed my photos from my iPhone, and drove back toward the site where the police cars stood, though the car was gone, along with the white van. I spotted Dolly talking to an officer I didn't know so I parked and waited, hoping this would be the end of it for her, that whatever evidence the car held would tell who'd hurt her baby or was getting even with her for something.

She opened the door and climbed in as I was about to take a

nap.

"Belongs to a Stephen Wentworth," she said. "Lives over on Elk Lake. Reported stolen Saturday night." She settled her gun off to the side where it wouldn't dig into her hip. She clunked her muddy boots down on my recently cleaned floor mat. "I don't know why in hell me and Lucky didn't get a bulletin before now."

"Fingerprints?" I asked.

She nodded. "Could be anybody's. Won't know until the techs process what they found."

She sat thinking while I waited for more.

"You mind?" she said.

"Mind what?"

"Going over to see this guy? The owner of the car?"

I shrugged. "'Course not."

"How about that 'Thou Shalt Not Steal' thing now?" She made a noise. "What do you think of that? Go figure, eh? A stolen car."

"I think it's nuts," I said without a lot of thought. "Find anything in the vehicle? I mean, anything to tell you who did it?"

"Jellybeans." Disgust dripped with the words.

"Jellybeans! That's all?"

"Three bags. Black jellybeans. Like some little kid was driving."

So, an angry guy popping black jellybeans was out to settle a score with a dedicated cop.

I backed around the last of the police cars, made an illegal U-turn, and took off toward Elk Lake.

THIRTEEN

"Wentworth lives on the lake." Dolly looked over at me. "Told Lucky he went to town to talk to some people at the coffee shop and never thought a thing about leaving the keys in the car. Nobody steals a car in Elk Rapids. Trust me. Nobody locks their houses, let alone their cars. Just not done. Never heard of. Why the heck did this person take that car to come after me, like it was a spur-of-the-moment thing? Something smells bad about all of this."

She settled back and rubbed at her eyes. "You know, Emily, usually we get incidents like a hit-and-run and a neighbor calls before I'm back to the station. Somebody saw something, somebody suspects the kid down the block. But here we've got nothing. Where'd this person come from, anyway? How much do they hate me that they'd steal a car in Elk Rapids to come after me? And why wait until I was out at a cemetery to hit me —when I wasn't even in the car?" She leaned her head against the back of the seat and sighed. "You get it?"

I said nothing.

"Okay, so Lucky called this Mr. Wentworth and told him I'm coming out in an unmarked car—just so he knows I'm official."

"I'd say that uniform . . ."

"Yeah, yeah, yeah. Anyway, we'll talk to him and then I got another idea. Something I've been thinking over."

I turned south and then east, along the lake.

Stephen Wentworth had a very nice house. The two-story log home faced Elk Lake at the end of a long strip of neatly kept lawn with garden beds filled with spring flowers. He came to the door, an affable gray-haired man in his sixties. He pushed the screen door open and invited us in.

"Terrible thing. Never would have expected it to happen in Elk Rapids. All I did was go in for a cup of coffee and to talk a little bit. So many of the folks who winter in Florida are back now. We like to get together, see how the world's been faring. My keys were in the car. Down in Boca I'd never think of being so lax, but Elk Rapids! For God's sakes, what's this world coming to, is what I'd like to know?"

I got introduced and he winced when he heard "reporter."

"I'm helping out in this where I can," I explained, hoping it was enough to let me squeak under his radar.

He nodded.

"So the keys were in the car," Dolly said.

He nodded again.

"And what time of day was this, would you say?"

He thought a minute, pulling his bottom lip in thought. "Must've been about five. I was meeting a friend at six thirty for dinner but I thought I'd go in early. As I said, to sit and talk awhile."

The two of them got the time narrowed down while I looked around, marveling at how the other half lived. Or, in my case, how the other two-thirds lived. Windows sweeping across a wide wall looked out on to manicured grounds and then a swath of blue lake water with painted on waves—all the same height. A long half circle of white sofa stretched in front of the window. Daffodils stood in crystal vases on almost every table in the room. But no Mrs. Wentworth in sight. A beautifully feminine room and Stephen Wentworth was a decidedly not-feminine man. More an auto executive type. The "at ease" clothes he wore probably cost as much as my yearly allowance for jeans and T-shirts, with all my new underwear thrown into the calculation.

"I see you're a big fan of jellybeans," Dolly said, giving a light laugh.

Wentworth looked perplexed. "Jellybeans? Why, no, I don't think I can remember the last time I ate a jellybean."

Dolly kept her eyes on her notebook, writing down every word.

"Then you didn't have bags of black jellybeans in your car?"

"What?"

"We found three bags of black jellybeans in the back of the car."

"Well, there you have it. Kids. I don't care where you live or how careful you are—if wild kids want to cause trouble . . ."

Dolly shook her head. "This wasn't a kid," she said. "We have reason to believe it was someone with a definite purpose in mind for your car. An adult."

"Care to say what that purpose was?"

Dolly shook her head. "Not right now. Our investigation is too preliminary. Nothing's sure at this point. Sorry you got mixed up in any of it. Just the way things are."

We were back at his front door. I complimented him on his yard, thinking I'd hear about his gardening service.

"Gardening's what keeps me sane," Stephen Wentworth said and seemed embarrassed. "Something about digging in the dirt . . ."

"Me, too," I said. "And the flowers. Especially after winter."

He looked at me as if noticing me for the first time. He

nodded. "Life," he repeated. "When I lost my wife . . . this whole place was her doing. I couldn't let it go."

He cleared his throat and held the door wide.

His last question to Dolly was about getting his car back so the insurance adjuster could get a look at it. He said nothing more to me but took my hand and held it a minute, as if dirt and worms and yellow flowers had made us automatic friends.

"Where next?" I backed down the long driveway to the road.

"Lucky said he told you about Ariadne Wilcox?"

"Spider lady."

"Yeah, whatever. I've been thinking and thinking. No way can I say for sure it was a man rammed into my car like that. I couldn't see him. Or no, maybe I saw something but it was just the shape of a person's head behind the wheel. By the time I got from Grace Humbert's tombstone out to the road, the car was squealing away, almost out to 131. So, who says it was a man? Huh? You tell me that."

"I think everybody just assumed . . ."

"See what I mean? Assuming isn't proof of anything. Big car. Powerful engine. Man. Woman. Kid. All they had to do was turn it on and come at me at a pretty fast clip."

"This woman hate you that much?"

"Who knows? Barely said a word at the trial. But she wouldn't testify against her boyfriend. Women like that, just as bad as the guy they let hurt their kid. Maybe worse because they're supposed to take care of their babies."

I thought awhile. "This one kind of makes more sense, when you think about it," I said finally.

"Nothing makes sense, you ask me. Who'd want to hurt

Jane to get even with me?"

"Maybe a woman who lost her babies," I said and took off around the bottom of Torch Lake, through Alden, over to 131, north up to Alba, then east again.

We were heading for a place close to Gaylord, and a conversation with a spider woman who thought mothering stopped at the delivery room door.

FOURTEEN

This part of northwestern Michigan rolled gently and opened wide with fields turning from brown to green. We drove through Mancelona, passing potato farms with rainbows hovering over automated sprinklers rolling and shooting mists of water across acres of growing plants.

I wasn't looking forward to meeting the spider lady and seeing Dolly embroiled in combat with a woman who'd had her babies taken away from her.

Beside me in the Jeep, Dolly was quiet, slouched down so her gun pushed up almost into her lap, hands draped over her knees, face blank, eyes staring out the front windshield.

We turned at Alba, a small, crossroads kind of town, then headed toward Gaylord, down a side road, and another left at a hand-painted sign reading:
PRIVATE
KEEP OUT
The house was small, set in the middle of a white pine forest, as if a Christmas tree farm had gotten away from whoever owned the place. I pulled in a dirt drive that wandered off beyond the house, ending in a sea of rusted-out cars and abandoned engines.

A young woman in jeans and a shirt that stopped just below her sagging boobs was hanging clothes on a line that ran from one corner of the house out to a skeletal tree, big dead limbs threatening to tumble. The woman stopped, hands reaching up to hang a gray undershirt on the line, mouth filled with clothespins, as I parked the car.

"That her?" I asked.

Dolly nodded. "Her all right."

The woman, who couldn't have been more than twenty-three (from the look of her a rough, mean twenty-three years), bent slowly to take up her wash basket and pull a clothespin from her mouth. She crossed her arms, canted her hips to one side, and stood where she was, with no intention of coming to us as we got out and stood, side by side, in her yard.

Dolly slowly pulled a pad of paper and a pen from one of her buttoned-down shirt pockets, buttoned the pocket back up, flipped the pad open, studied an empty page for a long minute, then looked over at me. "Might as well go talk to her," she said, but reluctantly, as if she had misgivings of her own about facing this Ariadne Wilcox again.

We'd only taken one or two steps toward the back when the front door burst open and a man in his late twenties came out, yelling before the door closed behind him.

"What the hell you want?" the man demanded, hands closing over the crooked railing around the tiny porch. "Get the hell away from here. You got no right . . ."

Dolly was taken off guard for only a minute, stepping back, hand going to the snap that held her gun in place. She left her hand where it was and looked up at the angry man with long sideburns, wearing only a sleeveless undershirt and khaki shorts that hung to below his knees. He was barefoot and spitting mad.

"Thought you were still in jail, Jerome," was all Dolly called out, one hand up, shading her eyes from the bright sun.

"Been out three weeks. Don't owe you a damned thing. Don't need to explain nothing. Why don't you get back in that car and leave me and Ari alone?"

"She let you back in the house, eh? After what you did to Carol Anne? Should have been castrated . . ."

Dolly walked toward the man, not away. As she approached him, he grew more anxious, his discomfort turning into rage. The white-knuckled hand released the porch rail and hung in the air. He nervously lifted his left shoulder again and again, then stretched his neck one way and the other, took swipes at his mouth with the back of his hand, but stood where he was, eyeing Dolly as she approached him.

"Mind yer mouth," he said, his voice lowering.

"I'll mind my mouth when you stop hurting babies and stop moving in with dumb women who don't know how to take care of their own little girls."

"You trumped up those charges. I never did nothing . . ."

Ariadne Wilcox approached slowly from around the back of the house. Her almost colorless hair was held back at the front by a plastic headband and at the back by a rubber band pulling her hair into an uncombed tail. She had the face of a poor young woman—no makeup, probably never could afford it, and the pasty look of bad nutrition. Her blue eyes were already lost in wrinkles as she squinted over at us, head skewed to one side. As she watched, I noticed the yellow of a passing black eye along the right side of her face.

"Ari's got no other kids for you to take away," Jerome spit out. "So, what you want this time? Come for me? I kinda thought you was thinking about you and me . . ."

"You let this . . ." Dolly turned to the silent woman and pointed at the man on the porch. "This *thing* back in your house?"

Ariadne said nothing, only stared at Dolly with dead eyes.

"He burned Carol Anne. Put her little hands on top of a stove burner to teach her not to grab food off the table." Dolly was pushing hard.

Ariadne looked at her feet, shuffling one dirty tennis shoe in the dirt. She said nothing.

"Clumsy kid. That's what I told you before. I never touched her," Jerome, leaning back against the screened door, yelled.

"You been out three weeks?" Dolly asked him.

"Yup. But I wasn't out running into that patrol car of yours, if that's what yer asking. I saw the newspapers."

"That is exactly what I'm asking. Found the car you stole. Looks just like something you'd think to do, Jerome. Something truly stupid."

He shrugged. "Think what you wanna think. I don't wanna go back to jail. Not even to teach you a good lesson. Yer not worth it."

Ariadne stepped from the shadow of the house overhang. "I heard you got a baby of yer own, Dolly." There was an attempt at friendliness in her voice. "A girl, right? Just like my Carol Anne. You know where Carol Anne and Susie Q got to? I'd like to see 'em . . ."

Dolly put up a hand, ignoring the woman and tightening her focus on Jerome. "You'd like a big car, wouldn't you, Jerome? Maybe an SUV? Maybe over in Elk Rapids? Be surprised they even let your kind in Elk Rapids. I heard they got some kind of crud detector there at the light on 31."

He curled his lip and smiled. "I had a car like that you think I'd waste it running into any piece of crap you drive?"

"I think you'd be dumb enough to think you were getting

even. Just your kind of thing."

Dolly turned to Ariadne, as if the woman had just entered her radar. "You and that creep up there have anything to do with what happened out at the cemetery in Leetsville? You think jail was bad last time? You wait and see what the courts will do to you for this kind of thing. And not just eighteen months this time. I'll see to that myself. I can come up with a lot of charges . . ."

Ariadne had a hand over her mouth. She shook her head. "I would never hurt . . ."

Dolly said nothing back to her. I'd seen that tight little body before and wouldn't want her coming after me right then. I took a step toward my car and reached out to touch Dolly's arm. She shook me off. She was in killing mode. Her hand was on her gun. He shoulders were up, almost touching her earlobes.

I whispered, "Dolly, let's go."

She stood still a few long seconds then shook herself.

"I hope you two were the ones who ran that car into me," she yelled toward both people. "I can't tell you how much I want to come back here and arrest you and save the pictures the newspaper will run to show to your little girls someday. Show 'em the kind of trash they got away from. You know what I'm going to say to your little girls, Ariadne? I'm gonna say they are two lucky girls, Carol Anne and Susie Q. I'm gonna say this is the woman who pushed you out into the world, but was never your real mother."

Ariadne said nothing. One hand went to her mouth and stayed there.

"I'm gonna tell Carol Anne and Susie Q that real mothers

don't let dumb jerks touch their little girls. And they don't let dumb jerks move back in after they go to jail for touching and hurting their little girl. Real mothers don't leave their kids. A real mother would put a gun to this lowlife's head and blow his brains out before she let him back in her life. So, you see, Ariadne, you got nothing to complain about. You never was a real mother to the girls, and I'm gonna be around to remind them of that. And remind them I was the one who put the two of you in jail for a long time, if it was you who tried to hurt my baby."

Ariadne shifted the laundry basket to her other hip. Her eyes didn't change. Not a muscle moved in her face. It was a face long beyond dead.

We walked to the car, but Dolly kept stopping to turn around and yell at Jerome Ordway, who screamed for us to get off his property.

We got in the Jeep. I turned the car and went out the rutted driveway. In my rearview mirror I saw the two of them standing where they'd been. Neither had moved nor turned to look at each other. Somehow, deep in my brain, I was hoping that just a little bit of what Dolly said was sinking into Ariadne Wilcox's head. Not a spider woman after all, I was thinking, more like a woman caught in somebody else's web. I'd seen these backwoods girls many times. Dropped babies because they had no other way to live. Moved in with any guy who would put a roof over their head. Sad women, growing old and more beaten down by the year until they came into the Save-A-Lot on Fridays when their welfare check came, a line of snot-nosed kids behind them, and filled their basket with on-sale sweet cereals and beer and hot dogs and swatted any kid who dared to ask for one of the cheap toys at checkout.

• • •

On the way back into Leetsville, I asked Dolly what she thought of Jerome Ordway and Ariadne Wilcox as suspects.

She shrugged. "Not her. She's like twice-ground cornmeal. Nothing to her. But him, he hates so many people I bet you I'm not even near the top of the list. We'll see what turns up on the SUV. Jerome's fingerprints anywhere on it and he's a dead man."

"But the 'Thou Shalt Not Steal.' That could fit. I mean, he's the kind of man who'd want to get even for taking his prey away from him."

"Yeah, but he wouldn't know how to write something biblical like that. His note would've been more like 'You piece of. . .' Well . . . I think you get it." She gave me a rueful look, saving my tender ears from the ravishes of a string of curses.

FIFTEEN

Back at EATS, Jane sat happily in her car seat atop a back table where Omar Winston sat, Jane's fingers wrapped around his pudgy pinky.

Dolly's greeting wasn't warm but Omar ignored it and simply said he needed to talk to her in private. Dolly called over to Flora Coy, who came to flutter at Jane with a napkin, then wipe spit from her chin, while Dolly went outside with Omar. I settled in a back booth, away from everyone, and ordered a cheese omelet and toast because I liked eating breakfast whenever I felt like it.

There'd been something about Omar's set face that didn't bode well for Dolly. I was hoping it was a break in the case, though why it should come from a Gaylord officer I couldn't figure. Maybe a suggestion, something Omar thought of that the rest of us hadn't. It was always good to have a fresh eye take a look at facts but I doubted a new idea was going to come at us from Officer Omar Winston.

Dolly came back in alone. No Omar in sight. Without a word she grabbed up Jane's car seat, with Jane in it, turned, and stomped back out the door without a word.

I followed because as far as I knew I was Dolly's only means of transportation. She went to my car and strapped Jane in the back.

"Where to?" was all I asked.

"My house," Dolly mumbled. "Gotta clear my head. I've got to think. That guy is driving me nuts."

I didn't say a word, figuring whatever was going on would

spill out after just a block or two anyway. It didn't take that far. Dolly sputtered, then she swore, then she looked over at me with her teeth clenched.

"You know what he wants? He wants to take Jane home with him. Says his mother can take care of her until this is all cleared up."

I didn't say a word. I thought plenty. Like how that wasn't a bad idea.

"Next thing he'll want to share custody. You watch. That's what's coming. I guarantee it."

"He's her father. He's worried."

She glared at me. "Yeah, well . . . He's not getting his paws on her."

"You might have to think about that someday."

"As if I'm gonna trust him to take her all the way to Gaylord where I can't be with her all the time. No sir."

"But . . ."

"That's enough, Emily. I got other things on my mind right now."

We left it at that. I went into the house with her to go over some items for my next story. She called Lucky, but there was nothing new beyond the jellybeans. Prints on the note turned up nothing. And the blood from that broken headlight wasn't typed yet. No DNA test unless it was deemed necessary for a prosecution. The tests were costly, and took a long time.

Cate was happy enough to take Jane from Dolly's arms and lay her on the sofa to change her diaper, which made me look off into a corner of the room so I didn't have to watch. Something about a diaper full of baby poop made my stomach turn. The one thing I couldn't avoid was the smell. All the baby powder in the world couldn't cover that smell, so I made my way out into the kitchen and sat down at the wooden table Cate had recently painted white, one of her many improvements to this spare and stripped-down house Dolly thought just fine the way it was.

Dolly followed me out to rummage through bottles in the refrigerator door, coming up with a Mountain Dew she offered to share with me. I shook my head, figuring I didn't need any more sugar in my system than I'd already put there with a candy bar I'd found at the bottom of my purse as dessert, after the cheese omelet and whole wheat toast.

Cate brought the sweet-smelling Jane out and pushed her at me. I put up a hand. "Gotta go," I said and started to get up.

"Take her." Cate scowled at me. "I've got something I want to show Dolly. Gotta go get it in my bedroom."

So I took the baby while Cate went back to her room. I got her settled on my lap as she looked at my face, seeming to worry about who I could be and what was expected of her now. I smiled down into that concerned little face and got a deep, Dolly-like frown in return.

Cate was back with something in her hand.

"Just wanted you to see this, Dolly. I've been looking for it. Knew I put it somewhere and this morning I opened up an old book and there it was." She handed a photograph to Dolly, who took it, stared down at it, then looked up expectantly.

"Who's this?"

"That's Audrey. My sweet little doll baby. That was a couple of years before she had you. Thought you'd like to have it."

Dolly held the photo out toward Cate. "No, thanks."

"Now Dolly. That's Jane's grandma. And that's something

you gotta care about."

"I'm not doing this again." Dolly stood, snapped the photo into the air toward her grandmother, and stomped out of the kitchen. "Told you before." Her voice was deep ice. "I don't want anything to do with that woman. Hate her!"

Cate bent slowly to pick up the picture from the floor and look at it again before tucking it into her skirt pocket.

"If only Dolly would listen," she sighed. "Audrey Delores was always such a fragile girl. You know, Emily, everybody's got faults. Why, look at me. What kind of mother must I have been to my own sweet little dolly that she turned away from me so bad?"

I didn't say anything. I held Baby Jane tighter, feeling baby warmth against my arms. It was almost hard to let go when Cate took her but I wanted to be someplace else right then, where people didn't hurt each other, and babies didn't come along to make a sorry life even worse, and "hate" wasn't a word that leapt so easily to mind.

SIXTEEN

I walked up Harry's darkening driveway with picker bushes pulling at my jeans and the sound of baying hounds sending prickles up my spine.

The overgrown drive was a tunnel leading to the crooked house and the crooked doorway, and inside, there sat Delia Swanson at the kitchen table in that small room kept warm year around by the ever-present mystery stew bubbling on the stove. Delia's round pink face and round pink mouth and round blue eyes lit up as she clapped her hands in happiness after I followed Harry in through the house and stood in the doorway, taking in the changes wrought since Harry'd announced their engagement: an African violet in a painted pot at the center of his enameled table, an iridescent blue dish hanging in a metal frame next to the back door, white ruffled curtains at the two narrow windows, and a prettily flowered dish towel hanging over the oven handle.

"We were just talking about you, Emily." Delia rose clumsily from her straight-backed chair. "Weren't we, Harry? Just talking about Emily."

I hurried to hug Delia and stop her from getting up to greet me. I'd seen the look of pain on her aging face when her arthritis was on her and didn't want any more pain today.

"Congratulations," I said, meaning it and feeling the palpable happiness in the little house. "Harry's told me about the wedding . . ."

"Well, yes. I heard you're our wedding planner." She grinned at me. "You don't think June second's too soon, do you? I mean, too soon after Mother passed. Some people said things to me . . ."

"You waited all this time to marry Harry so I think your life's up to you from here on in."

She thought hard, then nodded. "I'm over eighty, you know. Got a few years on Harry here. Who knows how much time the two of us have left? I can't say Mother would be happy for me. She never was. But I can say I respected her wishes as long as she was here. One hundred and one. That's a long life, I'd say. By my calculations, if I live that long, that means me and Harry's still got twenty good years ahead of us."

By my calculations, whatever time they had it would be well deserved. Happiness was what I wished them.

"You got an answer from Eugenia?" Harry asked. "I was at EATS the other day and she just said to talk to you."

"She said eight dollars a head. Oh, and she can't do it on the second. She's got a wedding to go to. She said she can do it on the third, if that's okay."

He thought awhile, looked over to Delia, who only raised her eyebrows at him. He cleared his throat. "That the best she can do? Eight dollars?"

I guessed the date change didn't bother him. "That's hot dogs and rolls, all the condiments . . ."

"Condiments?" His eyebrows shot up.

"Catsup. Mustard. Pickles."

"Chopped onions?" Harry asked, nodding as he spoke.

"I'll ask."

"Any salads?" Delia put in.

"Potato and macaroni salad, cucumbers in sour cream, chips and dip, beans and franks, and two sheet cakes. One chocolate and one white. Things like that. That's what she said. Sounds pretty good to me."

"I'll make a half dozen apple pies," Delia said.

"It's your day," Harry turned to protest. "I don't want you working."

Delia shook her head. "You don't know a thing about women, Harry. Seeing people enjoy my apple pies will be a wonderful thing. No work at all."

"What about dressing for the ceremony? You'll be busy with that."

She made a face at him. "I've been dressing myself for over eighty years. Think I can do it one more time and make pies, too."

Harry looked over at me. "What do you think for drinks? Keg of beer? Too early for cider. How about iced tea? Think that'll do?"

I told him beer and iced tea would be fine.

"No hard liquor," he said. "Delia wouldn't approve . . ." He glanced over to see if he was getting a go-ahead to serve anything stronger than beer.

He wasn't. Delia shook her head. "One keg of beer's all right. Iced tea. Maybe a fruit punch for the children."

"We havin' kids, too?" Harry seemed surprised.

"What's a wedding without children?" Delia said.

"Music?" I pictured all of Leetsville tripping through the tall grasses in front of my house but "in for a penny, in for a pound," as my father used to say.

"Sure. You got a phonograph over there? I'll get some records."

"Don't worry. I'll play music off my phone. I've got a

speaker dock." One of the perks of my divorce.

"What do you mean 'off yer phone'? What's a speaker dock?"

I sighed. "Don't worry. I've got lots of music."

"Country?"

"Sure. Country. Anything you want. Oh, and Eugenia needs a count. The number of guests."

"Tell her to ask around for a number . . ."

"Now, Harry," Delia spoke up. "We can't invite just everybody."

"Why not?"

She couldn't answer and gave in, lifting her hands in the air and then laughing.

"Eugenia said she'd hang a sign-up sheet at EATS. Get some idea of who's coming that way."

"Good thinking," Harry said. He turned to Delia. "So, how about June third, honey? Sound like a good day to tie the knot?"

Delia blushed as she nodded.

I offered to take care of setup and maybe decorate an empty arbor, if somebody had such a thing and could transport it, so they could get married under it. Harry was off to talk to Pastor Runcival and I needed to get back to my house, hoping for a phone call from Jackson. A phone call telling me something important came up, he wasn't coming; or maybe he found solace with a more consoling lady; or his Porsche shot a piston; or he'd just received an invitation to a White House literary dinner.

I'd have settled for anything, then told myself, as I walked back out the driveway, I was being mean and all he wanted was a quiet place to come and rest before going back to the wars he faced daily in his long march toward fame and eternal renown as the writer of all writers of all time. Which wasn't far from my own daydream.

It wasn't until I slipped the key into the lock back at home that I remembered I'd left Sorrow inside the house and I'd been gone all day. He'd finally taught himself to lift his leg, of which I'd been very proud when we were out in the woods, but now I thought about my kitchen table legs or, even worse, the coffee table in the living room, or one of my stools at the counter.

I pushed the door open while telling myself that a little pee on the floor was a small price to pay for a friend without piles of old baggage; a friend who greeted me with face licks, when I let him; and a sorrowful, eye-rolling head in my lap when I was having a good cry over how crappy my life was.

I got a leap and a yip or two but not a drop of pee anywhere. Not a pillow chewed. Not even his water dish stepped in and flipped. Sorrow had become a gentleman. Even he seemed proud of his new status and was careful not to hit me in the chest, or knock me back against the door so that the knob left another dent in my spine.

I fed him and praised him before checking the answering machine. Two calls again. Almost getting to be a habit, this newfound popularity.

"Faith Cardoni here," the woman's soft voice said. "Your editor. I'm so happy to be working with you, Emily. I really like your book and think we will have a fine professional relationship. I've been thinking of the next book in the series. I hope you're considering writing another and maybe another after that. We're all excited about this project. Maybe you could call tomorrow and we'll talk about your wonderful future with Crestleg Publishers."

A *future*. I hadn't dared think of such a thing in the last few years of bare subsistence. *Future*. No, no, no: *Wonderful future. More books. Happy. Excited. A fine professional relationship.*

After another happy dance around the room, I let myself take out my checkbook and figure how I was going to live for the next year or two. With that ten thousand coming in, I was in good shape. Still a little money left from my dad's estate, and a little from the divorce settlement. I had a few hundred a month coming from the newspaper. Maybe I could get some magazine work.

I told myself I was going to make it. Not a lot of space between me and the electric company and the gas company and the telephone company — if only I didn't need a landline, but I did since I had no cell service at my house. And car insurance. There was always food, and clothes, but the Goodwill had better stuff than I could afford in the stores and I could eat as cheaply as any grad student on a ramen noodle budget.

I was going to make it. I could stay in my little cabin, on my little lake, with my big dog, and live the kind of solitary life I'd always dreamed of living.

When the phone rang I wasn't even afraid to answer. I didn't owe anybody anything at that moment so nobody was politely enquiring when I might send in my payment and I wouldn't have to pretend to laugh, and lie that I'd forgotten, and I'd have it in the morning mail.

It was Dolly Wakowski.

"Didn't you get my message? Word's already out. Got a

couple coming into the station about that SUV first thing in the morning. Say they think they might know something but they're coming up from down below and won't be here until ten o'clock. I think you should come on along. Maybe it'll be your next story. Got to keep it going. Oh, and stop and pick me up first. Me and Jane'll be ready about quarter to."

SEVENTEEN

I called Faith Cardoni's number in the morning and got an assistant who said she'd have Ms. Cardoni call me later that afternoon.

Next it was the trip to town, getting held up by two flocks of turkeys rumbling in the middle of the road. Two old hens were having a dispute over something and didn't care if my car was big enough to flatten both of them, or if I was in a hurry, or if I honked until my head blew off. I sat and waited while one turned her back and walked to the side of the road, where her sister hens let her have it, sending her back to take up her quarrel again until I nosed my Jeep toward them, ready to nudge them out of the way if I had to. They gave up and, with more than a few cackles and lots of umbrage, went their separate ways.

I got to Dolly's house just after ten, which she let me know was late. We dropped Jane off at EATS and got right over to the police station, where an older couple sat waiting on the two scarred chairs in Lucky's office.

Well-matched, late sixties, nervous smiles for each other and for us. She had short gray hair neatly cut and styled. He wore a tan cashmere sweater and khakis. You saw their kind a lot around Petoskey and Harbor Springs. Not the ostentatious types dripping with gold necklaces and thick makeup, but more the old money of Petoskey's Bay View. Polite people. Kind people.

People who couldn't turn their backs on something they thought might be wrong.

That's what they were saying to Lucky as Dolly and I walked in and were introduced.

"Probably nothing." The woman, Janice Celrice, smiled a confident smile at us as we stood to one side of the room. "But I read that story about the baby being put in danger and haven't been able to get it out of my mind. Awful."

"My baby," Dolly said.

Tears sprang to Janice Celrice's eyes. "We're so sorry."

Tom Celrice put a hand out, then pulled it back. Embarrassed.

Dolly nodded, thanking them both.

Lucky said, "They've been telling me about a woman they gave a ride to. They met her outside a gas station down in Grand Rapids. She said her car broke down and she had to get up to Elk Rapids. That was Saturday morning. Then they read about the SUV being stolen there that afternoon . . ."

"As I said, probably nothing," Tom said. "Just that we decided we couldn't let it go. Only because it's so unusual for anything like that to happen in Elk Rapids—that's where we have a summer home. We dropped her off right at the middle of town. I offered to take her to her house but she said no, town center was fine. It seemed to both Janice and me that she would have had us drop her off at her home since she didn't have a car and had just taken that long trip. Seemed odd."

"Odd enough to bother us afterward," Janice said and nodded.

"What'd she look like, this woman?" Dolly asked.

The couple exchanged a glance. Janice shrugged. "Sort of, well, very quiet. Hardly said a word the whole way up. I'd say somewhere in her fifties. Not very well dressed. Kind of sad,

I'd guess you could say."

"What made you give her a ride?"

Tom shrugged his shoulders. "She needed help. Very upset about her car breaking down. For a while, at first, I thought she was going to ask for money, but it never came up. It was more . . . well, something else."

"I did ask her what she did—I mean for a living, since I hadn't seen her around Elk Rapids before," Janice said. "You know what a small town it is. She said she sometimes worked at the market there."

"But then she said she was having some kind of family trouble. I took that to mean a husband but she was silent after that," the man added.

"Shame to say, Tom and I did pity her. We just wanted to help. A middle-aged woman, stuck down there in Grand Rapids . . ."

"What was she doing there?" Dolly asked.

"Something about seeing a doctor," Janice said. "She did look as if she could be sick. I wouldn't have offered a ride otherwise. We're probably way off base here. She had faded blond hair. About shoulder-length. She tied it back with a black scarf. Can you think of anything else, Tom?"

He thought awhile. "Had on a kind of shapeless red sweater and black slacks. Think she had a blue or black purse. That right?" He turned to his wife. She nodded.

"And a name?" Dolly pressed. "She give you a name?"

"I never caught it," Janice said. "She mumbled. I didn't like to ask her to repeat it 'cause, to tell the truth, I'm a little hard of hearing."

"And where did you drop her off in Elk Rapids?"

"That's the thing," Tom said. "We dropped her off on the main street, right near where that car was taken. Still" — he gave a small laugh — "I'm sure she wasn't a car thief . . ."

"What makes you think a woman couldn't do that?" Dolly demanded, eyes narrowing.

Lucky stepped in. "What the deputy means," he quickly said, "is that it's not hard to steal a car. The guy left his keys in it, you know."

Tom shook his head. "No, I didn't know. Careless. Still, in Elk Rapids . . . well, you don't expect . . ."

"Was it a woman who hit your car?" Janice turned to Dolly, sympathy in her voice and in her eyes.

Dolly shrugged her shoulders. "I didn't see who it was. Could be either one. I thought a man just because of how violent it was, but that doesn't mean anything."

"I hope she wasn't that person," Janice said. "I don't really think she could have been. More . . . You know, not the violent type. More the type to have violence done to her. I'm really sorry if we helped cause . . . well, I'd hate to think we were instrumental in what happened to you . . . in any way."

Dolly smiled finally. "Nothing's your fault. Like me being out at the cemetery. If I hadn't gone or if I didn't bring my baby with me . . ."

"But she's all right?" Janice asked and Dolly nodded then mumbled thanks, again, for her concern.

Tom stood and helped his wife to her feet.

"If we can do anything . . ." Janice said.

"Don't hesitate to call us. You have our information," Tom added.

They left.

"You think there's anything to it?" Lucky looked to Dolly.

She made a face. "Probably not. Still, I'll go back out to Elk Rapids, see if I can find her."

"You don't have a name," I put in as I made notes on what we'd learned.

"Got a description. Said she worked at the market. Only one out there that I know of. Plenty to go on. You want to come with me?" She was talking to me.

"I've got cleaning . . ."

"Crap. That ex of yours isn't coming up, is he? That's the only time you clean."

"I have other friends."

"Yeah, sure."

Lucky said she could take the patrol car. He planned to stay in the office and get paperwork done.

Dolly turned to face me. "Jackson be gone by Monday?"

I didn't feel I had to answer anything but nodded anyway. "Sunday morning."

"Might need a ride into Traverse Monday morning. Jane's got an appointment with the pediatrician. Just to check her out, make sure everything's still okay."

"Call me," I said, and hurried out before I got the usual lecture on letting an old and dusty ex-husband walk in and out of my life and mess up who I thought I was, and then getting my head all mixed up over whether I should have ever left because the life I led now was a lot harder . . .

And on and on until I'd tell her to mind her own business and storm out, even as I suspected she was telling me a few hard truths, and I'd admit to myself I had no idea why Jackson and I were still so easily connected. Over and over, I'd asked myself, was this the way love went? Or was it just a bad habit neither of us could break?

EIGHTEEN

I spent the rest of the day cleaning. Alone, I never saw the stuff I left laying around, the piles of accumulated laundry on the floor of the washer and dryer closet, the newspapers that grew to teetering stacks. When I looked at my cabin through Jackson's eyes—a very particular man except when it came to bimbos—it looked messy and unloved; the refrigerator was growing odd experiments in little plastic containers; the bed in the spare bedroom was piled with winter clothes; and boxes with unknown content filled what would be Jackson's closet. Laundry had to be done, newspapers put in my car trunk to recycle in Mancelona, and basic things like coffee and milk were needed, which required a trip into Leetsville, to the Save-A-Lot.

When Dolly called late that afternoon, after I made a trip to the market and spent hours scrubbing things, I fell on the couch, rubber gloves on my hands, happy to take her call.

"Can't find that woman anywhere in Elk Rapids. Nobody seems to know her."

"You check the market?"

"Never heard of her."

"You mention the black jellybeans?"

"Huh?"

"The black jellybeans. Seems a cashier would remember selling three bags of black jellybeans. Or maybe a cashier there just loves jellybeans."

There was a pause. "Didn't think about that."

"Can you go back?"

I could almost hear her nodding at the other end of the phone.

"Darn it," she said, upset with herself. "Should have thought of those jellybeans. Could be a gas station or a convenience store. I'll get to all of them."

"Bags of black jellybeans? I doubt it. I don't remember ever seeing just black jellybeans. Seems like it would be a special place. Almost like a candy store."

"Then I'm going back to the market. I'll talk to every one of those cashiers." There was a pause. "Anything else I missed?"

I thought a minute.

"Be honest, Emily. You think I'm too close to this to do a good job?"

"Because of the jellybeans?"

"Yeah."

"You would have thought about it sooner or later. It's just that so much is happening so fast."

Again there was a pause. "I'm glad you're working with me," she said, the nicest, most accepting thing she'd ever said to me. I figured I had Baby Jane to thank for this softer Dolly.

"You know what?" I said after my surprised silence. "I am, too."

"I'll let you know what I find. You got enough to do another story?"

I said I had and hung up, then pulled off my gloves and wrote the new story, focusing on the stolen car. I called Bill and told him I was emailing a follow-up and he told me again to stay with it.

It was good to talk to him, a pragmatic, kind editor who always seemed to wish me well. I told him about the sale of my novel. He congratulated me and said when I next came to Traverse City he wanted to take me out for a drink at Red Ginger. At that—what sounded like it could be a real date—I giggled like a sixteen-year-old and gushed that I'd certainly take him up on it.

His voice went just a little lower, down into what I thought might be the "I'm really interested in getting to know you better" register, when he said, "I mean it, Emily," and I hung up, happier than I had any right to be.

When the house was clean and I was thinking about making a mushroom pasta for dinner, the phone rang again and a languid female voice said, "Emily Kincaid?"

My new editor. Faith Cardoni. So happy to finally talk to me. She was going over the book at that moment and would get notes to me as soon as possible. "Nothing big, you understand," she said and gave me one of those light, trembling laughs. "Just a few minor suggestions."

And then she went on, asking about another book with my same women. "They are so very, very droll, Emily. I'm sure women around the globe will simply fall in love with them."

To which I outlined, as best I could, the book I'd just begun—the human skull found at the edge of a shrinking lake—and promised to get her chapters as soon as I had anything.

And that was that. I had joined the inner fold of writers—one with an agent and an editor and wide possibilities ahead of me.

I got out a large pot for the pasta water and banged it happily on the stovetop, making Sorrow leap up and bark before settling back into a deep, paw-peddling sleep.

I chopped mushrooms, unscrewed a jar of spaghetti sauce,

and poured it into another pan, then diced up some garlic and some onions and cooked them in olive oil until they were soft. I finished the dish as I merrily skipped around my kitchen, setting the table with two place mats and my two best dishes. I dug out knives and forks and spoons, which didn't match but had to do, I told myself, with my "eclectic" decorating skills.

The table looked nice. Yellow daffodils from the garden stood in a green glass pot at the center. My yellow tablecloth was short at one end but the yellows and greens were pretty and my two blue dishes clashed enough to make the table interesting, and, anyway, that's all I had so who cared?

The whole cooking experience was one of the happiest I remembered and I knew the pasta would be perfect, my salad a miracle, and my dessert, of dollar-fifty sponge cake and the first fresh strawberries of the season, a sight to behold.

Except that Jackson was late and the pasta was gummy. The mushrooms shrunk down to nothing.

He drove down my drive in a swirl of dust and gravel, pulling his Porsche to a stop beside my arbor already covered with green leaves and leaping out to wave at me as I stood on my side porch, holding Sorrow back while trying not to frown at the thought of my shriveling pasta. I wanted to remain upbeat, happy to see him . . . *and aren't we off to a wonderful start of a marvelous weekend . . .*

We hugged. He was his usual delicious self in open-necked sport shirt and beautifully ironed pants. He gave me a peck on the cheek and I pulled away only slightly because I knew that snare too well. Jackson was a charmer — maybe a little too much like a snake charmer: beguiling with words and smiles and eyes that crinkled when he leaned close. A tall man, Jackson had a languid way about him that tall men effect: ambling walk, loose-jointed arms and legs, long hands reaching out easily to cup my chin and stare deeply into my eyes.

"Ah," he said. "You look happy. Exactly what I need right now, after that devastating review."

He brought his leather bag into the house and set it on the neatly made bed in the spare room. He hung enough pants and shirts for at least a week in the closet then set toiletries on top of the small dresser.

He was back outside, pulling a flat of purple and yellow pansies from his trunk, where he'd spread sheets of plastic to protect the carpeting. He set the pansies on the brick walk in the garden then was back to his car for a bag of groceries. He unloaded white wine and containers of food into my nicely emptied and cleaned refrigerator.

All that activity made me tired so I produced a bottle of Pinot Noir (one of his favorite wines, along with Moet & Chandon—which I couldn't afford), then hurried to serve the pasta and salad, but he said not to worry about dinner because he'd stopped in West Branch to eat.

I served myself and murmured what good food he was missing as he leaned back in his chair and patted his stomach. "Got to watch the waistline." The smirk that followed suggested maybe I should think about doing the same.

I ate and put the rest of my dinner away. We settled on the living room sofa to catch up with each other's lives, except I had that one thing on my mind: my good news, and it was eating at me.

Jackson had one thing eating at him, too, so we talked about the bad review the *New York Times* gave him. I read it three times before he would discuss it or let me be consoling.

"Would you call that a fair assessment of my work?" he demanded when I set the article down on the coffee table. "You, of all people, know my book inside out."

Of course I said "No," emphatically. Though I'd typed the entire book at least twice, I'd forgotten it as soon as it popped out of my printer so my "No" was made louder due to guilt.

I said "No" again and meant it because this was a different Jackson, a chastened man, and I wasn't taking any pleasure in seeing him diminished in his own eyes.

"I knew you would understand the unfairness of this. I can only surmise that it's jealousy. The man thinks he is the greatest Chaucer scholar in the world and is afraid of having to share that distinction. Do you think a letter of rebuttal to the *Times* is in order?"

His good-looking face wrinkled with the question. His dark eyes were intent, staring into mine. I knew he didn't really want an answer, only a nod, but I couldn't do that to him.

"I don't think so. Writers make fools of themselves when they charge back at a reviewer. Remember Joyce Carol Oates's unfortunate replies to bad reviews in the *Times*?"

"Ah, but wasn't she right? That woman never gave Oates a single good review. She should never have been handed another of her books. I think I'm facing exactly what Oates faced."

"But no one wins, Jackson. You could jeopardize future reviews."

"Future reviews!" he huffed at me. "If this—my book to end all books—is relegated to the trash heap, how can I ever write another?"

One of those unanswerable questions.

"Do what you feel you have to do," I said and poured myself more wine. It was going to be a long weekend. I'd spent time with academic egos in the past. The narrowness of that kind of conversation would make the hours stretch into weeks.

Jackson set his glass down carefully, looking for a napkin to put it on rather than chance a moisture ring on my table of patterned moisture rings. He sat back, keeping the glass in his hand. He sighed. "I suppose you're right. What good would it do me? My editor said we'd get around it by a few well-placed ads in journals. I suppose I'll have to settle for that. But, oh, Emily, how I hope that someday I'll be given a book by that man to review."

I smiled at him. "I know you, you'd be honest."

Jackson frowned. "No, I wouldn't. That's the nature of the game—we tear down others to build our own reputation. You play the game to win or sit on the sidelines."

Ah, I told myself, now we were into sports metaphors. He'd be okay, having given himself a sense of grievance repaid. I threw one of my favorite female ploys into the pause in our conversation, asking if he might be tired, could I get him anything, and telling him where his one towel and washcloth hung in the bathroom.

He didn't take the hint. Too revved up for sleep. I was in for a long night. I figured, since I had my good news to deliver, I might as well skew the conversation my way, which would probably drive him to bed anyway.

I settled back on the sofa, downed the last of the Pinot, and took a deep breath.

My brief silence gave Jack time to make his next move. He

leaned over, leaning in to kiss me. I almost let him because my skin was aching to be touched and my brain was telling me that it was okay, that nobody but me cared what I did anymore. But I pushed him away, picked up our glasses, rinsed them in the sink, and set them upside down to dry on a towel. I didn't tell him my good news. It seemed somehow smaller than I'd thought it was. Quickly, I wished him a good night and went to my room, closing the door behind me and climbing into my own, lonely bed.

Well, lonely except for Sorrow.

NINETEEN

I took my child-care book down to the lake while Jackson slept in the next morning. Most of what I read wasn't aimed at me—the know-nothing caretaker—but more for anxious mothers. All I needed to know was how to feed and burp the kid and when to recognize that something was really wrong or if she was just being a pain.

It didn't take long to get bored and set the book facedown on the folding chair beside me.

A beautiful May morning. The kind of morning I dream about all year but couldn't slow up and hold on to, no matter how I tried.

The loons were out there. Nineteen of them. I counted once and then again. Nineteen. Nine pairs and one extra. I couldn't tell which was the odd man or woman out, but it was obvious one had lost her mate over the winter. Usually it was a lucky year when if I got a couple pairs. This was a bounty of loons, though I doubted they would stay. If it got hot they'd head further north, up into Canada and the lakes back in the bush. If not, I won all the way around: it didn't get hot, the loons stayed and raised their babies here, and I'd hear their haunting calls all summer.

Morning on the lake was a sleepy and quiet time. The beaver didn't stir. The birds swam noiselessly, diving to come up far out in the water.

I picked up the book again, since I might be called upon to know this stuff, and read about a child's expected development. So many ways to judge a baby's progress.

I was into "Neurological Development" when I heard steps on the dock behind me.

"Didn't mean to sleep so late," Jackson said and straightened his open-neck shirt. He was dressed neatly, well pressed, a bright white, cashmere sweater tied around his neck. "How about I take you out for breakfast?"

As the alternative to cooking eggs and ham and stuff, I agreed it might be fun. I picked up my book, followed him back through my rushes and blueberry bushes, changed into a cleaner T-shirt, and we were off.

The rest of Saturday was actually fun. After breakfast at the Manistee Lake Inn, where I got the best omelet I could ever remember, we drove to Traverse City. We walked Front Street, stopping to see my friend Peter at Brilliant Books, then down to Horizon Books to visit Amy and check out the new Patricia Cornwell. Then it was to the Brew, for a latte. Fustini's for local oils and vinegars. Murdick's for fudge. We checked out the Opera House for upcoming writers in Doug Stanton's National Writers Series.

I had hours of fun. Jackson spent his money — his credit card flashing at every store. I carried packages, deciding which I was going to lay claim to when we got back to my house, then deciding I wanted everything, for which I was already practicing arguments in my mind about how I couldn't part with even one of the books, nor one oil, not even the so very special box of fudge.

After the latte and a scone we drove along Lake Michigan, up to Charlevoix, stopping to walk along the beach. I was blissfully happy. The hordes of tourists weren't due to arrive until Memorial Day. We had the beaches and the stores almost to ourselves.

It was late when we got back. Jackson offered to cook dinner. A couple of manly steaks with a tomato and fresh mozzarella and basil salad.

The day had been a day out of time. Maybe a day set aside from our own history. We'd been at ease—no tense moments when Jackson let something awful slip. No phone calls from Dolly, though I couldn't help thinking about babies and wrecked SUVs.

I pushed all of that to the back of my mind and told Jackson what a nice time I was having.

We spent the late evening with a bottle of Chateauneuf du Pape Clos St. Jean, 2009, which Jackson found at the Blue Goat in Traverse for an amazing forty dollars, outstripping my screw-top Pinot by a few thousand miles. Later, we went to sleep—separately, because I passed out in my lounge chair on the deck from too much food and too much expensive wine and he left me there.

Early Sunday morning as Jackson prepared to leave, bringing his suitcase to the door, I poured us a last cup of coffee.

He stood at the kitchen counter, mellowed, I thought. Maybe ready to go back to town and get over the tongue-lashing that critic had given him.

I lifted my cup to him. He saluted me in return.

"I have something more to tell you," I said hesitantly, knowing I wasn't going to let him go without my news. Not and keep my self-respect.

He smiled slowly. "I thought there was something," he said and then, out of character for Jackson, he moved over to put his arm around me, hugging tightly.

When he pulled back, he looked down into my eyes. "I want to support you in this," he said.

"Well . . . Really?"

"I'm not a bastard," he said. "Just not an easily married man."

"And?" I looked up at him. "What does that mean?"

"That means I can understand when a woman . . . well . . . things happen."

"This didn't just happen."

"Oh, don't get me wrong. I understand perfectly. I hope you'll be happy and whoever the father is will be the right person . . ."

"Father?" I asked. "Father of what?"

"Your child, Emily."

"What child?"

He pointed to my child-care book on the coffee table.

"You think I'm pregnant?" I didn't laugh. Odd, it was almost as if my real news would be a disappointment after this.

"You said you had something to tell me. I assumed, by your reading material, it was a pregnancy. Your age and all. That ticking clock."

I put my hands up between us. "No. No child, Jackson."

"Then? What's the news? Couldn't be half as astounding as what I was thinking." He laughed, stood back, and gave me one of his superior smiles.

"My agent called. My book sold. It'll be out next summer. My agent is very excited about its prospects. She says it should do well. Then the editor called and is asking for more books. A series."

For maybe the first time in my life I saw the real Jackson Rinaldi—a series of odd expressions crossing his face, smug to sorry to sentimental to falsely happy and all the way back through, ending in a confused frown and a shake of his head.

"You don't say. Well, how nice for you. Hope you got a good advance. You know these publishers don't put advertising dollars into a book they aren't heavily invested in already."

I smiled my own happy smile. "A very good advance," I lied.

At this, his face paled beneath his tan. "Then," he said, still thinking hard for a way to mitigate my news. "I suppose congratulations are in order. That's very good news."

I told him who the publisher was, which caused more consternation.

He shook his head a few times. "They aren't exactly known for fostering best sellers. You really shouldn't expect too much, especially from popular fiction. So much of it out there, don't you think? I mean with this populist Internet publishing going on. But still, I'm happy for you. I hope I'm not in it. The novel, I mean." Here he gave a short, nervous laugh. "No male characters based on me, I trust."

I assured him he wasn't in the book though I was, of course, lying and should have simply told him he was a part of my life and my life was mine, every bit of it, and that a writer only had her life to use for material. But I didn't.

"And," he said, leaning back to give me a royal sniff, which usually predicted good news. "I'm a bit of a fraud here. I said I wanted to see you because of that singularly unfair review. And you've helped me so much, as usual, Emily. But I, too, have news. At least a mitigation of that awful man's opinion."

With my shoulders back and a phony smile stuck in place I waited for Jackson's "news."

"As it turns out, Emily, I'm not a completely lost cause. Though you may deny it, I know your hopes for my Chaucer work were always high. My editor, too, stands behind my scholarship and has asked me to take on a new project. Now, this is a secret. A very deep secret at the moment. Word, down through the ages, has it that Geoffrey Chaucer was murdered on the order of Henry IV. Can you imagine a book investigating such allegations? There's one out, but I'm hoping now to add my expertise to what has always been mere gossip. I'll be going to London soon. Me, a veritable Sherlock Holmes." He threw back his head and laughed. "Perhaps a Meerschaum pipe will be in order."

With that he was out the door and to his car, all the packages from our shopping trip firmly in hand—except the fudge. He offered that as congratulations on my good news then left with a wave of his hand. All the books I'd coveted, and all the local oils went with him

My grudging mumbling followed him up the hill and lasted long after the sound of his car faded.

TWENTY

I called Dolly.

"He's gone?" she demanded, then made a clucking sound deep in her throat.

I assured her he was and hurried on to news, any news, she had for me.

"Blood type from the broken glass is O negative. Kind of rare, I guess, but same as mine."

"Mine, too. Not too rare."

"DNA won't be done unless we get us a suspect. Oh, and the tread on the SUV matched the casts from the cemetery — not that I had any doubt."

"So? What's next?"

"You taking me and Jane tomorrow?"

"Where?"

"You forgot already." Disgust lay between us. "Must've been some weekend. Remember, I asked you to take us into Traverse? Jane's got an appointment with her pediatrician. Just a checkup. See how she's doing."

"Sure, I remember," I lied — yet one more time. "When you want me to pick you up?"

She said by ten.

"I think I'm going to stop by the cemetery first." The thought had just hit me.

"What for?"

"Take a look at that gate. Maybe figure the angle the car was coming from. You ask people along that road if they saw anything?"

"First thing Lucky did. He got nothing. Oh, and Emily, say hi to Grace for me, will you? I've just got this feeling the woman's looking down and trying to send me some kind of message."

"Sure, Dolly," I said. "I'll do that. If she throws me a thunderbolt or two, I'll pass it on."

I spent the rest of Sunday cleaning again, kind of like "washing that man right out of my hair," though I had no bitter feelings toward Jackson this time. It was as if we were equal. He had no pedestal to look down from and had been almost gentle when he left. Except for his penurious squirreling away of all the items I'd coveted, which I considered a hostile act on his part since I'd been the one to pick them out.

By late afternoon I got over my huff at losing books I really wanted to read and took Sorrow for a long walk, then came back to the house to warm leftovers and take them down to the lake, where I chewed and yawned and laughed at the angry beaver and was surprised by one of the usually leery loons swimming up to the dock to get a good look at me.

Sorrow and I were exhausted and in bed by ten o'clock.

• • •

Monday morning I went to the Leetsville Cemetery first though I had no idea why I was drawn there. A quiet, old-fashioned place. One of so many small cemeteries found along our country roads. The crooked gate had been only partially straightened and supported, hanging at an odd angle off to the side from where it once stood. I photographed the gate again and photographed the deep tire gouges in the grass. Nothing else to see.

Except Grace.

I found her grave easily and felt a kind of tug at the name and plain little tombstone. So like Dolly to have replaced a woman she hated with a bearded circus lady few people remembered. The grave was weedy and unattended except for some dead daisies strewn through the grass. Something brought the words "Thou Shalt Not Steal" to mind.

Maybe Dolly'd stolen somebody's reputation.

What do you think, Grace? I bent over the depressed grave.

Maybe Dolly busted some pillar of the community for selling porn out the back door of their candy shop.

Or maybe she stole somebody's Publishers Clearing House entry.

Or beat somebody out to be next in line at the Save-A-Lot.

I got nothing back from Grace.

Who knew what people valued enough to seek revenge? I thought. And that's what this was shaping up to be: somebody mad about something. Somebody spending the long winter months simmering over an imagined slight or a score to settle.

Or maybe it had nothing to do with Dolly after all and that had been only a blown-around note at the towing service. Two and two didn't always make four, at least in this new world where I lived.

Yes, they do, I scolded myself and frowned down at Grace. Immutable addition. Two and two always made four and that's what we had: a car deliberately coming after Dolly, a warning note, a lady from Grand Rapids — or was she a red herring? Still there was that car parked back exactly where it had been parked.

And black jellybeans, I reminded myself.

I looked down at Grace's weedy grave. Something about standing there, being with the woman who'd withstood stares and laughs and made herself into a circus star, cleared my mind. Maybe that was the power Dolly'd found here, talking to Grace Humbert. An ability to see clearly.

I gave up thinking inane thoughts, said good-bye to Grace, and went to EATS for breakfast, where I avoided Eugenia and Gloria for as long as I could and ordered French toast with thimbleberry syrup and sat alone, enjoying every minute of the feast I shouldn't have ordered. Not after putting away half of Jackson's fudge the night before.

Eugenia slid in across from me. At first it was all about Dolly and Jane and what was going on with them.

"I'm getting back into doing genealogies for people. Thinking of giving Harry a family tree for a wedding present."

I said that was a creative gift and asked Gloria for another pot of tea water when she came by, pad and pencil in her hand.

"Lots of old families up here, you know," Gloria said, hair bouncing so she pushed at it to keep locks from falling into her eyes. She nodded in Eugenia's direction. "Bet you Harry goes right back to the *Mayflower* or something. Hope I can come up with a gift like that."

I agreed, that would be some wedding gift. A stellar family tree to hang on the wall of his odd little house. Then I was struck with the idea of coming up with a gift of my own for the happy couple. If Eugenia wasn't going to bake the cakes, maybe that could be my gift. Except that I'd never made a cake in my life and was afraid to try such a feat for such a momentous occasion. Maybe my garden would be far enough along and I could do all the flowers for the wedding. My climbing roses should be out, which led me to think: "Gather ye rose-buds while ye may, old Time is still a-flying. And this same flower that smiles today, tomorrow will be dying."

On that happy note Gloria was back with my hot tea.

Eugenia lifted an eyebrow at me. "So funny, about Cate. I mean, all Dolly's got . . . well, beside Baby Jane. And won't lift a hand to help. After all, Dolly gave her a home. You'd think . . . Well, just can't figure her."

I shook my head and sipped my tea.

"We've been talking about it, in here." she nodded toward Gloria and some others. "Gloria thinks it's some kind of phobia. Can't take care of a sick person, something like that. She said she had an aunt had that problem, didn't you, Gloria? It doesn't seem quite right, you know. Baby Jane here so much of the time. Germs in a place like this. Babies need to be where it's quiet, not so stirred up. We're glad to do it. Don't get me wrong. Just that . . ." She sighed. "I liked Cate before this. Maybe a little funny — the way she dressed — but still we were all happy when I traced her and had her come to Leetsville as a surprise for Dolly. No knowing, is there? I mean, you think you're doing good and look at now. She's living off Dolly and refuses do to a simple thing like watch poor little Jane."

Gloria added a few tongue clucks from where she scrubbed a table down behind us. "You never know about people, do you, Emily?"

I agreed, getting ready to leave. "You just never know."

I got out of EATS and was over to Dolly's house at twenty to ten.

Jane was in her swing when I walked in, dressed in a pretty

pink dress with matching bonnet. Dolly had her quirks, dressing Jane in little cop uniforms, but today Jane was pure little girl.

Her face lit up when she saw me, which was good for my ego. I knelt down in front of the swing then picked her up when she stretched her arms out and gurgled at me.

"I didn't hear you come in." Cate stood in the kitchen doorway wiping her hands on a dish towel. There was no smile. Her frown was dark. I figured maybe she was feeling guilty for letting Dolly down the way she was. Usually the two of them would take Jane to the doctor. But whatever it was bothering Cate, she was sticking to her hands-off policy.

"How are you doing, Cate?" I held Jane, who smelled of baby lotion and a yard-dried dress, though when she saw Cate she put her arms out to her.

Cate shook her head slightly at the baby. Jane snapped back to me, examining my face intently, ending with my eyes, which she reached out to poke except I was too fast for her, having been poked before.

"I'm fine, thank you, Emily." Her voice was chilly.

I looked at the woman, dressed in a long flowered skirt and green peasant blouse, and tried to say nothing.

"I suppose you're as mad at me as the rest of 'em."

There was nothing to say to that. Mad wasn't the word I'd have chosen. More confused. More wondering at her motive—almost punishing Dolly for Baby Jane's accident.

"I don't blame Dolly for being upset with you, Cate. Nobody gets it, the way you're acting. You're Dolly's only family, except for Jane."

"Guess it's everything coming at me all at once. And the

way Dolly talks about my Audrey Delores. She's her mother, Emily. Audrey deserves to know she's got a granddaughter. I mean, everybody should get a second chance. Who knows but this would be the best news for her? Might even straighten her out. Be the happiest day of my life, I tell you. If Audrey came here for a visit. It's been such a long time."

"You said you didn't even know she was pregnant. Not until it was too late."

Cate's wrinkled face colored up. "Just between us, that wasn't strictly the truth. I knew she was pregnant. Then she just disappeared. Wasn't until later, when it was too late, that I learned about Dolly. Maybe I could've tried harder to get Dolly back. I don't know. With Audrey . . . er . . . gone, the way she was. And me not in the best financial situation. Sometimes life is just what it is. But look, I got a second chance, here with Dolly. What about a second chance for Audrey?"

I couldn't think of much to say to that. This world of women who were mothers and daughters and granddaughters was way beyond me. Thinking back to Grace Humbert's clarity, I told myself that "A spade was a spade," "What was done was done," "You can't go home again," "As ye sow so shall ye reap," "The sins of the father" . . . and on and on, bouncing clichés through my head until I felt better.

Dolly, fresh from a shower, hair wet and slicked back, came into the living room dressed in a short-sleeved uniform shirt and lightweight pants; same shoes she wore all year long: shining black brogues. She pinned her badge to her chest, grabbed her hat and a diaper bag, and we were off for Traverse City with Jane tucked into her seat in the back of the Jeep.

We didn't talk much. Dolly was deep in thought. From time

to time she unbuttoned her shirt pocket and took a small notebook out to jot down a note or two.

As we passed the Indian casino on M72, she asked me how my weekend had gone.

"Not bad. I told him about selling a book."

"He happy for you?"

I said, "Yes."

She snorted. "I'll bet."

"He was very supportive."

"Yeah." She turned to look out the side window at the shore of Lake Michigan as we drove through Acme. She made a comment on how low the water was.

"You sleep with him?" she asked after a while.

"That's none of your business."

"Oh, really? Guess that means you were as dumb as you always are."

I burned for a few minutes before telling her it was a good thing Jane was with us or I'd pull over and put her out at the Speedway station.

"Yeah, sure you would."

At that silly impasse we started laughing and laughed all the way to the other side of town to the doctor's office.

We got taken in right on time and Jane enjoyed the attention of a stethoscope to her heart and fingers feeling gently over her head as the young doctor asked questions about her appetite, sleep, and general mood.

With everything checking out fine, we had Jane dressed and out of there in twenty minutes. We stopped at the newspaper to show Bill the baby, since we were in town. Being the kind of man who was always a little rumpled, like an old-fashioned editor, Bill's office wasn't the tidiest but he pushed files from a couple of chairs and asked us to sit.

Dolly wanted to call Cate to tell her everything was fine with Baby Jane. She stepped into the hall but was back in under a minute.

"She's not home," Dolly said, sticking her cell into her pants pocket. "Probably went to EATS."

"Wanted to talk to you, Bill." Dolly leaned forward now.

"I've got a little money put by," she said, sitting on the edge of her chair, Jane bouncing on her lap. "You think maybe some kind of reward would help here?"

Bill pushed his glasses up his nose and thought awhile. "Couldn't hurt, Dolly. But what kind of information are you looking for? You've got the car. From what Emily says you've got fingerprints, blood. You asking the public for names? That it?"

"Yeah, sure. Names. Proof. An eyewitness. It's this whole thing. Like something poisoning my life. My grandmother's all upset; probably just thinking about what happened to Jane. She really loves her, I know that much. And I can't sleep for wondering if it was me, directly, he was after, or some kind of mistake. Whatever it was, I need to know."

"I'd say better not have it come directly from your department. More an anonymous donor, seeking justice for the baby. Something like that. Or"—he looked over at me—"you could say you're putting up the money, Emily."

"Me! You're kidding, right? My creditors see I've got a couple thousand dollars and I'd have everybody after me."

"A couple thousand!" Dolly leaned back and shook her head. "I was thinking a hundred or two. I don't have a couple of thousand to throw away. Got doctor bills from having Jane. Still paying. No health insurance. Now I got the three of us to see to."

She shook her head again.

Bill had a hard time keeping his face straight. "Why don't we just say 'reward'? Say it's for information leading to the arrest of the person who stole the SUV in Elk Rapids."

Dolly agreed that would work and Bill shifted back to me. "You're getting a story turned in this afternoon, right? Put the reward info in."

I agreed and we were out of there, off to stop at Wal-Mart's for diapers and formula and a couple of Onesies, then back on the road to Leetsville without Dolly mentioning lunch at McDonald's or any other stops. I was left with the rest of the day to myself and thought I'd go home, make a sandwich and a cup of tea, and take myself out to my studio and that new book I was outlining for my agent to look at before sending it on to Faith Cardoni.

Back at her house, I helped Dolly get the car seat and diaper bag out of the car, along with the Wal-Mart bags, while she carried Baby Jane.

"Cate, we're back," Dolly called as she stowed the bags on the sofa and laid Jane down to change her.

"Cate?" she called again when the diaper was changed. She held Jane, wobbly as a scarecrow, in her lap and mugged at her.

Nothing. Not a sound in the house.

"Guess she's not home." Dolly held Jane out to me and went to check the kitchen and then around to Cate's room before coming back to where I sat dandling Jane in my lap. "Not here," she said. "You might as well go on home."

"Want a ride to the station?" I offered, knowing she'd be antsy about getting in to work.

"I'll call Lucky. He'll come get me. Probably's got a car waiting for me by now."

"You taking Jane along?"

She said nothing though her face crinkled. "Guess I have to. I'm looking into a regular sitter. A couple of girls in town called me last night, offered to sit and not charge an arm and a leg."

"Sometime you've got to have a long talk with Cate. I can kind of see her point. But it sounds to me like she heard from Audrey and she's using Jane to maybe get you to change toward your mother."

Dolly took the formula into the kitchen and I heard a cupboard door slam. She came back for the diapers and headed back to Jane's room while I hung out with Jane.

Sometimes you can sense something in the air before it happens. This was one of those times. Like a missed heartbeat. Maybe it was a footstep that didn't happen. Maybe an intake of air that changed everything.

I knew before Dolly screamed.

I was up and running down the hall.

She was in Jane's nursery. I took everything in at once. I understood nothing. Dolly knelt in the middle of the ruined room with her hands clutched at her cheeks. She was down on one knee beside Cate, who lay on the bare floor in a pool of blood.

In what had been a pink and white room with white curtains and framed photos of puppies and kittens on the walls, Dolly bent over Cate Thomas, feeling for a pulse at the back of her neck, holding her breath, then looking up at me.

Terrible, terrible, was all I could think as I touched Dolly's back, my other hand on the cell phone in my pocket. What we needed, I told myself through my shock, was an ambulance. EMTs saved lots of people with their defibrillators. They knew how to get a heart started again — if that's what this was.

Dolly pulled carefully at her grandmother's shoulder, rolling her toward us. The woman, so obviously dead, came over slowly. Her eyes were open, face almost serene, but blood pooled under her chest, and neck, and soaked the floorboards beneath her.

I held my breath and turned away. The room had been destroyed. Clothes were thrown everywhere. The crib was torn apart, pieces of it laying in corners. The mattress had been gutted as if stabbed again and again. The changing table was overturned and broken. Someone had smashed the legs into crumpled sticks.

This isn't real, was all I could think. Nothing could look this terrible — ruined pink and white and ruffles and teddy bears and . . .

On the wall between the front windows someone had scrawled a message. Hard to read words done in what looked like red crayon. Bloody words.

"Thou Shalt Not Steal."

TWENTY-ONE

Everything, after those long, agonizing minutes we waited for Lucky to get there, was a whirl. Jane cried out in the living room. Dolly knelt beside Cate's body. I knelt beside her, my hand on her shoulder until she shrugged me away as if her pain was too personal. I left her alone and went to the front room to get Baby Jane and bounce her until she stopped crying, then stepped out to the porch to listen for Lucky's approaching siren, alerting Leetsville that there'd been another tragedy.

When Lucky pulled up and jumped out of the patrol car, I led him into the house without a word, then set a strangely quiet Baby Jane in her swing. I took him back to the nursery.

Lucky looked to where Dolly knelt beside the dead woman and then to me.

"Can you get her out of here?" he asked brusquely. "I've got officers coming, and techs. I called an ambulance but . . ." Here he shrugged toward where Cate lay. "I can see it won't do any good." He leaned in close and tapped his friend's bent shoulder. "Dolly, I need you to leave now. I'm . . . this looks really bad. Why don't you go outside and let me get to work? That okay?"

Dolly, head down, stayed where she was on her knees beside Cate. But it was only a few minutes before she nodded, grabbed Lucky's offered hand, and got slowly to her feet.

She took a last look at where Cate lay, her long gray hair tainted with blood, eyes wide but empty, before she turned and left the room.

Lucky, after bending over Cate, making a cursory

139

inspection, looked back at me. "Seems pretty clear, doesn't it?" His dark eyes were angry. "This was about Cate to begin with. Something followed her up here. That'd be my first guess. Nothing to do with Dolly or Baby Jane which, in a way, is a comfort. Hope Dolly will focus on that when she can think straight."

I nodded, but thought Grace Humbert thoughts again. *Clarity. Clarity.* "Or this could be another terrible way to get even with Dolly," I said, putting things together in my head and coming up with a straight path, no forks to mislead us.

The house filled with techs in their white suits and white booties, like a group of fairies from *Peter Pan*. The horror of murder was set aside in favor of order and jobs to be done. I stayed on the front porch at first, taking care of Jane when she needed a bottle or a clean diaper. A surprisingly easy job.

Dolly was the hard part—her face so set, her eyes filled with something like death, or maybe the promise of death to someone, whoever did this to Cate. She didn't talk. She said nothing about where she and Jane would go—not being able to stay in this house now. There wasn't even speculation as to who could have done it. None of the usual Dolly attention to detail or motive or innuendo was there. She was silent, sitting in a wicker porch chair then walking to the railing and back.

Dolly ignored the crowd gathered along the sidewalk and didn't answer when people shouted out their sympathy. Dolly was a zombie. Her head turned at a noise. She nodded or shook her head when Lucky came out to speak to her. She looked straight ahead and through people most of the time. I was ready to suggest a trip to the hospital—maybe to be treated for shock, but then I figured I'd just leave her alone, let her handle this in her own way. Dolly would be back, eventually. And when she did come back I pitied whomever had done this to her family.

Within the hour, Bill was there. I moved Dolly and Jane to the front seat of my car when Cate was carried out to the waiting ambulance. She would be autopsied in Grayling.

Dolly didn't turn to watch. She stared out the front window at nothing and only came back to where we were when Jane let out a tired little cry.

Bill caught sight of us huddled in the Jeep. He raised a finger in the air and made his way over slowly, head down, deep in thought.

"Dolly." Bill nodded to her through the open door. "God, I'm sorry. Awful stuff going on."

Dolly looked at him but didn't seem to understand.

Bill looked to me. "Anything yet?"

I shook my head. "Nobody's saying a word. Lucky told me to hang around. He needs a statement. But I didn't see anything. I didn't know anything was wrong until Dolly screamed."

Bill nodded, blinked, then pushed his heavy glasses back up his nose. "Everybody at the paper sends their condolences," he said to Dolly, a hand on her bent back. Baby Jane, in her mother's arms, reached out and grabbed his finger, giving it a shake.

Dolly's eyes were bloody red; her nose was swollen. When she looked at me, she blinked hard. "We're gonna get 'im, Emily."

I nodded.

Bill stood within the crook of the door saying nothing. He

motioned to me and I got out to join him at the back, near the trunk.

"Maybe you don't want to write this but I've gotta get something in tomorrow's paper . . ."

"Don't worry. You know that sliver of ice that the writer Graham Greene talked about at a writer's heart? I've got an iceberg in me. I'm not just mad. What he did to Dolly . . . let alone that Cate got involved. If I ever wanted to get somebody . . ."

"I'm sure Dolly feels the same way. She's got the law. You've got the newspaper. I'll stand behind you. I want a feature every day: what's happening, anyone questioned. Information. Keep it in the reader's face. Let's stay on top of this, Emily."

I nodded, not needing to be told what I had to do. "I'll send what I can. I've got a photo of Cate on my iPhone. I might as well be doing something. When's the latest I can get it to you?"

"No more than a couple of hours. I'm heading back to town now. I'll save room on the front page. You okay with that? Give a recap, cover speculation, every fact you've got . . . Lucky said something was written on the wall . . ."

"'Thou Shalt Not Steal.'" I shuddered.

"Can you get in there to get a photo?"

I shuddered again but settled down into my big-girl pants. I nodded.

"You have any idea what's going on? Was it about Cate all along, the way Lucky told me on the phone?"

"Who knows? It just . . . seems . . . like there's no real reason to it. Go after Dolly and Baby Jane to get at Cate? Or is Cate's death to get at Dolly?"

I fell quiet, thinking about Dolly's family. Abandoned by her mother. A grandmother who'd let her be carted off to one uncaring home after another. Then the hit-and-run. Now a murder. There was so much to look at. None of it made sense.

Bill touched my arm because I'd drifted off, thinking how unfair life could be to some people and wondering how those innocent people got chosen and telling myself I didn't believe any of the good church folks who said we had to grit our teeth and bear it because that was God's will, reducing God to some kind of Nazi general sending one to one line and the next to another.

"You okay?" Bill asked, obviously knowing I was anything but okay.

"Look, if you need me for anything. Even if you think Dolly should stay at my house for a while. I mean, somebody's after her about something . . . Stick with Lucky, look into Cate's background. Use the other reporters. Everybody wants to help any way they can."

"I don't know where to begin. Guess we should go through Cate's things."

"Lucky's got resources you don't have, at least on the forensics end."

"Cate didn't talk much about her life before coming here. Southern Michigan, I think. I heard her mention Dexter once. And Ypsilanti. She said she'd lived there." I tried to clear my head. "Now I'm wondering why it was so easy to talk her into coming to Leetsville, and then moving in with a granddaughter she didn't know and who didn't know her. There could be any number of enemies or old troubles buried in her past. Or in any of the towns she mentioned."

I thought awhile longer. "Maybe Lucky's right and the murderer is somebody from Cate's past. Still, the cemetery thing . . . how was that a threat to Cate?"

Bill shrugged. "Maybe go for her loved ones first. Some vindictive payback. Who knows?"

"We've got to find out before he comes back for Dolly, or for Jane."

"Imagine the mission she'll be on," Bill said. "And Emily, that 'Thou Shalt Not Steal' business. Think that's some kind of cover-up, a distraction?"

I shook my head. Who knew anything in this upside-down, *Alice in Wonderland* world we'd been drawn into?

As he was leaving, Bill leaned over to kiss my cheek in a not-so-brotherly way I almost didn't notice.

When, three hours later, Lucky asked Dolly and me to come over to the station while techs finished up at the house, Dolly put her head down and gave a single deep sigh. She was giving Jane a bottle, leaning protectively over her baby, looking down into the perplexed brown eyes looking back hard at her. She nodded.

I started to lay out plans for after we talked to Lucky. I was telling her that there would be no going back into that tall, plain house—maybe ever.

"Anything we need for Jane we can pick up on the way out to my house," I said, and was about to add that I needed a few groceries and hoped it would be all right . . . when one of the techs came to the door of the house and called Lucky back to him.

We watched as Lucky cut across the grass, then up the steep front steps, broad back hunched. The tech walked out to the porch to meet him, handing him something that looked like a small plastic bag. The two of them talked for a couple of minutes. Lucky nodded, hurried back down the steps, and over to the car. Whatever he held in his hand, he'd palmed so only the clear plastic edges of the bag showed around his fingers.

"Found something, Dolly." He leaned in. "I don't know . . . Think you gotta take a look."

He held out his hand. Whatever was in the bag wasn't large. It lay under his thumb so it was difficult to see.

Dolly took the bag, holding it up toward the sun. She squinted to make out what was at the bottom.

She shook her head slowly, beyond comprehending anything. "What is it?" she asked Lucky.

"Look again," he said, as if reluctant to name what she was seeing.

I leaned in, peering over her shoulder.

Dolly shook her head. "I don't get . . ."

"A black jellybean, Dolly," Lucky almost whispered. "They found it on the floor of the nursery. Just that one black jellybean."

TWENTY-TWO

It would have been one of my favorite May days if it weren't for Cate's funeral.

When I awoke my bedroom was dim. I could hear rain softly hitting the windows. A perfect day to sit at my desk and write and drink tea. And maybe entertain myself with thoughts of other writers in their garrets all around the world, plugging away at their hard and thankless tasks—suffering for our art, the lot of us.

All I had were a couple of hours to kill before picking up Dolly and Jane at their motel in town, where they'd moved after one night with me.

Not nearly enough time to develop a good case of rainy day self-pity.

I put on a crinkly old yellow slicker and whistled for Sorrow, who never minded the weather or let much of anything interfere with his boundless happiness. He pounded past me, out the door and into the drive, then stopped to look both ways. He chose the lake, beating an ear-flopping lope down the sand path to the reeds, where he sniffed and searched for loons or geese—interlopers in his world—while I stood watching the dimpled lake and listening to the dripping trees behind me. Spring, and all that new life. I smelled the wet earth smell of stirring worms and wondered about living and nonliving until it was time to give up thinking dark thoughts and get into town for Cate's funeral.

• • •

146

The rain kept up all morning. The service graveside was short, people separated by nodding umbrellas. Dolly and I stayed on after the others, though we were soaked through and our shoes were shiny black from the damp grass. She wanted to stop and talk to Grace a minute.

"I'm here anyway. Might as well say hi," Dolly said as we tramped over to Grace's grave and bowed our heads, both dumping our woes on the poor soul who probably only wanted to rest in peace.

I asked Grace to straighten this whole thing out so we knew which path to take. She had a way of cutting crap, the way she'd probably done in life—with her red whiskers and shaped mustache. Like Dolly, I could think clearer after having a short heart-to-heart with Grace. Things were falling slowly into place, facts lining up like guests at a wedding: groom's side; bride's side. Jellybeans and blood on a headlight and a wrecked SUV returned as if borrowed for only a moment.

Things were just beginning to gel when Dolly turned, head bent, and headed back toward my car. I scrambled after her, waving to Grace over my shoulder.

"We've got to go back in there," Dolly announced on the way over to EATS for the funeral luncheon.

"In where?"

"My house. Got to face it. Eugenia said everything's cleaned up in the nursery. Jake Anderson and some guys from the Skunk painted the walls. They left Cate's room alone. We've got to take a look. There's got to be something."

I said I'd help and she gave me a grateful look. "But I don't know if I can live there anymore. And I'll never put Jane back in that room."

I understood. Who knew what anyone would feel about the house where their grandmother had been murdered?

I wasn't ready for what came next.

"I asked Lucky to see if he could find Audrey Delores in France," she said. "She needs to know her mother's dead."

There was nothing to say. I could only imagine the long nights of misery this decision brought Dolly.

Eating began when Dolly and I walked through the front door. Baby Jane, who'd gone ahead with Gloria, gurgled in her seat at the middle of a long table filled with bowls of chicken salad and extra-large homemade rolls, and lettuce and tomatoes and home-canned pickles, and chips with dips and berry pies townswomen had baked. Lots of conversation. Lots of laughter. Lots of offers of help to Dolly:

"You need me to watch Baby Jane for you, all you gotta do is ask," one woman with four children of her own offered.

"I'm home every afternoon—if you want to drop the baby off," another said.

"Dolly, whatever you need. You go after whoever's doing this to you. Get 'im."

"Dolly, you ever need a man over there to help you with anything at all, why, you just give me a call," Jake Anderson, a kind man with troubled eyes, said.

And one that made Dolly angry. Deputy Omar Winston came in shaking rain off his plastic-covered hat and from his black slicker. He found Dolly in the crowd and stiffly came to express his condolences. His offer of help had to do with Baby Jane.

"I already told you, I'll take her any time," he said within earshot of everybody. "You know, I'm gonna have to see a lawyer if you won't give me visiting privileges. Hate to bring it up, but I'm figuring she could come stay with me and my mom until this thing going on with you is over. I mean, until you catch the guy. My only concern is the baby's safety. That's all I care about . . ."

"She's fine," Dolly, beside me at a center table, growled and turned her back. He put a hand on her arm.

He cleared his throat. "All I'm thinking about is Jane. Her safety. She got hurt once in all of this. I don't want it to happen again."

Dolly reared back to fix him with an angry glare. "You think I do?"

"I think you're a stubborn person."

Dolly opened her mouth then snapped it shut. She gave him a long, thoughtful look, swallowed hard a time or two, turned, and got up to go back to the ladies' room.

TWENTY-THREE

Next surprise through the restaurant door was Bill Corcoran, apologizing for missing the funeral. "Tried to get here on time but a couple of things at the paper held me up. Had a reporter quit. No explanation. Just packed his stuff and left this morning."

He greeted Dolly, even hugged her, and wished her good luck finding the person doing these things. He asked a few questions about the investigation, grabbed a dish of chicken salad, then took a chair at our table, across from where Baby Jane held court with a yawn, a sleepy smile, and a nod of her head.

When we finished eating Bill asked me to come outside to his car a minute.

"Got some things we should talk about," he said, getting up slowly, shoulders hunched.

I told Dolly I'd be back and followed him out while Dolly watched, turning around to comment to Eugenia, who looked after me and smiled.

I climbed in Bill's pickup and slammed the door behind me. The nice soft day had gotten colder and damper. Bill turned the motor and then the heater on when I shivered and wrapped my arms around myself.

"So?" I asked, aware people inside the restaurant were discussing us by now.

"Couple of things. First: can you handle this or do you want some help on it?"

"You mean Cate's murder?"

150

"That and the hit-and-run at the cemetery."

"Of course they're connected," I said. "I don't care who this is aimed at, Cate or Dolly. It's all part of the same thing. Not two separate incidents."

"No response on Dolly's reward," he said. "A couple of psychics from down below. One UFO nut. That's all. I'm beginning to think whoever's responsible isn't from around here. If he was local, somebody would know what's going on."

I agreed. Another vote for somebody from Cate's past.

"Dolly's started hunting for her mother in France. Finally. She wants to tell her about Cate and, I guess, see if she's got any idea who would do this to her. She just doesn't know what part of France she's in."

"French government will know. Even if she's a resident alien, they'll have records. Can't go there and just disappear. Unless you really want to. I mean, on purpose. I could help, if you need me. Got a good friend over there. A journalist. He'd find her."

"Lucky already started searching. Before she even asked him to. Told me he contacted la Sûreté. French form of the FBI. Doesn't expect a problem, locating the woman. He was anxious, though, about going ahead and searching behind Dolly's back. He figured it would be hard on her, with the history she has with her mother," I said. "Or lack thereof. But now it's okay."

I hesitated only a minute before bringing up something else Lucky had confided to me. "Another thing is, Lucky thinks this is getting to be too much for Dolly. What with the baby and now her dead grandmother. He's wondering if he shouldn't turn the whole thing over to the state police and keep her out of it."

"Good luck with that," Bill said, knowing Dolly well by now.

"That's what I told him. He couldn't keep her away if he tried. Would you expect Dolly to sit out a hunt for somebody after her family?"

"Still, maybe the state police should take over."

"She'd be at the center of things anyway. And driving them crazy."

He thought awhile. "You know what defense lawyers can make of overzealous police."

Bill hesitated a few minutes, looking off toward the rain-dotted windshield. "There's this thing with the reporter who left today. I wanted to talk to you about it."

"About what?"

"The job. I know you've got a book deal but that won't bring you any money for over a year."

"I get an advance."

He shrugged. "Well, the offer's there if you want it. I mean, the job is yours."

I drew in a long breath. "I have rewrites on the manuscript. I'm starting a new book. The editor talked about a contract on a second . . ."

He shook his head a time or two. "It's up to you. Let me know in a couple of days, all right? I've got to fill the position."

I agreed and got out of his car, running back into the restaurant through the rain and muddy tire tracks, thinking about taking that "road" just offered—safety of a full-time job, benefits, security.

Or go on as I was. Writing mysteries that still might not sell.

Fooling myself that everything would be okay and ending with nothing.

TWENTY-FOUR

We were back at Dolly's by three o'clock. The house felt abandoned. Chilly and damp. The chemical smell of paint layered the air. The stink of incipient mold floated up from the basement. Any spirit of welcome this old house used to give was gone.

Dolly laid Baby Jane on the couch to finish her nap. We went back together to see what the men and women had accomplished in Jane's room. I could only imagine Dolly's stomach must've been turning fast. Mine was.

If you didn't know what had happened in there, the room looked new and untouched. It had been scrubbed and polished; the air was thick with fresh paint. All traces of blood were gone from the floor. Pictures on the walls were straightened. The broken crib had been removed. Bedding gone. Order restored and almost nothing left behind. Even that terrible scrawled message had been painted over — the spot turned into a large rectangle of blue with a painting of the Au Sable River done by Mardi, a local landscape artist, hanging at the center.

Dolly said nothing. She closed the door behind us then went into Cate's room. More a sense of dread here, in the simply covered single bed, in a lamp draped with a yellow scarf, in a closet half filled with sad clothes, like leftovers from a Gypsy troupe, or remnants of a woman with very limited means. Some were almost rag-like: long skirts and peasant blouses and jackets that were much too large and hung from their hangers like the dejected backs of prisoners.

"I'll do this." Dolly pulled a large old trunk from the closet.

154

"You take the dresser."

"Am I looking for anything in particular?"

Dolly shook her head. "You'll know. Something from her past. Names. Letters. Things like that. Something from Audrey Delores Thomas, I guess. Or anybody else Cate kept in contact with. You got a question, we'll talk about it."

I settled into searching a dead woman's dresser drawers and found the pathetic collection of useless things not only sad and poignant, but instructive. Here was a life traced in Lily of the Valley bath powder, in old underwear and rolled-up nylon stockings, in a drawer filled with nightgowns washed so thin the patterns were gone. I opened the bottom drawer and found an ancient Bible held together with a large blue rubber band. Beneath the Bible there were three letters in the original envelopes, the return address to a Mable Todd in Washington, Michigan, and postmarked June, 1981; January, 1985; and September, 1989. In one drawer I found a pile of yellowed newspaper clippings held together with a paper clip. These were tucked under a stack of bras stained at the underarms. I riffled through the clippings but they were only recipes and stories about old movie stars.

Tucked inside a book of poems by Christina Rossetti were fifteen twenty-dollar bills. I counted the bills then read the poem they'd marked: "When I am Dead, My Dearest," but didn't read it to Dolly because it was so sad.

I handed the money to her. She took it without a word and stuck it in her uniform shirt pocket.

I pulled the drawers from the chest, one by one, and turned them over, checking for anything stuck underneath. Nothing.

"Got this," Dolly said and pulled a red, plush-covered

photo album from the trunk. She set in on the floor beside her. "Guess we'll take a look later."

I was done with the chest and had nothing to show for it but three old letters, a decrepit Bible, and a book of poems.

Dolly leaned back on her legs and leafed through a stack of papers. "Paid bills," she said. "Stubs and receipts. Nothing going back before last year, far as I can see."

When we finished going through everything in Cate's room, even turning the bed to see if she'd stuck something between the mattress and box springs, we had a sum total of a pile of old clothes, three letters, a Bible, and a photo album.

"And this." Dolly pulled a last thing from the trunk.

She handed me a pincushion stuck full of pins and one needle. It looked like something made by a child: raveling raw edges of the overlapping chintz material sticking out around the sides. I turned it over and found, written in small stitches on the bottom: *Love from your little Dolly.*

"You give her this?" I asked.

She shook her head. "I didn't even know her when I was a kid. Or that's what she said. Who knows? Never got any real truth out of the woman."

"You have a relative named Dolly?"

She shook her head. "Got no relatives, remember? Probably just a coincidence. Somebody's kid she used to know."

Dolly crossed her legs and drew the photo album to her. I settled beside her, watching the faces of long-ago people drift by as she turned the pages.

"There's your Dolly," she said and jabbed a finger at one of the old photographs. She pushed the album toward me.

In the picture a girl stood at the end of a dock. A teenager with long blond hair. Skinny. Squinting back at the photographer behind a hand up to shield her eyes. She wore a bathing suit from the 1960s or 1970s. Maybe sixteen years old. She wasn't laughing, more annoyed at the person taking her photo. Beneath the picture the words "Dolly at the cottage" had been hand-lettered.

"Not me," Dolly said.

"Could she be your mother?"

Dolly made a face. "No clue. All the women in these pictures look alike."

"And isn't your mother's name Audrey?"

Dolly nodded. "Far as I know."

"Then why 'Dolly'?"

"Her middle name's Delores. Guess that's what it is. When Cate talked about her sometimes she'd call her 'My sweet little Dolly.' I always thought she was just using a pet name. You know, like Baby Doll, or Sweetie, or something like that."

"Your mother named you after what her mother called her? Sort of like naming you for herself."

"Doubt it. That's somebody else there." She jabbed at the fading photograph of the young girl on the dock. "Nobody to me."

Dolly flipped more pages, bending to squint over photo after photo. I sat back and watched the old photos go by.

"Lots of that girl in there," I said. "Pretty."

"Pretty is as pretty does. One of my foster mothers used to say that to me." There was a bitter laugh. "All she meant was that I wasn't pretty and didn't act pretty."

There wasn't going to be anything soft coming out of Dolly that afternoon. I could sense her mood darkening. Hatred for her mother ran too deep, for too long a time, with too much blame attached to be healed by a single photograph of a young girl about to leap into a lake somewhere in time—if that really was her mother.

I pulled out the three letters and opened them, oldest to youngest.

Nothing much beyond the usual "It was really good to hear from you again. We were wondering what happened to you after all that fuss you went through. We're still hoping things will get better one of these days. John says hello and hopes you are feeling okay. He went through a bout with the flu last winter and still has a leftover cough that gets to him every so often." All the nothing stuff people used to write to each other and now tweet or email by way of reaching out and holding on to friends and family. The letter was signed, Your Cousin, Mable Todd. The next letter was almost the same except this time Mable wrote they were going on vacation to Florida and were looking forward to that. She asked Cate if she was doing okay and if there was any news of Audrey, then added she prayed for both of them every night.

The last letter only said she was sorry things weren't going any better with Audrey and she wished there was better news.

I handed the letters to Dolly, who examined the envelopes and the return address first, then read through the letters quickly. "This all there is?" She looked up at me. "Cousin. What do you know? Must be my cousin, too."

"But the last letter is postmarked 1989. Guess they lost touch after that."

"Still, who knows? Maybe I can find her. Sounds like she knows about Audrey going to France. And things about Cate, too. Might be all I need."

"There's a return address." I tapped the envelope.

"I'll write her. Or better yet, I'll see if she's listed and give her a call."

I carefully pulled the rubber band from the old Bible and opened the book. The name inscribed on the first page had faded beyond reading. I turned to the list of family members, a page of fading scrawled ink notations, ink faded to brown leading down to small, handwritten listings: A Catherine Linden was listed. Born March 5, 1938.

"Is this Cate?" I pointed to the listing.

"She told me she was sixty-six."

"Then maybe it's not her."

"Naw. She probably was seventy-four. Crotchety as anything sometimes. Probably lied to me."

"A family trait," I said under my breath. "That 'crotchety' business."

Dolly ignored me. "Here, look at this one."

Audrey Delores Thomas. Born July 18, 1959.

"And here's me." She pointed to a listing for Delores Flynn, born in 1979.

Dolly pulled the Bible from my lap and rested her hands on the open pages. "Guess I should put a death date in for Cate."

She ran a hand across the page. "This is all I've got." She rifled through the pages then, turned to places marked with death notices and rotting newspaper articles and funeral cards with long-gone people's faces and small prayers, but nothing more about who they were.

As she turned the fragile pages the book fell open to a place where a small brown envelope lay. She pulled the envelope from where it had indented a space for itself and held it up to the light.

"What the heck?" Dolly said, opened the envelope, and slid a medium-sized key out into her hand.

"Got numbers on it: 2341. Nothing else. Not even the name of the maker."

"House key?" I asked.

"House key's in her purse, on a ring with what looks like a post office box key. Had a wallet with a few dollars, and her last Social Security check stub."

"Didn't she have direct deposit? Most seniors do it that way."

"Never asked." Dolly stuck the key into the pocket where she'd stuffed the twenty-dollar bills. "First thing I'd better do is get over to the post office. Check that box."

Out in the living room, Jane awoke and began to cry. Dolly pushed the dresser drawers closed. She closed the strapped trunk and toed it back into the closet.

We picked up our meager finds and left the room, closing the door firmly behind us.

TWENTY-FIVE

The rain stopped on my way into Traverse City the next morning. Puffs of warming moisture played across M72. The sun came out from behind dark clouds as I drove past the casino then turned at US 31, toward town. I still didn't know what I was going to say to Bill about the job.

No woman living on the edge of financial disaster has any right to turn down an offer like the one Bill made: full-time work in my old profession, regular pay, benefits — so I could actually afford to get sick once in a while.

And, after all, lots of writers worked full-time jobs and still found time to write.

So. I shouldn't kid myself. The book I'd sold might be the last. I passed Burger King and resort after resort. Lake Michigan was so far down its marshy shore stretched out farther than I'd ever seen before.

At the newspaper office, Bill stumbled to his feet to greet me. He took my hand in both of his and immediately asked how things were going. "If she needs somebody to watch her baby. Like a safe house. We've got people here in town who'll be glad to step in."

I shrugged and promised to pass on the information while assuring him she had an army of people back in Leetsville helping already.

Sitting there, in his office, I thought how nice it would be to come into this place every day, be part of the turmoil of a newsroom again. He added to my problem by taking me out to introduce me to Cathy, the City Editor, a beautiful woman with a smile that lighted her whole face. She wished me luck with this thing going on in Leetsville and offered any help she could give. "I'll back you out there, if you need me," she offered as Bill moved me around the room.

"Giving you a flavor of our operation," he leaned in close to murmur after introducing me to Anne, one of the reporters, who got up to hug me and say everybody was pulling for me and the deputy.

"You want me out there with you," Anne offered, "Bill says this is our top story until the guy's caught. Tell Dolly we're all so sorry about her grandmother."

I met women in Advertising, and an older woman in Circulation before Bill led me back to his office, where I cleared files from a chair.

"So, what's going on out there?" He leaned back, hands behind his head, then shot out that middle finger to push his slipping glasses up his nose. The only time this gesture bothered me was when he left the finger there to think. A person could take that gesture personally after a while.

"We cleaned out Cate's room. Found letters from a cousin down in Washington, Michigan. Back from the 1980s. Dolly's following up on that. Nothing to help us find Audrey Delores Thomas in France or much of anything else. I don't see how a woman could live for more than seventy years and leave so little behind her."

He made a note of Audrey's name again. "You know for sure she went to France?"

"Right after Dolly was born. That's what she understood."

"So? What year?"

"Seventy-nine."

"Lucky will probably come up with something soon. Nobody just drops off the face of the planet," he said.

"Some do," I said. "We all do eventually."

He smirked at me. "I've got that friend in Paris. Gave him what I had. One of them will get us information."

"Dolly would sure appreciate it," I said.

"Now, about the job?" He leaned back. "I'm going to need to know pretty quick."

"Just a couple of days, all right? I've got to talk to my agent and my editor." Then I approached an idea I'd come up with on the drive in. "Would there be the possibility of more stringer work?"

Bill bit at his lip. He shook his head. "You know what's going on with newspapers. I'm actually going to cut down on outside writers and lay more on my staff. I could keep on with what I've been giving you. You're over there: Kalkaska, Leetsville, and Mancelona. That's a long way for my people to go."

He considered. "Maybe a few more stories. You like covering teacup collections? That's about all I've got."

"Love teacup collections," I assured him.

"Let me know soon."

My phone rang. I bent to burrow in my shoulder bag.

The first thing I heard was a baby crying and Dolly's voice talking baby talk.

"Hello? Hello? This you?" were her first coherent words.

I assured her it was.

"Think Jane's getting sick and tired of being on the go all the time, like we're homeless or something."

"You could go back to your house." I wagged a finger in the

air toward Bill and went out into the hall.

"Not safe."

"How about my house?"

"Hard to get babysitters to go out there."

"Bill said he knew people here in Traverse City who would be happy to keep Jane until this is over."

"Not letting her out of my sight. But that's not why I called. Got a couple of things. I went to the post office. Only thing in the box is an ad for hearing aids. But Lucky came up with a phone number for that Mable Todd. I called her."

"What'd she say?"

"I'll tell you, but you don't write up anything unless I say it's okay."

"Fine. What's going on?"

"She sounds kind of old. Probably like Cate. Anyway, she said she hadn't been in touch with Cate for a long time and was sorry to hear she was dead. Then I told her Cate was murdered and the woman could barely speak after that. She said something funny."

"What?"

"All she said was, 'Does Audrey know?'"

"That's understandable. Audrey's her daughter."

"So then I said that I'm Cate's granddaughter and she acted flummoxed. I told her I'm an officer with the Leetsville Police Department and that Cate had been living with me. The woman said: 'Granddaughter?' Like she never heard of such a thing. So, I said, 'I'm Dolly,' and she said what a surprise it was to hear from me and she went on to say something about thinking I was 'out of the picture.' Whatever that means."

"Maybe because you went into foster care."

"Yeah, could be that."

"So, what else?"

"Well, then she said, 'You must be doing all right after all. Glad to hear it.'"

"What?"

"Yeah. Hung up on me. Sounded nervous, like she wanted nothing to do with a murder. Maybe that was it. People get funny. Scared. But I'd told her I'm her cousin, too. You'd have thought . . ."

Jane cried and Dolly took time to rearrange her, probably to her other shoulder.

"What'd you do then?" I asked.

"What'd you think I did? Called her back. She answered and I said this was official business and I was calling for information on Cate. She took a long time to say anything and then her voice got stiff, kind of, and she said something like, 'I don't mean to be harsh, Dolly. But, well, with your history—I don't think it's a good idea to go on talking about this.'"

"What history?"

"No clue. She hung up again. I've got to get down there, to Washington. Somewhere in the thumb, I think. You want to come with me? I could use the help with Jane."

Of course I was taking a road trip with Dolly and her baby. Nothing like a little time away to think over a job offer that could ruin my life.

TWENTY-SIX

Even with so much to talk about, Dolly and I were silent for the first few hours of the trip, keeping inside our own heads, with our own thoughts.

I'd already learned that the baby's room had been full of fingerprints—attributable to no one but Dolly and Cate and one other set that couldn't be found in any of the databases. There was blood on the knife that killed Cate. Cate's, of course, but blood belonging to someone else, too. This time DNA testing was ordered on both the blood from the broken headlight and the blood on the knife.

But that could be weeks away—knowing for sure the blood came from the same person. Neither Dolly nor I believed we had weeks to wait. And that single jellybean was beginning to feel like a hook left to draw us in a direction we didn't want to go, an over-the-cliff direction into crazy-land with no real markers to follow.

That jellybean seemed at first childish, and then diabolic. Someone with a motive buried in his own head. Someone who didn't know Dolly or Cate but had latched on to them as targets. This route could lead to a man living in a shack back in the woods with nothing to focus his hatred on beyond a woman he'd spotted at the supermarket, or a car he saw parked at a cemetery. Which would mean my newspaper stories led him straight to Dolly and Cate.

That wasn't a thing I wanted to think about, so instead I thought long and hard about mental illness and crime and how if we, as a society, would only put some of the money spent on prisons and prison personnel and law enforcement into curing all forms of mental illness we would, in the end, be one step closer to a perfect world.

Another thing to be thankful for: that I wasn't born with a glitch in my brain. At least not one that threatened anybody but me.

Then, since Dolly still wasn't talking and she was driving, I decided I had more immediate things to think about—like summer taxes coming up and whether I wanted to take a full-time job so I could pay them . . . or not. And—way in the back of my head—was Bill showing an interest in taking our friendship a step further? Or was it just me again, imagining things that weren't there due to an excess of imagination.

Jane slept until we were down to Bay City, where we stopped for her to take a bottle and get her diaper changed and her bottom creamed because she was getting red from sitting. We grabbed a drive-thru hamburger and were back on the road in fifteen minutes.

"I've been thinking," Dolly finally said. "Isn't it kind of funny how I get one new family member at a time? I mean—my mother, and then she's gone before I even know her. My grandmother—now she's gone. Now a cousin—God help her."

"You've got Jane. You'll always have her."

"Yeah?" She turned worried eyes on me. "That's what's scaring me."

I said nothing because I didn't have easy words for the fear she felt.

After a while, she launched into a different problem. "I got a call from an attorney last night. Omar hired him to get visitation rights."

"Are you going to fight him?'

She sighed deeply. "I don't know. I don't see why he should have any rights at all."

"He's Jane's father."

She rolled her eyes at me.

"So? A father has rights, Dolly."

"My father didn't have any. I never saw him. Not one story about him. Not one word from him — my whole life long."

"You want that for Jane?"

We fell silent again.

Another stop — this time at a rest area, where Jane smiled and cooed at everyone she saw, even flat on her back, legs in the air, with a new diaper slipping into place.

Down around Flint, Dolly said she was going to call Mable Todd, to make sure she was home and would stay there. I thought the arrangements had been made before we left Leetsville but didn't say anything. I hoped the woman was home and this whole thing wasn't a wild-goose chase.

I listened as Dolly identified herself and said she would like to see her this afternoon, sometime around three. Evidently there was pushback from the other end and Dolly stuttered a couple of times before agreeing to have Lucky call the Washington police and confirm the appointment.

She hung up and called Lucky.

"Won't meet with me unless you call the police department there in Washington and have them call her. She said she's got no idea who I am and won't let me in her house unless the local police say it's okay."

She hung up and looked over at me. "She doesn't trust me. Thinks I'm a murderer coming after her. Lucky'll take care of it."

"Is Lucky going to mention that the cop coming to call will have a baby strapped to her chest?"

"What do you mean? Why'd you think I brought you along? You carry Baby Jane. What would it look like for a cop to go on an interview with a baby?"

"What will it look like for a reporter to show up on an interview with a baby?"

"Hey. I'm the one in charge here."

We both stewed awhile and then made a deal. I'd carry Jane in her holder as long as I could go in with Dolly. We'd make no mention of the baby and hoped Mable Todd wouldn't notice.

The house, on West Road, in Washington, a tiny village I'd once visited in apple season because of the orchards dotting the main road, was a spare, white farmhouse now lost in a line of newer bungalows. We climbed the steps to the wide front porch and rang the bell. Jane felt warm against my chest. I looked down into her open and considering eyes and smiled at her. She smiled back and wiggled in her Snuggie as the door opened and a woman, who looked like Cate Thomas, frowned at us, taking in the uniformed Dolly and me with a kid strapped to my chest, a shoulder bag tossed around to my back, a reporter's notebook in one hand, a pen in the other, and a silly smile on my face.

"You're Dolly?" the woman said and motioned us into the house. When Dolly introduced me as a reporter from a Traverse City newspaper she looked long and hard, then muttered, "Don't go putting my name in any newspaper. I've got nothing to do with what happened to my cousin. Hope that's clear right up front."

I assured her it was clear and moved Jane a little to the right so my boob wasn't flattened.

The living room was one of those comfortable places where people kicked back in La-Z-Boy chairs in front of a redbrick fireplace and glass-framed photos of angels ranged around the walls. Mabel Todd, herself, was dressed like a peasant woman straight out of a Rumanian wheat field: blue headscarf covering her hair, narrow face without makeup, red cheeks. Her eyes were Cate's eyes—far spaced and deep set, with tiny lines radiating from their corners.

"So?" she demanded after indicating we should sit on a brown micro-suede sofa with a multicolored afghan thrown over one arm. "You're here about Cate."

She shook her head slowly. "Don't know why you made the trip down from . . . where'd you say? Leetsville? I haven't seen or heard from Cate Thomas since the . . . oh . . . let me see." She rolled her eyes heavenward. "Maybe late eighties. I had no idea she'd moved up north. She ever marry again?" She went on without waiting for Dolly to answer. "That husband of hers. One day there. Next day out for cigarettes and never came back. That was your problem, I always thought. No father. Grew up like a weed, you did."

Dolly, confused, made a face. "I think you've got me mixed up with somebody else."

"You said Cate was your grandmother . . . Oh . . ." The woman put a plump hand to her cheek. "For heaven's sake. You said 'grandmother.' Here all along I thought you meant Cate was your mother. So, that means you're not Audrey. You're Audrey's baby. Well, what do you know. I thought you were lost and gone right from the git-go."

"Lost and gone?" Dolly's confusion deepened.

"You know what I mean. Cate was having so much trouble with Audrey and then you were born and your father took right off. Cate found out all this later, you see. And then, well . . . your mother wasn't exactly the dependable type."

"She signed me over to the state."

"That's what I figured though Cate never came out and said. Just a lotta trouble, is what she told me in her letters. I kind of thought . . . well now . . . I thought your mother ended up in a hospital or something."

Dolly shook her head. "She's with a religious group in France."

"Well, what do you know. You don't say. Know a lot of people saved by religion. I'm glad to hear it. Better that than where she was headed."

Dolly pulled one of the photos from the album out of her shirt pocket and passed it to Mable Todd. "Is this Audrey Delores?"

The woman took the picture, thought over it a while, then shook her head. "I really wouldn't know. Even though we were writing letters, me and Cate weren't close. I don't remember the last time I saw her. You know how it is with families."

Dolly gave her a tepid smile. "In the album I took that picture out of, somebody wrote in 'Dolly at the cottage.'"

"Well." She looked down at the photo again. "Could be your mother, I suppose. Cate called her Dolly. Guess that's what confused me when you called. You know, the name and all. And being my cousin."

"What about the cottage?"

She shrugged. "Can't help you there. Probably some

friend's place."

"And this." Dolly pulled a small envelope from her pants pocket. She emptied it into her palm and held it out to Mable Todd. It was the key we'd found in Cate's Bible. "Would you know anything about this?"

The woman took the key into her hand and looked it over, both sides. She shook her head. "What is it?" she asked.

"Something we found among Cate's effects. Just wondering if it was old. Maybe a key to some house where Cate used to live."

"Doesn't look like a house key to me. Look, there's numbers on it. You ask me, I'd try a bank. I got a key looks something like that, to my safe-deposit box here in town."

The woman warmed as we got up to leave, believing us— that we were no threat to her. She patted my shoulder and remarked what a beautiful baby I had. There was no use correcting her at that point so I puffed up and thanked her and said she looked more like her father than me and got a menacing look from Dolly.

At the door, the woman hugged Dolly. "So we're related. What do you know? I guess you're my second cousin. Isn't that how it works? You keep in touch now. Imagine, they called you Dolly, too. Guess Audrey named you for herself. That's kind of nice, you think about it. Nice to meet you. Me and Cate were the last of the family, far as I knew. There was Audrey—but with her troubles, well, who knows where she got to? So you say she's in France?" The woman looked away, thinking, then back to Dolly.

"I don't suppose you know much about your father," she said.

Dolly shook her head, agreeing.

"Well, no harm in telling you now. You see, when Audrey went into labor her husband or whatever he was—never sure about that marriage—his name was Harold Flynn, dropped her off at the hospital and was never seen again. Cate told me all this in a letter. She just needed to tell somebody, is what I suspected. Later, she didn't say much about Audrey, just that there was this baby. Gone, is what she said. Nothing else. That's the same thing Cate's husband did to her. Be your grandfather, Dolly. Up and left. My own husband was a good man. But he died at fifty-two. Guess women in our family don't have a lot of luck picking men that last."

I watched as Dolly absorbed this news then gathered herself to leave.

TWENTY-SEVEN

I dropped Dolly and Jane off at their motel about seven. All I wanted to do was get home, thank Harry for letting Sorrow in and out all day, and go to bed. Emotions, with Dolly, were rarely raw and open things. She didn't talk about much, only let her feelings simmer inside her then boil over in anger at the counter girl at Burger King, who didn't get her change right; or the driver who forgot to turn his right turn signal off; or the poor soul (me) who had the temerity to suggest maybe we had to stop for gas.

So I was mad. She was mad. Jane was cranky and whipping up that little "Waa-Waa" into a full-out cry against riding in the car for so many hours and visiting people she didn't recognize and having to put up with a tense mother who stayed silent hour after hour.

I let Sorrow out and then back in and noticed the answering machine signaled four missed calls. I ignored them. Being thrilled at popularity was beyond me now. All I wanted was to be left alone.

I laid down on my bed and threw an arm over my eyes until a warm, wet tongue swiped my face and I looked up into a pair of chocolate brown eyes with more love in them than most people see in a lifetime. I hugged Sorrow's big shaggy head until even he got sick of me and pulled away to lie down, going off into one of his Doggie-Disneyland dreams that brought snuffling yips of joy.

In the morning I didn't want to get up, though Sorrow needed to go outside before he had an accident that would sour

our seemingly perfect relationship.

The message light still blinked. Four messages that made me groan. I didn't want anyone to want me or need me or have things to say to me. I hoped for a chide from the electric company over a late payment when I pressed the playback button and wasn't too unhappy to hear the robot voice of someone wanting to help me with my dire financial situation— if I'd only call this attorney's office . . .

The next message was from Bill, telling me to call him first thing in the morning.

I checked my watch: six a.m. wasn't "first thing" to most people so I figured I'd wait until nine on that one, a decent hour for Bill to get to the office. If he was pressing for an answer on the job offer I guessed I'd say no. I couldn't give up everything I'd struggled for this long, just when I'd had a breakthrough with my writing. Maybe—later . . .

The third call was from my editor, Faith Cardoni at Crestleg Publishers. This one made my heart race. "Emily, this is Faith Cardoni. Could we talk sometime today or tomorrow? I'll be in my office tomorrow, although it's a Saturday. I look forward to hearing from you."

So. It was real. I had at least one book bought and coming out sometime in the next year. But—talk to me . . .? Somehow I wasn't expecting this to be good news. Hesitant phone calls from publishers were never good news. Maybe there was a quality in the woman's voice, a kind of forced cheerfulness, that alarmed me. I sat at the table with a cup of Earl Grey and ran everything over in my mind. I prided myself on being able to read people, to protect myself in advance just by picking up signals. I always thought this was what women's so-called intuition was all about: the need, because we were smaller than that other sex, to protect ourselves, to be ahead of the game.

By eight o'clock I was convinced she wanted out of the contract and was about to ship my book back to me. By nine I knew she wanted to take back the offer of the advance and would probably want me to pay for . . . I didn't know . . . something. Maybe the whole thing was a scam. Millions of scammers hustling writers now—with the ebook explosion. *We'll get your name out there. We'll publish your book. We'll handle your legal affairs. Oh, we just love your book. For fifteen thousand dollars we'll get it into print . . .*

It wasn't until after I'd planted the flat of pansies, after I took Sorrow out into the spring woods and stumbled on a patch of white and blue and yellow violets prettier than anything in my garden, that I sank to my knees and reminded myself of real problems. Problems like Dolly's, protecting her baby from an unknown enemy who struck whenever he felt like it; losing her grandmother to murder; living in a motel room, virtually homeless.

Real problems.

Sorrow and I went back to the house and I called Bill.

"I got a call here at the paper yesterday," Bill said without more than a grunted hello. "Not really coherent. All I got out of it was that the police officer in Leetsville should be investigated for baby stealing. And that she was glad it happened."

"Is that what she said? "I'm glad *it* happened?"

"That's it. I don't have a clue what the woman was getting at. Things like this can sure bring out the nuts."

I thought awhile. "I'll talk to Dolly," I promised. "A woman? Hmmm. Didn't get a name, did you?"

"I asked. She hung up. Probably nothing. Somebody Dolly gave a ticket to who wants to get even. Get a lot of that when a cop's name is in the paper."

I promised another story that afternoon, one about the cousin and a little bit about the search for Audrey Delores. Dolly and I had agreed I could start telling how she was hunting for Cate Thomas's daughter and print all that was known about her whereabouts.

Then I had to call the state police for anything on the forensics. I needed a quote.

First—Faith Cardoni. Saturday morning. I wasn't sure I'd really reach her.

"Oh, Emily." She answered herself. "I wanted to talk to you about the next books in your 'Dead' series."

I took a long, deep breath, and waited. No rejection. No chiding me for even thinking my work was good enough to publish. She was talking about more books.

"I'll need the next two titles right away. I want to get the contract drawn up and out to you. If you could get back to me by Monday or Tuesday—we'll get it all sewed up."

I promised. Of course I promised. No idea of what the next books would be about. No titles. No plots—well, one. No new characters. But—sure, Faith, I'll get you titles. "How about Tuesday?" I said.

I celebrated alone again because I didn't dare call Jackson, who would probably be reduced to tears, and not Dolly—who had deeper things to think about, and not Bill, and not any of the friends I'd left behind in Ann Arbor and hadn't heard from in months.

Me and Sorrow. A whoopee and a couple of jumps in circles,

then a cup of tea, and a punch to the answering machine. One last message yet to listen to.

There was silence at first. A deep breath. A woman's voice came on: "Rockabye baby . . ." the voice sang. More silence. A long, slow chuckle.

Then nothing.

TWENTY-EIGHT

She shook her head over her cup of coffee. "I stole somebody's baby? What the heck! You think it was the same woman called you, called Bill?"

"Unless everybody's going nuts."

"You get the number from your call log?"

I nodded. "Bill, too. Same number."

We sat across from each other in her tiny office. I nodded and handed her the piece of paper with the number on it.

She frowned hard. "I'll check right away. Bill said the woman claimed I stole somebody's baby, eh? Whose baby? Sure not Jane. Got the stretch marks to prove I produced her myself."

"No clue. She hung up on him. Didn't give a name."

"And that was all? That I should be investigated for baby stealing?" She thought awhile. "Don't people know by now that their phone numbers are left right there on the call log?"

"Unless they buy one of those disposable things. Then we wouldn't know."

"But you and Bill got numbers."

She bit at her lower lip as she reached out and automatically rocked Jane in her car seat set on the desk. Soon Jane was jumping with the rocking. I reached over and stopped Dolly's nervous hand.

"Think it's that Ariadne Wilcox?" she asked. "You know the one. We went to see her and her boyfriend, the guy that abused her kids."

I shook my head. "She seemed abused herself, if you ask

me. This woman was taunting—like, 'I'm glad it happened.'"

"She knows you're working with me, from your stories. That's why she called you. Means somebody local, don't you think?"

I shook my head. "Could be anybody."

"Well, I say we get back out to that spider lady's house and face her down."

"If it's her, I'd say her boyfriend made her do it. He's the cruel one. That poor soul—not enough to lose her little girls, but did you notice the black eye on her?"

Dolly nodded. "I told her she'd be better off putting a gun to the guy's head instead of giving up her kids."

"You think she could've murdered Cate?"

That stopped Dolly. She shook her head from side to side. "Not Ariadne. But him. Yeah. You know what, I'm bringing him in for questioning. Maybe her, too. See if she'll give him up."

"Why don't you trace this number first?" I waved the paper at her. "See who it belongs to."

"Okay. Good idea. Then we'll know."

"What about that key?" I reminded her.

"Took it to the bank in Kalkaska. Lisa there said it's definitely a safe-deposit key, just not one of theirs. Guess I'll have to take it around to some other towns. But how'd Cate get anywhere? She didn't have a car for the last couple of months. That one she came to town in lost an axle. I never took her to a bank. But she was always bumming rides from people."

"From whom?"

"Whom?" Her face broke into a wide smile.

"I'm educated, remember."

"Yeah, well, I'm not sure who gave her rides. You know people around here. You need something they're there to help." She thought awhile. "Why don't we ask Eugenia? She knows just about everything going on in town."

"Okay. But to start with why don't I call this phone number and see who answers?"

"Worth a try. Then I'll trace it."

"Not many public phones around anymore . . ."

I dialed the number. The phone rang on and on. Not even an answering machine. I hung up and gave the number to Dolly.

"So what's next?" I asked.

"Let's talk to Eugenia about anybody giving rides to Cate. Then I'm heading out to do something about that Ariadne Wilcox and Jerome Ordway . . ."

"And trace that number."

She nodded as she started to get up. "Yeah. So? You coming with me?"

"You've got the patrol car now. Why don't I talk to Eugenia while you go back to the station and trace that number. After that we'll see about Ariadne and the jerk."

We had a plan that almost felt like progress.

Eugenia was taping new numbers over some of the prices on her big wall menu. She looked down from her ladder and smiled.

"You ready for the wedding? Got about a hundred signed up already. I think some of them just want to see where you live. Some like a good party. Some are really happy for Harry and Delia."

She climbed down to lean in close. "And some of the old

biddies are shocked the wedding's so soon. What with Delia's mom barely cold in her grave. I asked a couple of 'em if they thought she was pregnant."

"Geez," was all I could think to say.

· "My word exactly." Eugenia nodded with a knowing look in her eye. "There's some people got nothing better to do."

She leaned back. "You ready for all of this? Sure hope it doesn't rain. I never been out to your place but you better have plenty of room."

I wanted to groan. "I have lots of room in the front, between my house and the lake. We could put up tables. I just don't know where to get them. If it rains—well, I can fit a hundred in my house. That's if they all stand and don't move."

Eugenia waved a hand at me. "I talked to that Reverend Runcival from that Contented Flock church. Said they got plenty of tables and chairs. And a truck to bring them in. He's doing the ceremony so it has to be in the afternoon after morning services. Sunday, you know. He said to make it around two o'clock. You tell Harry it was on the third?"

"All set," I assured her, then went on to list other things I was only then beginning to think about. "How about tablecloths? Napkins? Serving dishes? Serving pieces? Coffee urn? Cups? Glasses?" I started counting on my fingers. Not even possible!

"What the heck have I done, Eugenia?" My mouth hung open. "There's no way I can do an event like this one's shaping up to be."

Eugenia patted my back a few times. "Sure you can. I got everything. Jake and the guys from the Skunk will cart it out and back. I just need a few plugs for the coffeepots. Some running water. I've got extension cords. And don't worry, Emily, if things aren't perfect, nobody cares. We just like to get together. Especially at some new place."

She patted me again. "You'll do fine. Just be there to point out a flat place on your property and me and my helpers will do the rest."

"You'll need a barbecue for all those hot dogs." I was almost wailing.

She shook her head. "Got a big one on wheels we'll be bringing."

"For eight dollars a head?" I knew this was impossible and getting worse.

Eugenia laughed hard. "Some things in life you just gotta do. Can't look at the money. Kind of like a present from me and my waitresses. Jake and the boys, too. You're doing flowers, right?"

I nodded, thinking I'd go home and take a look at the daffodils. Maybe my early roses would be out. At least I'd have buds.

"Got room for a bower? They can stand under it for the ceremony. The reverend said he's got a member of his flock has an old rose arbor she's not using anymore."

I nodded. Sure. A wedding arch. Bouquets of flowers. Room for tables and chairs and a rolling barbecue cart. Why not? The grasses in front of the house weren't too tall yet. Area down to the lake was flat enough. If all they needed was room—I had plenty.

With plans in place, we went on to other things.

"What's going on with Cate's murder?" Eugenia asked as if she'd been waiting for the right moment.

I shook my head. "All kinds of things. Dolly and I went through Cate's stuff back at the house. We came up with a safe-deposit key but we don't know which bank it might belong to."

"You ask at the bank in Kalkaska?"

I nodded. "Dolly did. It's not from there. Some other bank."

"What's Dolly think could be in it? Not like Cate was rich or anything."

I shrugged. "At this point we just need something. She ever tell you about her past? Where she came from?"

"All I know is where I got ahold of her. Down near Ypsilanti, if I remember right. She said she'd only been there a few months. Seemed she was moving around a lot but always in Michigan. Different towns."

"That's what I thought from the few times we talked."

"And she mentioned that daughter of hers, Dolly's mom. The one over there in France. I don't think she ever visited her though. Think she would have mentioned going to France."

"We're looking for her, too. Lucky contacted the French police. My editor at the paper is checking with a friend of his, a journalist who lives in Paris."

"Poor Dolly. I know she doesn't really want to meet the woman. Giving her to the state the way she did."

"Still, Cate was Audrey's mother. She should know."

I let Eugenia think awhile then asked, "What we need to find is the bank that key goes to. Dolly says she never took her anywhere to do any banking. Do you know if anybody here in town did? I mean, was there somebody she asked for a ride?"

Eugenia thought awhile. "Well, Flora Coy mentioned going places with Cate. I hated to think of it, not with the thickness of those glasses on Flora. Shouldn't even be driving, you ask me.

And . . . let me see. I think Antigone Jones picked her up here a couple of times. Going to Traverse, if I remember right." She thought a minute. "No, maybe not Traverse. You want me to ask?"

"If you see Antigone Jones, ask. I don't know her. I'll go talk to Flora. It's kind of important, finding the bank she used. Tell people, okay? We need to know who took her to a bank, any town around here."

I called Dolly from the car on my way over to Flora Coy's house.

"We traced that telephone number," she said, then turned from the phone to talk to someone in her office. Then she was back. "Kind of a dead end. It's the number of a summer home over in Norwood. The place belongs to a downstate doctor. I just got off the phone with her. She hasn't been up in a couple of months. Keeps the phone on because she comes when she can and needs to stay in touch. Cell service out there is kind of spotty. The state police are on their way over to take a look at the house. Somebody got in somehow. Could still be there. I'm just hoping it can be this easy."

"Me, too. Still, just because a woman's making ugly phone calls doesn't mean she's the killer. You know how people latch on to stories like this."

"Yeah, well, we'll see. Let 'em get there and take a look around. That doctor said she'll come up as soon as she can to see if anything's stolen. But not until next week at the earliest. One thing, though, she said she keeps a car out there. White Volkswagen Passat. The key is in the house. She wanted to make sure that's still there. Nothing else of any value. I got the license number for the car."

• • •

Flora Coy lived in a pretty little house almost as quirky as Flora, herself. Windflowers and daffodils and purple hyacinths stuck up everywhere behind a white picket fence. No flower beds. Just a riot of flowers. Banners flew around the house, some stuck in trees, some attached to porch pillars, some hung in windows — all happy banners wishing people well; admonishing everyone to embrace spring; banners with Easter bunnies; banners with bright flowers, one banner — maybe the national flag of the gardener — sported a seed packet and a hoe.

Flora opened the door and seemed happy to see me, inviting me in and offering tea, which I turned down since I had other places to get to. The house was filled with birds in cages that hung and sat everywhere. It was a house filled with birdsong. A little tough to talk in, especially with Flora hard of hearing, but I finally got across what I wanted to know — about Cate and trips to a bank. Flora thought awhile then shook her head. "I only took Cate to market with me," she said. "Never anywhere out of town. I don't like driving much. You talk to Antigone Jones?"

I said Eugenia had mentioned her.

"You try Tiggy. Saw the two of them together more than one time."

I thanked Flora and was out to my car, ears ringing with a hundred tweets and trills.

I headed home to write the story of our search for anyone who might have driven Cate Thomas anywhere in the last few months and to shut a couple of windows I'd left open. The sky was almost black off to the west. A storm was coming.

• • •

As I drove down to my house the rain hit hard and then settled into to a steady drizzle. I closed my two bedroom windows just in time and let Sorrow out.

Later, with a wet and smelly Sorrow leaping around me, I called Dolly. I told her Flora never took Cate to a bank.

"Both Eugenia and Flora mentioned Antigone Jones. Do you know her?"

"Yup. I'll give her a call." She hesitated a long minute. "Heard from the state guys. Looks like somebody broke in, out at that house in Norwood. They're taking fingerprints. Can't figure it. Norwood. That's way the heck over there by the big lake. Nice homes. Quiet. I'll bet they haven't had a break-in in the last twenty years."

"Do you think we should get out there?"

"I was thinking . . . maybe. Not my jurisdiction but we have this reciprocal agreement. You know, between all the departments up here. They'd let me take a look around."

"Especially with the murder."

"Yes, I suppose." She was distracted, as if she didn't quite hear what I was saying.

"Want me to pick you up or are you driving?"

"Why don't you come get me? We got something else to do first."

"You mean Ariadne Wilcox. You still want to go out there?"

There was a long pause. "Don't have to."

"Why? I thought . . ."

"Just got word. They brought her to the hospital in Kalkaska about an hour ago."

"What?"

"He beat her up pretty bad."

"Crap. Hope the creep's in jail."

Another long pause.

"Dead," she said. "Ariadne shot him straight through the head."

TWENTY-NINE

Raining again, dark clouds moving like thick blood clots overhead. Sheets of rain, the color of red sand, poured down across the windshield, wipers barely keeping up. I took this as an omen, since I lived my life by signs—though they usually stood for nothing—and didn't want to get to the hospital. All of this business with Ariadne felt not just tragic but personal. As if I had something to do with bringing the woman, with her children gone, to a hospital bed and probably to a prison.

Dolly got a town girl in to watch Jane. I waited while she told the girl what she had to do and couldn't do and shouldn't do and better not be caught doing. She told her what was in the motel fridge she could help herself to and how to heat Jane's bottles and when to give her cereal. She pointed out a pile of clean diapers and clean clothes and mentioned that the TV only got three channels. After all of that, we left.

We had nothing to say the whole way down to Kalkaska except for the one time Dolly said she'd heard from that woman Antigone Jones.

"Guess Eugenia told her to call me. Said she took Cate to church a time or two but that was all."

Another dead end.

For myself, I just wanted to merge with the beat of the driving rain and the occasional clink of Sorrow's name and vaccination tags—I'd brought him to town with me because I was tired of apologizing every time I came home late and he'd tried to be good but there was another puddle just inside the door.

There were few cars in the hospital's main parking lot. Bad weather kept people at home. I knew I didn't want to be there dragging a long shadow of guilt behind me. I'd made fun of the woman. I'd blamed her. God only knew what was waiting up in a sterile hospital room to haunt me.

I walked Sorrow around the car a few times then locked him inside with a window cracked.

We stopped at the desk and were told to go on up. The room was on the second floor. I knocked at the closed door only to have it opened by a man in a white coat who said he was almost finished with Ms. Wilcox and would be right out.

Dolly shuffled around looking at the pictures on the walls of the hall while I shuffled around looking down at my sneakers.

Dolly came to stand beside me. When she spoke, her voice was muffled and troubled. "You know I didn't mean for her to really shoot him," she said.

I made a face in her direction.

"Well, maybe she took me seriously. I'm feeling . . . well . . ."

"Yeah," I half whispered back. "And I made fun of her."

The tech, with his vials of blood, came out, and told us to go on in. He held the door wide.

I didn't recognize the person in the bed. I hoped it was the wrong room. This woman's face was mottled red with blue bruises, and swollen to twice the size of a normal face. The eyes were slits with something dark behind the lids, something going back and forth from me to Dolly. The thin lips were puffed and cracked and shiny with ointment. Ariadne Wilcox was bandaged around her head, down across her ears, and under her chin. Her right arm, lying on top of her light coverlet, was swathed in bandage. I didn't want to know about the rest of her body. Ariadne licked at her lips with the tip of a swollen tongue. Her head didn't turn toward us. Only those dark irises under the gapped lids followed me and Dolly as we came in close, to stand over her.

She focused on Dolly.

"Is he dead?" she asked in a voice that sounded like something trapped in a box.

Dolly nodded.

Ariadne tried a smile but winced. She settled for an almost imperceptible nod then added a few words that weren't clear. She tried again, licking out at her lips and holding her breath.

"Good," was what finally came out.

Dolly leaned down closer to her. "I'm sorry. I'm really sorry . . . I didn't mean for you to . . ."

Ariadne half lifted the bandaged arm from the blanket.

"Don't . . . sorry," she said. "No kids . . . No life . . ."

Dolly and I both nodded, catching on; knowing now what her life had been like back at that plain little house.

We'd blamed her for letting her kids be taken.

How cheap blame was.

Ariadne took a couple of deep breaths. "His gun. Beat me with it. Grabbed . . . it. Fell down." She took more deep breaths though she winced and groaned before going on. "Turned around. His face right . . . down by me. I just . . . shot."

"That's self-defense," Dolly whispered. "I sure wish you'd said something that day. Told us to get you outta there."

I took Ariadne's movement to be a shrug. "Nobody . . . believe me. My . . . own mama . . . Me. Somethin' wrong with me."

"I'll be there to testify," Dolly said. "I saw that bastard in action a couple of times."

I added "me, too" because I had to say something supportive to clear my conscience. I'd seen the remnants of that black eye the day we were out there but went on to believe what was easiest to believe about her.

"Was he the one who ran into my car?" Dolly asked. "Was he trying to kill my baby?"

Ariadne shook her head very slowly. She tried to clear her throat but it hurt too much. She remained still without speaking.

"Did he kill my grandmother? Maybe 'cause he was still mad that I got your two little girls away from him?"

She shook her head again. A single tear leaked out from the ruined eyes. "Wish . . . almost . . . be over for you, too."

Dolly put a hand on her shoulder, squeezing just a little to let her know she understood, maybe felt the same way.

After a while, Ariadne licked hard at her lips. "My . . . kids? You think . . . someday?"

"You take care of yourself first," Dolly said, barely containing herself. "Get better. Me and Emily, here, we'll get you help. You've got to get your GED, get a job, make a home for the girls to come back to. That's what you've got to think about right now. And . . . and . . ."

Maybe there was a smile. So hard to tell smiles when a face doesn't look like a face. "No death . . . penalty . . . in . . . Michigan."

"You've already been to hell and back. Nothing more's going to happen. Me and Emily . . . we'll . . . see to it."

Outside, I ran through the steady downpour to the car then put Sorrow on his leash and walked him around the drenched parking lot until he found just the right place to lift his leg. Dolly waited in the passenger's seat.

There wasn't much to say after what we'd just seen. I didn't want to think about anything Dolly'd committed us to. I had no money for lawyers. She sure wasn't rolling in cash.

Still, some tragedies simply take your breath away. Some tragedies stand outside ordinary worries. I was with Dolly. And Ariadne. Whatever it took.

THIRTY

Because neither one of us wanted to do any real work that afternoon, we drove toward Norwood to take a look at the house where the woman made those phone calls.

For myself, I was glad to leave my usual places behind. In my head the usual had become contaminated by a woman's dark and terrible life. I needed to be away from town, away from home, away from the work I should be doing. Here I was driving along black and shining roads with the misery of a dank rain all around me, and happy for it.

We had a lot to talk about but words were small, compared to what we'd witnessed back in the Kalkaska hospital.

Dolly called her sitter, then, satisfied all was well, settled way down in her seat, pushing her gun around to her right side. "Lets him out," she said.

"Lets who out?"

"Lets Jerome Ordway out. She wouldn't have lied to me. He didn't do it. Guess I've got to rethink some of those others who've got it in for me. You know, like that Roman Valderez, the wife beater, except usually wife beaters are drunks and cowards and I don't think the guy even knows how to write let alone copy out one of the Ten Commandments."

"What about Claudine Worfman? How about her? She could be the one making the phone calls. Just to add to your misery."

Dolly shook her head. "I don't see Claudine going all the way out to Norwood to break into a house and use the phone."

"Okay. There's still that bulging garage at the Throes

194

brothers house."

"So what? We found the SUV. What else do we care about?"

I shrugged. "Could be stolen goods. Could be they're afraid you'll find out what they're doing."

Dolly gave me a disgusted grunt.

"You going there to have a look?" I pushed.

She stuck her bottom lip out and shook her head. "Who cares if they're growing a little pot?" She burrowed farther down into my front seat while putting a hand up to push Sorrow's head, sticking through between the seats, away from hers.

"Let 'em do what they want. No skin off my nose," she said with un-Dolly-like resignation.

At US 31, I turned north. Norwood was beyond Elk Rapids, about halfway to Charlevoix. A picturesque little village I'd been to many times. It sat on the shores of Lake Michigan, off by itself, away from the main highway and far from other towns. Old houses, new McMansions, horse farms, and tiny shoe boxes—all old money and new money. Quiet places with screened porches and expansive lawns. And little huddled houses where fishermen and hunters used to make a subsistence living before selling off to people from down below, in southern Michigan, to use as their getaway cabins on the big lake.

I turned at the sign to Norwood. A narrow, two-lane road curved through woods and fields and up and down hills. The rain let up a little but the sky was still odd, the threat huge, even mystical overhead.

"You think she'll go to jail?" I asked when I made a left turn at a white church, as Dolly indicated.

"Ariadne? Not if there's justice anywhere in this world. And just to be sure, you mean what you said back at the hospital? That you'll testify for her?"

"Of course. I saw her black eye when we went out there. And I saw his rage — that we'd dare question him."

"But he wasn't the one who ran into my car. And he wasn't the one who killed Cate. Would have been good if he had been. I'd have liked to send him back to prison. Men up at Marquette don't like child molesters."

"He's dead anyway," was all I could answer.

Along either side of the road, heading down toward the lake, were thick woods or old barren fields where someone once tried to farm. The road, the trees, the fields — everything glistened darkly with the still dripping rain.

"Ominous," I said, shivering.

"Yeah, you see the lake?" She pointed through a stand of weedy trees. "Mad as hell."

I saw roiling water and waves breaking on a rocky shore. I saw whitecaps rolling from as far off as I could see.

"How does something so beautiful get so ugly?" she asked, an unusual question for Dolly. "Seems wrong. You know? If a thing's beautiful why does it have to have this other side?"

I had no answer to a philosophical question from my pragmatic friend.

"Where's the house?" I asked to deflect the anger she was working up to.

"Straight," she nodded ahead.

I drove until she pointed to a white farmhouse set back from the road under tall maple trees. Far behind the house, across a wide, fallow field, stood an old barn, large corrugated roof partially fallen in, red walls gaping. The sturdiest thing about that building was a solid white stone foundation. Evidently the property hadn't been farmed in a long time.

There were no cars in the drive beside the house. The state police had come and gone.

"Nobody around," I pointed out the obvious.

"I'll call the post, see if there's a way to get inside."

I got out, Sorrow on his leash, and left her to her phone call while Sorrow sniffed out the perfect tree to lift his leg.

I got him back in the car and went up the steps to cup my hands at the front door glass, looking in at a still-life room: a curved-arm sofa with big, fringed pillows and rocking chairs set in front of a well-used stone fireplace.

"Said there's a key over the door," Dolly called up the steps to me, slamming the car door behind her. "They put cardboard in the window where she broke in."

She found the key and, with the help of a pushing shoulder, got us into a living room colder and damper than outside, though I heard a faraway furnace snap on, probably set very low back before winter. The place smelled of must and an earthen cellar. Not a place I wanted to hang out in, unless we were going to build a fire and stay to see if the phone lady returned.

On the far side of the living room, in front of a wall of bookcases, a log staircase climbed to the second floor. Dolly headed there and I followed.

Upstairs, there were two bedrooms. Each had an old canopied bed with dusty curtains hanging over the canopies. There were very similar old dressers in each room. No closets, but tall chifforobes stood along a side wall—one empty and one with a pile of what looked like old jeans, a chenille bathrobe, and a worn, wool plaid jacket. Typical summer visitor gear.

There was a bathroom but nothing looked as if it had been touched in quite a while except that the toilet was running. All I could think of was the electric bill the owner was going to get as her water pump ran on for months. I jiggled the handle until the ball inside caught and the water stopped.

"Hope the state police got some prints off that handle before you messed it up." Dolly stood behind me, in the bathroom doorway

"Think of the bill."

"Yeah, well, think about catching her."

Properly chastened, I followed back downstairs to check out the kitchen. A painted wood table with six high-backed chairs stood at the center of the large room. An expensive industrial-type range and a double-door refrigerator took up one wall. Cabinets and a double sink took up another. Under one counter there was a built-in dishwasher. All the appliances were new and more what I expected in a doctor's house.

A tall window on the back wall had been closed with cardboard taped over broken glass.

Dolly nodded to it. "That's how she got in," she said. "State boys fixed it as best they could."

When I opened one of the cupboards I found a stash of can goods and a can of coffee.

The woman had helped herself. An empty chili can stood in the sink, along with an opener, a dried-on pot, a dirty dish, and a glass.

"She was here for a while," Dolly said, pointing to the mess in the sink.

"Not today." I examined the dried-on chili.

"So, maybe she hasn't been back since she made those phone calls. Look for a car key. The doctor said she kept a car up here and that the key was in a cupboard. It was the only thing she could think anybody might want to steal. I didn't see a car out there anywhere. Did you?"

"Could be in that barn."

"We'll look when we finish here," she said and opened the refrigerator to find it empty.

I searched everywhere for the key but found nothing. No key hung on the little pegboard by the door. No key in any of the cupboards.

We finished the kitchen and went through the living room, checking bookshelves and even shoving our hands down between the cushions of the sofa and chairs. Nothing anywhere but a little dust.

We looked over the place a last time then went out the front, locking the door behind us.

The rain had turned to mist. I let Sorrow out to run, nose to the ground, snuffling ahead of us around the side of the house, where he stopped to sniff at the double-wooden doors to a Michigan basement sticking out from the stone foundation.

Dolly hurried up behind him to check the padlock on the doors. "Nobody been down there," she said.

"Such a big place." I pointed to the empty fields surrounding the house, then back to where the derelict barn stood. "Think it was a dairy farm at one time?"

"Who knows? People come up here with crazy ideas about going back to the land. Soil is nothing but sand. Still—cows. Suppose that could be." She shrugged.

"Man over by Mancelona grows potatoes. He's got a great business."

"Potatoes have to be easier than cows."

When we got to the barn, we stood in one of the door-less openings. The old tin roof hung halfway to the floor in places. The cavernous building was empty except for piles of timber and the rusted skeleton of an old plow. Rain dripped from jagged roof edges. Nothing looked safe: not the gapped walls, not the roof, not the hanging hayloft.

"Nobody here," Dolly declared and we gladly headed back as I whistled Sorrow out of the field. "And no car."

"And no key to a car inside the house."

"I better get that license number out to all departments across the state."

"I'll call Bill. Maybe he can get the make, model, and license number into my story. It would help to have a lot more eyes looking."

Back at the car, Dolly bounced the house key in her hand as I started my engine. "I'm keeping this key," she said. "In case the woman comes back. She'll have to break in again if she wants to hide out here."

The ride back to Leetsville was a little better than the ride to Norwood. As Dolly called Lucky with the information on the Volkswagen, the sky cleared, rays of late day sunlight shot down like spotlights, then a broad halo, and then the sun broke through and the woods and rolling hills shimmered.

When we were almost back to town, Dolly sighed, sat up, and twiddled her fingers on the dashboard. "You know what's driving me crazy right now?"

"Everything?"

"Yeah, well, especially two things. That 'Thou Shalt Not Steal' business, like I've got some crazy preacher after me. And those damned jellybeans. You know, maybe Audrey isn't the only one who loves black jellybeans . . ."

I didn't look over at her. I had my own ideas but didn't feel I had the right to say a word to Dolly.

"And you know what else? It's Omar. He's serious about wanting to be in Baby Jane's life. Don't expect I can stop him. I been thinking maybe I'll call him tonight, invite him to my motel. Let him play with Jane awhile. I guess what you said is right: 'It's only fair.' He's her father after all. And sometimes I can be a little bit hardheaded."

On that monument to understatement, I dropped her off at the motel and headed home. Now it was just Sorrow and me.

Happily, Sorrow couldn't talk.

THIRTY-ONE

I was happy to be home and to be alone.

I was happy to pour myself a glass of Pinot and settle in my faux leather recliner with a blanket pulled up to my chin against the May chill in the house.

Something was telling me this murderer we were chasing was laughing at us, dropping clues like black jellybeans and phone calls and biblical taunts while holding his sides with merriment. I'd figured out that the target, all along, had been Dolly. What better way to get at her than to hurt her baby? Then kill off the only family member she had? So—who was next? The only friend she had?

Which was me. I got up and double-checked the locks on the doors and went around making sure the window locks were in place. As it got dark, I crept, on hands and knees, pulling a curtain aside to look out, thinking I'd surprise someone sneaking toward the house.

Then I had another glass of wine and sat down to have a long talk with myself, about bravery and cowardice and real things to be afraid of. I fell asleep in my chair in the middle of the talk so I'll never know which side I came down on, though in the morning I had a good laugh at my childish fear of the dark and got more than a little worried over the empty wine bottle. Which brought a resolution to stop consoling myself with alcohol and grow up.

Dolly called at seven thirty Monday morning. I was on my second cup of tea and thinking about a poached egg and toast.

"We've got the make and license out to every department in the state."

"Great," I said, though I figured this was old news.

"They'll get her."

"Unless she holes up again."

"Could be the Norwood house, if she does. No way of knowing we're on to her there."

"Unless she saw ten squad cars in the drive."

"Hey, what's your problem this morning? I could use a little support here."

"I'm supportive. It's just . . . I don't know. All this . . . stuff . . . and then Ariadne killing her boyfriend. Right now I'm not pleased with the world I'm in—where a guy like that can hurt kids, then hurt their mother—and she goes to jail."

"Wish she'd killed him when he was hurting the kids," she said. "But then, I never walked in her shoes. Don't know what I'd do. Guess I'm out of the people-judging business."

"You kidding? That's your job. You go out of the judging business, you might as well retire."

"Yeah, suppose so. Just maybe a little more thought behind the judging."

Time to change the subject.

"You talk to your neighbors? I forgot to ask before. Anybody see anything when Cate was killed? Hear anything?" I asked.

"Nobody was home. Most of the women from around here go to the Kaliseum to swim in the pool. They go out to lunch and don't get home until the afternoon. Oh, by the way, I called the hospital about Ariadne. Still the same. I'm gonna run down there and take a statement. Her doctor says she's up to it and wants to get everything on the record."

"You don't need me for that."

"Nope. Stay home and write that stuff you write. Oh, and thanks for yesterday's story in the paper. I'm thinking that jellybean business will jog somebody's memory. Somebody they know or maybe somebody they saw buying bags of black jellybeans."

"I'll keep them coming until there's nothing left to write."

"Good." A long pause. "Omar came over Saturday night."

"How'd that go?"

"Okay, I guess." I heard a shrug in her voice. "We're going to work something out between us."

"That's good for Jane." The thought actually made me smile.

"Think so? Said his mom offered to watch Jane if I got in a bind."

"Hope you take her up on it."

"I'm keeping it at the back of my head."

"Now there's a lonely place."

"What?" she asked as if she hadn't heard me.

"Nothing." I quickly moved on. "Have you ever thought about your friend Grace Humbert?"

"What do you mean: 'thought about her.' I go there every Mother's Day."

"Yeah, but, like, what would Grace do in the situation we're in?"

"Huh?"

"You know. She suffered sneers and jibes and people's fear of her all her life. Had to have handled it all some way."

"What do you mean 'fear'?"

"I saw an article about her down at the museum once."

"Lots of newspaper articles down there. She was famous."

"No, this was after she came back here to live. When she retired from the circus. All that hair didn't go away. There was this little article about how the town's people asked her not to walk the streets without a veil because she was scaring the pregnant ladies."

"Geez. Scarin' people." Dolly thought awhile. "You talking about me scarin' people? That's why somebody's after me or my family?"

"No. I was just thinking about Grace. What did she do when people came after her. I mean, did she ever back away from who she was?"

"How should I know?"

"Then why did you choose her as your stand-in mom?"

"Read about her. Liked her style. Figured she went through a lot and came out on top, famous in the U.S., maybe kind of wealthy, known around the world. All that with hair all over her body. Kind of like Cousin It from that old TV show. And I figured if she could do it I could sure get over whatever problems I have."

"Yeah, that's what I mean. It's like, in the situation we're in now, what would Grace Humbert do?"

"I still don't get it."

"Think about it. That woman had courage. She had a look to her like nothing was going to get in her way."

"You think I'm going to give up because this all seems so crazy? Is that it?"

"No, of course not."

"Then what the hell are you talking about?"

"Nothing." I gave in and decided I'd keep my "what would Grace do" strategy to myself.

I bundled up and took my egg and toast down to the lake to eat while the beaver harassed Sorrow and a pair of stately geese swam nearby, watching me as I huddled in a heavy sweater against the chilly morning and thought about titles for a series of books. I wanted to hang on to the "Dead" word, figuring that would keep all the books in the same place on bookstore and library shelves, then reminding myself I'd be shelved by my last name anyway. So all in the Ks. Since I wanted to start the next book with my main character out walking around that little wild lake, I thought hard about the skull she would stumble on and, in a few minutes, I had my two titles. As if they were dropped in my lap. I went back into the house and called Faith Cardoni. I told her: *Dead Floating Lovers* and *Dead Sleeping Shaman*. She said she was thrilled and couldn't wait to read the books. We talked about a book a year coming out and I got off the phone, suddenly hit with the real need to write a book a year and no real idea if they would make money. All I knew was that I had to give myself a fair shot at my dream.

My next call was to Bill.

"You're sure?" he asked when I turned down the job.

"I have to give this a try."

"I understand." He took a long breath. "I'll keep giving you as much freelance work as I can. I told you about the cutbacks here . . ."

"I know. And I know I'm crazy for turning this down."

"Maybe not crazy, Emily. Maybe it's Frost's 'road not taken.'"

"I hope so," I said. "I'd like to think I'm not self-destructive."

He laughed. "Doubt that. Oh, and don't forget our picnic. A couple of people around here would like a shot at getting you to join us, despite what you're telling me."

"Let me know when. I'll bring potato salad, for which I am justly famous."

"Don't bring anything. You're my date, remember."

I hung up not letting myself think about what Bill had said and what that meant.

Later, I put on my oldest clothes and went out to garden because I could think better out there with the worms. Sorrow sat dutifully beside me. I was congratulating him on being such a good dog, when a yellow setter came streaking through and Sorrow ran off barking, causing a commotion, until I had to stand, wipe the dirt from my knees and take off after him, up the driveway toward Willow Lake Road.

Since my drive heads straight uphill my legs gave out before I quite reached the top. I was swearing at a great rate when I finally struggled out into the road to see Sorrow standing next to Harry Mockerman, the very man I'd been avoiding for the last few days, along with any talk of his upcoming nuptials at my house, which was going to require strict concentration and days of housecleaning.

"So, how you doing there, Emily?" Harry smiled a rare smile. "See you're still havin' trouble controlling yer dog here."

I shook my head. "No trouble. Somebody's running setter. He's got no business on my land."

"Your land, eh? Well, now, you go show a dog a deed to property and see if he gets it."

"Not one of your dogs, was it?" I kept a little tight anger at the back of my voice.

"Nope. Got no setters." He let Sorrow slink over next to me, his shame apparent for all to see.

"Say, Emily, I've been wanting to talk to you about the wedding."

"It's all set."

"Well, yes, but I was going in to see Eugenia this afternoon. Delia says I should talk to her."

"What's the problem?"

"We been kind of worrying about something."

Feeling mean, I thought: Good. Maybe they would call off the whole thing and live together in sin.

"What's that?" I asked.

"Delia says I should come right out with it and tell Eugenia cucumbers in cream gives me gas."

"Oh." I leaned back, wide-eyed and trying not to laugh. "And that wouldn't be good for the honeymoon."

First he looked embarrassed and then he looked mad. "Getting old's hell, ya know, Emily. First one part goes and then it's another."

I agreed, and agreed he should go talk to Eugenia about omitting cucumbers from the menu.

"The franks and beans okay?" I thought I might as well check that gassy item out before we got to the big day and had a red-faced groom.

"Fine. Just fine. Though I think, for myself, I may be skipping the beans. Just in case."

I agreed that was a good plan and headed back home to have a close talk with some awakening lily bulbs and teach myself to be grateful that Harry's big event was going to be held in my own scruffy outdoors.

THIRTY-TWO

I felt guilty, taking a whole day off. So I was back at the Leetsville Police Station Tuesday morning looking for Dolly and talking to Lucky because Dolly was out beyond town where kids had been knocking over garbage cans again.

One thing I can never figure is the smell in all police stations, old or new. I don't care where it is or how big it is, they all have a distinct scent to them. Today I figured it out: wet leather. Not a bad smell, but something you don't always expect, especially on a dry, warm day when the sun's shining and the temperature is hovering around sixty-five.

Lucky sat behind the front desk taking calls from other departments and fending off anything that smacked of another garbage can complaint.

"Heard from France." He leaned back between calls, arms behind his head.

"They find her?"

He shook his head hard. "Not a sign of her. The department head I spoke to said they did everything, checked immigration, checked her name, even ran her through their wanted lists. Nothing. If she's still going by that name, she's not in France."

I was puzzled. "Cate told me directly that her daughter was in France."

He shrugged and spread his hands wide. "Who knows?"

"Let me call Bill. He asked a friend to look for her, too."

"Hope he's got better luck."

But Bill had nothing. "My buddy was going to go to the police until I told him you'd already covered that. He says he used all his usual tricks and even called religious leaders he knew, asking them to help. You know, that 'cult' business. Nothing. Anywhere. You sure this woman exists, Emily?"

I thanked him and got off the phone to tell Lucky. We gave each other the same odd look. I didn't want to say anything but Lucky wasn't as shy.

"You think she's really over there or is this some story Cate made up?"

"Why?"

"I don't know. Protecting Dolly."

"From what?"

"Who knows? Maybe she just wanted to hand her a mother —dead or alive."

"Makes no sense . . ."

We were deep into figuring out the mind of a dead woman when Dolly came in dragging two juveniles by the backs of their hoodies.

"Can I put these two in your office, Lucky? I already called their parents. They're on their way over. Somebody's got a lot of garbage to clean up. I told their parents to bring shovels."

"It wasn't me . . ." one of the struggling teenagers grumbled.

"Yeah," Dolly sneered down at him. "You always go around with a garbage can lid in your hands?"

"He did it," the other boy complained loudly. "I was only watching."

"Take 'em in back," Lucky said. "If they get off their chairs, handcuff them together."

"Sure thing." Dolly led the boys down a side hall, back to Lucky's office.

He gave me a smile, the kind of smile only people who know Deputy Dolly Wakowski give each other.

"So?" She came back grinning and brushing off her uniform pants. "What else is new?"

Lucky and I looked at each other. Neither one of us wanted to tell her the news.

"What's going on?"

"Heard back from France," Lucky said.

"Good," she said. "About time. How do I get ahold of the woman?"

"Seems you can't. The French authorities can't find her."

She nodded a couple of times then turned to me. "What about Bill? He have any luck?"

I shook my head. "No woman by that name anywhere in France, unless she's hiding from the authorities, or changed her name. Maybe she got married."

She thought awhile. "Think Cate was lying?"

We fell over ourselves mumbling and coming up with denials.

"You sure you told 'em Audrey Delores Thomas, or even Audrey Delores Flynn?" she said.

"Gave 'em both," Lucky said.

"Hmmp. So she doesn't exist. What was Cate talking about then? Why'd she have to lie?"

Nobody said anything.

After a while, Dolly drew in a deep breath, let it out, and looked over at me.

"You know what?" she asked.

I shook my head: nope, I had no ideas, no help, no how.

"It's about that jellybean thing. Like some kind of sign,

don't you think? I mean, somebody knew Cate would know what it meant when she heard we found three bags of 'em in the SUV. Then we got one dropped in the house after he or she kills Cate. Maybe a sign to me. This whole thing is nuts. I can't put my finger on anything . . ."

I clucked, or something, showing my concern and at the same time relieved to have the missing mother business behind us.

"You want to come with me, Emily?" She turned to me. "Got a call from Martie Sinclair out on River Road. Said maybe a friend of hers can help us. Said maybe this friend drove Cate places. They knew each other from garden club."

"What's the friend's name? Can't we go see her directly?"

She shook her head. "She won't give me the name until she talks to us first. Got it in her head she might be getting her friend in trouble."

"Sure, I'll go with you."

We were on the way out the door when Dolly stopped, turned, and looked hard at Lucky.

"So, Cate lied. Looks like I never had a mother after all."

"Everybody has a mother," Lucky said, his look fierce.

"Not me," she said. "And if this Audrey person is really my mother and maybe she gave me away and never got in touch with Cate the rest of her life, well, then I hate her more than any person should hate another person."

On that happy note we went out to Dolly's car as a van filled with angry parents pulled to a jerking stop in front of the police station. A man got out and yelled at Dolly. He shook his fist as Dolly saluted him and we drove off.

THIRTY-THREE

Martie Sinclair lived down River Road, back in the middle
of a forest on the banks of the Manistee, a winding river so
slow shadows of wild celery waved against the rippled sand
bottom. Minnows darted, silver in the sun. A deer came out to
drink at the other side of the river and looked hard at me before
deciding I was harmless.

I could have hung out there, outside Martie Sinclair's house,
and watched the water flowing around the banks and between
floating islands of vegetation, and not moved all day.

Up the bank from where I stood, Dolly talked to Martie, an
older woman with a puff of snow-white hair, while I watched a
stick float by the toes of my shoes.

Dolly scribbled notes while I took off my sneaker and stuck
my foot in the water. Cold. Very cold. And I had nothing to
wipe my foot on so I wedged it back into the sneaker wet. I
squished up the bank to where the two women stood.

Dolly thanked Martie and took my elbow, leading me back
to her car and shaking me from my river trance.

"You asleep or something?" she demanded, starting the
borrowed squad car, then lurching back up the drive to River
Road.

"Tired, I guess. What I really want to do is go home and sit
down in my studio and work on a book. I don't want to be
here, Dolly. I want to be in a world I make for myself where I'm
in charge and people listen to me and I know what's going to
happen, to whom, and who the killer is. I'm not liking it in this
real world. We've got some woman who thinks it's all right to

make creepy phone calls for kicks. We've got some jellybean-eating killer. We've got me creeping around on my knees at night because I'm scared. And you . . ."

"Yeah?" She waited. "What about me?"

"Just . . ." I was sorry I'd started the whole thing. "All the hurt thrown at you. Baby Jane. Cate. Now Audrey Thomas — nowhere."

"So? What do you expect me to do? Curl up and die?"

At the main road she checked for traffic and made a right.

"I'll tell you this, Emily," she started again. "Sure, I'd rather be someplace else. Maybe Hawaii or Alaska. And maybe I don't want a sixteen-year-old watching my baby. And sure I want to find out who killed my grandmother and I want to take 'em by the neck and throw 'em, hard. Maybe ten miles." She turned to look over at me.

"And maybe I'll get a chance to do all of that," she went on. "Maybe even a chance to sit in a corner and cry my eyes out. But, if I've learned one thing about living, it's that you don't give into bad stuff. You fight it and you keep fighting it until maybe — someday when I'm long gone — people will stop doin' terrible things to each other."

I didn't answer. Chastened, I sat up, pulled over the notebook Dolly laid between us, and read that we were headed to Bellaire, a town northwest of Mancelona. To Rodgers Road. To see a Ginny Schwartz.

"Does she know we're coming?" I asked sheepishly, tapping a finger on Dolly's notation.

"Martie called her."

"So she took Cate places?"

"She picked up Martie for garden club and met Cate there."

"Anything else?"

She shook her head. "Martie said Ginny would tell us all they used to do. Places she took Cate."

We were there in half an hour. Me, with a new resolve to concentrate, to keep my mind on finding this murderer, and put my life, my future, my choices behind me until this was over.

One thing I vowed: I was going to be a better friend.

Ginny Schwartz's house sprawled across a green knoll. Neat flowerbeds edged the walls. All shades of spring flowers nodded in a freshening breeze coming over the hills from the big lake.

Ginny Schwartz expected us, inviting us into a kitchen with tall, many-paned windows of sparkling glass. We sat at a table with a teapot in the center, kept warm by a knitted blue cozy. Three cups and saucers, sprinkled with blue forget-me-nots, were set on the table. Lace-edged napkins were folded, laid with shining spoons, and arranged beside the saucers. There was a silver pot of cream and one of sugar, and a plate of oatmeal cookies so warm steam rose above them.

Ginny, a woman in her sixties at least, indicated our places at the table and poured the tea. She passed the cookies. I took one—just being polite. Dolly took three then tucked one in her pocket, which, she explained, would be for later.

Ginny, a sweet-face woman, seemed flattered and didn't mind.

"Now, you want to know about me and Cate," she said, then smiled at Dolly. "Your grandmother."

Dolly nodded.

"She was a lot of fun to be with. Certainly she'd seen more

of the world than I could ever imagine. Not that she bragged about it or anything. Just that she had . . . I guess you could say she had more knowledge than I."

She put her cup carefully back into its saucer and wiped at her lips with her ironed napkin. "We enjoyed each other's company. I was so sorry to hear . . . what happened to Cate." She shook her head sympathetically.

The woman went on. "I'm surprised she never said anything to you. Why me and Cate would take off every couple of weeks. We called them our adventures." She hesitated. "But mostly we just went to Alden. Such a lovely little town. We'd have tea at a restaurant there. Walk through the shops. End up out on the dock, sitting and watching the lake, and enjoying the day.

"Oh, and, of course, our visits to the candy shop. Cate went to Alden especially to visit Spencer's. Always for the jellybeans. They sell the individual colors, you know. And Cate only liked the black ones. Heaven knows why. She did say once they weren't for her. She said they were for a friend, but I had a sneaking suspicion it was something of a secret pleasure, since she never opened a bag and passed it to me. But, as we all know, folks have habits of being. Cate's was to hoard those black jellybeans to her. Which, don't get me wrong, I thoroughly understood. I have little things I keep to myself, too. Don't we all?"

She laughed lightly and poured more tea.

I looked at Dolly, who kept her face blank, her eyes fixed on the woman.

When Dolly spoke, her voice was steady. "I never knew Cate to eat jellybeans," she said. "Or any other candy. Never kept it in the house. So, she ever say who this friend was?"

Ginny shook her head. "Never said. I figured it was somebody from her past. You know, somebody I wouldn't know, if there really was an old friend."

"Anything else?" Dolly asked. "I mean, any other place the two of you got to?"

She thought awhile. "Just the bank. Brought her to the Northern Community Bank here in Bellaire. Cate said she didn't like banking closer to home. Didn't want neighbors knowing her business."

Dolly and I stiffened at the same time.

"Which bank was that again?" Dolly smiled that odd, Cheshire cat smile of hers that said more about what was going on inside her head than that she was feeling friendly.

"Only one. Northern Community, right down in town. Can't miss it."

THIRTY-FOUR

The Northern Community Bank was downtown where Ginny Schwartz said it was. I'd never noticed it in all the times I'd driven through Bellaire, stopped at the Brewery, or went to Lulu's Restaurant when Jackson came to town and I talked him into going there because he could pay for the Sangiovese, and the Santa Margarita Pinot Grigio I couldn't afford to buy, and he could pay for the wonderful cheese platter of salamis and cheeses from all over the world, with nuts and slices of crisp baguette . . .

Painful to think about and, if I was ever honest with myself, one of the main reasons I let Jackson continue to visit.

Paraphrasing Dr. Seuss, I quoted to myself, "Oh, the places I will go. The places I will go."

Back to earth and Dolly pulling into the parking lot beside a plain redbrick building with a Northern Community Bank sign across the front.

"Did you bring the key?" I asked.

She held it up for me to see.

"You have a death certificate?"

She patted her breast pocket.

"Think this is it?"

"You mean, maybe I'll find out something truthful about Cate's life for once? Doubt it."

She gave me a skeptical shrug, opened the door, and jumped out.

A woman in a blue suit looked at the key and examined the death certificate Dolly handed her. She marked Dolly's badge number down on the form she had in front of her, slapped her hands on the paper, then pushed a button that zapped open the gate beside us. She led us back into a vault, walls lined with narrow, locked boxes. The woman used Dolly's key to open one lock and a key she took from her pocket on another. She pulled out the box to set on a table at the center of the room, then turned and left.

The top on the metal box slid back, exposing nothing but stacks of envelopes. Dolly picked one up, looked at it, set it on the table, and picked up another one.

"Mail," she said, looking perplexed.

"Mail? What do you mean 'mail'? Letters from people?"

She shook her head and took another envelope to look at closely. "This pile's from some hospital."

"Why don't we take them back to your place? She must have had a reason for hiding them. We've got to look at everything."

"Good, then I won't need Janie to stay with Jane. Her mother swore up and down she's reliable and she probably is. But *sixteen*! When I was sixteen I was sneaking out to drink beer with my buddies."

"No wonder you never lasted in a foster home."

"What do you think forced me into drinking beer?"

We got a bag from the lady who'd let us into the safe-deposit vault, filled it with tightly packed envelopes, some held together with red rubber bands, and headed back to town and the Rolling River Motel.

I drove the babysitter, Janie, to her house in town, dropped her off, then headed back out to the motel. Dolly had the letters lined in rows on the bed by the time I returned.

She was on the phone and motioned for me to take a look at what she had there.

"Yeah, well," she was saying, turning her back to me. "Let me think about it. Might be something coming up. I'll let you know."

She hung up, turned to me, and made a face. "Omar. Offering his mother up as babysitter again."

"I thought you said something close to 'no way in hell' last time he asked?"

"Not like that, I didn't. But take a look at what we've got and you tell me if we don't have another trip downstate ahead of us.

"They're all in order," she went on, pointing to the array on the bed. "All from the same place. Same address. A hospital in Kalamazoo. Different signatures on some. One signature on the earliest—goes back to the 1980s. Different on the middle letters. Different one on the latest. They're reports." She looked hard at me. "I think they answer a lot of things."

I skimmed over the envelopes, making note of the hospital's name and address.

"Oakwood Psychiatric Hospital," I read aloud from one of the envelopes. "Have you gone through them?" I asked.

"Some. They're all the same—just about."

"So?"

"Each one is a letter from the director of the hospital and a copy of a doctor's notes."

"Huh? Was Cate confined there? Is that the big secret about her?"

She shook her head and frowned hard at me.

"Come on, Dolly. This could be important."

"The reports cover the years from 1979 to 2012. The woman they're talking about was in that hospital all those years, with something called 'schizoaffective disorder.'"

"What? Thirty-three years? I didn't think they kept people that long anymore . . ."

She shrugged. "What I read so far, she didn't get any better. In a few of those later letters they said she had that 'schizoaffective disorder' along with something called 'comorbid anxiety disorder.' None of it sounds good. The doctor's reports I looked at had her always about the same. Recently, they used something called paliperidone on her, then something called lithium. But I guess the lithium made her confused so they changed that. You can read them all, if you want. But nothing's different until early this year . . ."

"God almighty." Dolly took a deep breath and dropped her head into her hands.

"Oh, geez, she died," I said. It seemed the logical conclusion. "Some relative of Cate's?"

Dolly shook her head. "No, didn't die. Changed. From what I understand they put her on a new drug—something called . . ." She looked down at the letter she'd just picked up and sounded out the word, "Aripi-pra-zole."

"Hope it helped, whoever she is. What a life of hell."

"Yeah." Dolly looked hard at me.

"Yeah," she said again.

"What's her name? Are you related to her, too?"

Dolly nodded, then nodded again. "I think so."

I made a face. "Not exactly the kind of family you wanted to find."

"That's for sure."

"So? You ever hear of her?"

She nodded. "I think we just found my mother."

THIRTY-FIVE

What was there to say? I could have been watching a puzzle fly apart in front of me. Dolly's mouth sagged. Her eyes stared off, the one lazy eye moving slowly left, as if there was something to see on the blank motel wall. All I could do was wait. I pulled out the desk chair, sat down, and watched Dolly for a cue—what I should do or say to help her. I prayed she could hold herself together one more time.

Baby Jane fussed in her swing, set up in a corner of the room, a few tentative baby protests. For a minute Dolly looked over at her baby as if she didn't quite understand what had made the noise. Slowly, as I held my breath, she stirred and got up from where she'd collapsed on the bed. She took Jane from her swing and held her tightly to her chest.

When Dolly turned to me, her baby's face pressed to her pale cheek, she said only, "I could have visited her. All these years. I could have known her."

It was as though some of Dolly's life force had leaked away. She was distracted rather than sad; thinking hard but thinking about things that didn't matter. She looked toward the refrigerator, then the TV, then the bed. As if she needed to inventory her world, make sure it was intact, she turned slowly around.

"So?" I prompted finally.

"Guess we gotta get down there. To that hospital. Looks like it's time I met the real Audrey Delores. If this is even her and not somebody Cate dreamed up to be my mother."

She made the phone call to the Kalamazoo hospital and was

connected to the director after a few minutes. I listened as she explained she was an officer with the Leetsville Police Department, investigating the death of someone who might be related to a patient there. She said she needed to come down and speak to him, and maybe see the patient.

I watched her face as she gave the man her mother's name and then listened quietly to whatever he was saying. Something was quickly agreed on. Dolly said she could be there by ten the next morning, hung up, and turned to me.

"He wants a court order," she said. "Patient privacy. Lucky'll get it for me."

She hesitated, but only for a minute. "I'm calling Omar. No more sixteen-year-olds watching Jane. We're going to his mother's house."

While Dolly called Lucky, who said he'd have that order by evening, I called Bill and told him what was happening. I helped Dolly gather up the swing, the diaper bag, plenty of bottles and clothes, and a portable bed.

"Omar's meeting us there," she said as we stuffed Jane and all her gear into the backseat of my car. "I've gotta leave her overnight. We need to get an early start tomorrow."

We headed toward Gaylord and the first meeting between Dolly Wakowski and Omar's mother.

• • •

The house wasn't easy to find, hidden behind tall bushes at the back of a long lot near the center of town. When I pulled in I caught sight of the back end of a blue state police car pulled off to one side. So Omar was there to ease the meeting.

I wanted to help Dolly with Jane's stuff, but instead Dolly pushed Jane into my arms. Of course, the first thing Baby Jane did was smile one of her lopsided dopey smiles at me and bobble her head against my shoulder so I was butter melting along the path to the house. I held on tight, watching where I walked across flagstones set down into deep turf. She felt like an enormous weight against my chest. Responsibility. Her need for protection. There was no spring to her warm, little body. No self-reliance. She laid her head against me and made noises I took for approval, and maybe surprise, that I hadn't dropped her yet.

Omar was at the door, smiling, holding the door wide then quickly reaching out to help Dolly with the swing and the diaper bag.

"Emily," he acknowledged me with a nod. "Good to see you. I'm really looking forward to this."

He nodded again and again. "My mother's out in the kitchen. She's all excited about meeting her granddaughter for the first time."

I caught a kind of bravado in his voice as he talked over his shoulder at us, leading the way through a house so clean it looked like shrink wrapping had just been pulled off for this special occasion. I followed Omar, baby still in my arms, taking in the number of religious icons hanging on the walls, candles in religious holders, candles wound in ribbons and sitting at the center of a lace doily on the polished dining room table.

"Myra's actually my stepmother," Omar murmured.

"Religious, huh?" Dolly said, noticing what I was noticing —a kind of excessive presence of God stuff.

He nodded and gave Dolly a tight smile. "A very good

person."

"Long as she's older than sixteen," Dolly muttered back.

"I'll be leaving her overnight," she raised her voice. "Picking her up tomorrow, when we get back."

"Where're you going?" Omar asked,

"Kalamazoo."

"About your grandmother's murder?"

"Sort of. Following up on some things. Things I didn't know about Cate's past. Have to check out every angle."

"Yeah, that's what I imagined it was about. If there's anything . . ."

"Your dispatcher's got the license number of somebody who stole a car out in Norwood. She broke into a house and made phone calls from there, then took the car. The phone calls were to Emily here." She indicated me with a flip of her thumb. "And Emily's boss at the *Northern Statesman*. We're thinking some whack job going after me, but who knows?"

In the kitchen, an older woman, with short, steel gray hair pulled back behind her ears, got up heavily from the table to greet us.

Another immaculate room, as if no one ever cooked a thing in there. No smell of fresh bread baking or soup simmering in this house. The watchword here was: Clean.

The woman came over to look closely at Baby Jane, getting within inches of the baby's face, narrowing her eyes, then shaking her head.

"Don't look like you," she said over her shoulder in Omar's direction.

He laughed nervously. "Don't worry, Ma. She's mine all right."

She glanced at me, taking in my hair, my shirt and jeans, my ratty shoulder bag, and even looking at my left hand—maybe searching for a ring, I thought.

"Women should be more careful," she said sourly in my direction. "It's the woman's fault. Babies are going to come when a girl doesn't respect her body."

Dolly, beside me, sputtered a time or two. Her eyes grew huge and round. I watched her face move from distracted to animated, then right on to mad as hell.

"Eh . . . Mrs. Winston . . . I'm Dolly. You're telling off the wrong woman there."

Mrs. Winston stepped back. "You?"

She spun around to face Omar. "This is the woman you had sex with? She looks like a man."

Dolly sputtered.

Omar frowned. "This is my baby, Ma. And Dolly's my baby's mother."

She made a noise and threw a hand in the air. "I raised you better than this."

I stood still, holding on to Baby Jane for dear life. It was a standoff at the O.K. Corral, or Eastwood making somebody's day. All I could do was watch Dolly's back hunch up, her neck disappear, and her head dip forward.

"Maybe we should leave," I whispered in the hope of staving off World War III.

Dolly looked at Omar for a minute, then back to me, mouth open. She shook her head.

Omar, in the doorway, put his arms out. "Please, Dolly. She doesn't mean things the way they sound. Mother's had a hard life. You've got to cut her some slack here. All this is a surprise.

I only told her about Jane a few days ago."

Dolly took Jane out of my arms, turned, then stopped on her way out of the room. Her little square body was hunched down tight. "You know what, Omar?" she said, a small smile running across her lips. "Lots of women have hard lives. They're still decent human beings. I'm not leaving my baby here. Not now. Not ever."

She was gone.

He ran after her, out to the car. The swing was still in his arms, diaper bag still canted off his shoulder. As we re-stowed Jane's gear, he begged Dolly to reconsider. "I'll call in sick, stay here all day and take care of her myself."

Dolly looked around at him. I heard her say, softly, "Omar. You've got problems of your own here. Jane's not going to fix anything. Get your own place. 'Til then, you're welcome to come over and visit but I won't let Jane spend a single minute in a house with a woman who's got a mouth like that on 'er."

He backed off from the car.

The next words Dolly uttered as we drove out were, "Damn. Who can I get to watch her?"

We headed back toward Leetsville while Dolly called Gloria at EATS and explained. I could hear Gloria begging off but not the reason why. Dolly hung up and said, "She's got a doctor's appointment this afternoon. Can't take Jane."

She thought hard while I took a couple of long gulps and offered to stay behind. "I'll watch her, Dolly. I'll be happy to."

She turned me down, saying, "Naw, you've got to be there. This'll be your story for the day."

I was about to argue when her phone rang. All I heard was "Uh-huh. Uh-huh. Be right there."

229

She looked relieved. "Eugenia's keeping her at the restaurant until three o'clock, then she'll take her home with her. Tomorrow she'll take her to the restaurant or maybe take the day off. If she needs help she's got a dozen women already offered to chip in."

That settled, she said, "You know I can't go on like this, taking Jane from pillar to post. I've got to settle on one babysitter."

I agreed. "And you need a stable place to live, not a motel."

"That, too."

I thought awhile. "I can understand you wanting company for this trip down to the hospital, but, Dolly, this isn't something I can put in any story about Cate's murder. I'd say this is personal business. Your personal business."

She looked over at me. "Yeah, maybe it could've been like that. Except for one thing. That director told me something that's got my head spinning. We're not going down there to talk to my mother. She's not there. That new medication they put her on changed everything. She improved, the man said. A few months ago she petitioned the courts to be released."

There was more.

"About a month ago, they released her," Dolly said. "She's been out of there ever since. Cate must've known and never said a word."

Back in town, we picked up the court order Lucky'd brought back from a judge in Kalkaska, and dropped off Jane.

THIRTY-SIX

I was happy I wasn't Dolly, driving up to the cluster of austere, small-windowed brick hospital buildings from another time. Everything so neatly lined across the front—narrow windows, roof edges. All topped with what looked like a dome.

I thought of my mother—during the twelve years I knew her—compared to this, the place where Dolly's mother had spent most of her life.

In my head were good memories of long, thin fingers gently brushing my face as my mother lay between blue sheets, sick in her bed. And gray eyes, echoing the colors everywhere in her room; the eyes narrowing to happy lines when I ran in after school to hug her and rattle on and on about my day.

And a voice that maybe I remembered or maybe only reflected my father's memories, but I knew that voice could say my name in so many different ways: joy, love, disappointment, laughter.

This was all Dolly had of hers, an icy institution and a web of lies Dolly's confusion would probably never work through.

We said nothing to each other as we parked in the lot beside the biggest of the buildings and walked in—one behind the other—to ask for the director.

Yes, we had an appointment . . .

We were ushered into an office as warm as the building was cold.

I liked David Heilman. He stood to greet us, his back to an ochre-colored wall with a huge copy of Monet's *Water Lilies* behind his desk. He shook our hands and smiled and waved us to comfortable upholstered chairs.

Dolly handed him the court order she'd folded and slipped into the breast pocket of her wrinkled blue shirt.

"Officer Wakowski." He took the paper, looked it over, then leaned forward, setting his elbows on the desk. "How can I help you?"

"It's about Audrey Delores Thomas. I called . . ."

He nodded. "I knew Audrey well. Everybody here was happy to see the new medication help her the way it did. Almost a miracle, how she went from a delusional state to as close to normal as she has the possibility of ever being. The Audrey I, at last, got to know in her remaining days with us was a very pleasant and loving person. Of course, I wasn't here when she first came to Oakwood, but that was thirty-three years ago. None of us were here then. I have only our records to go on and they tell a very different story of Ms. Thomas's state of mind."

"She had a mother. Cate Thomas."

He nodded. "From what I've been able to ascertain from the files, Mrs. Thomas was kept apprised bimonthly of her daughter's condition. We've had different addresses for her, but never had any of our letters returned, as far as I know."

"Could I get a list of those addresses?" Dolly said.

"I take it you have good reason for asking."

Dolly nodded. "Cate Thomas was murdered recently. Letters from here were found and that was the first anyone knew of Audrey's existence . . ."

I interrupted. "Well, not of her existence, Dolly. Everyone believed Audrey was in France. Cate said she'd joined a religious cult over there."

Dolly nodded toward the director. "I'm investigating Cate's murder and all of this is a surprise to everybody who knew her — that Audrey was confined here."

He nodded sadly. "Many family members choose to hide the existence of a loved one in long-term mental care. That's changing somewhat, but not fast enough."

He sat thinking a minute. "After Mrs. Thomas was told Audrey was improving and might possibly be released, she did write me a letter that wasn't quite . . . well . . . what I expected."

"Like . . . what'd she say?" Dolly asked.

He frowned. "It seemed she had her reservations about Audrey's ability to function on the outside. Well, actually she was adamant about it, though I called her to assure her Audrey was doing wonderfully. After all, two doctors, other than the doctor assigned to her here, attested to her ability to rejoin society."

"Why'd Cate want to stand in the way of her kid's getting out of this place? I don't see . . ."

"I suspect it was because Audrey would never answer Cate Thomas's letters. Never thanked her for gifts. Without that resolved, well, I'm sure Mrs. Thomas had grown embittered over the years."

Dolly turned to me. "That's why we didn't find letters from Audrey to Cate."

I didn't say anything. It was as if Dolly'd split herself in two — one treating these two women as strangers, the other wincing just beneath the surface.

"Did Cate ever visit here?" She turned back to Mr. Heilman.

The man slowly shook his head. "I've got a record of only one visit. That was back in the 1980s. It seems it didn't go well and Mrs. Thomas was asked not to return until there was significant change in Audrey's condition."

He cleared his throat, then moved a file in front of him to a far corner of the table.

"It was never certain, according to Audrey's files, what the problem between the women was. Her current doctor, who signed her out, thought it was due to a harmless quirk in Audrey. Something, no doubt, going back into her past. The doctor thought, as Audrey improved, that she had a good handle on that quirk. There were no more outward manifestations of it. Though I have to say, Audrey's . . . eh . . . special quirk had become almost a humorous aspect of her disease. A small thing, but here, at the hospital, I have to say — in our defense — that we do look for humor where we can find it."

"What was this 'quirk' that worried Cate?" I leaned forward to ask.

He waved a hand. "Audrey was always pregnant. Pillows, towels under her skirts, whatever she found to fortify her fixation. Sad, in a way. What with her history. But pregnant she stayed for most of her thirty-three years with us." He smiled as if we would get the joke. "Before she was released, the court-appointed panel that examined her were told about the fixation and decided that, as a delusion, this was a harmless one. It was felt Audrey hung on to the idea to counter something from her past and that once she was out in the real world the idea would simply fade."

Dolly made notes on the pad she'd laid in her lap. She pretended to read her jottings, gathering herself, then asking, "Why was she brought here to begin with?"

Dolly still called the woman "she," never letting on Audrey Thomas was her mother. At first I was surprised and then I thought I understood. Something about professional objectivity, maybe even something of her own embarrassment, maybe part of the anger she'd held in, still aimed at the woman.

"I have the complete file," the director said, pointing to stacks of folders, old blue boxes that must have held more files, and then battered files held together with cord. "It's all chronological, though it looks a mess. You have to understand — thirty-three years. Many different doctors. Many directors. Social workers. But I can easily pull out the initial diagnosis and the circumstances surrounding Audrey's hospitalization."

"I'd appreciate it."

He drew one of the stacks toward him. He stopped. "Oh, and don't let me forget, we found some things after Audrey left. We'll be returning them to her — when we get an address . . ."

He untied the cord on one of the stacks of folders and let the cord fall to the table. He checked one file after another until he had the date he wanted. At first he read to himself, nodding from time to time.

"You can read it, if you like," he offered to Dolly. "There's a police report attached. Evidently Audrey's initial breakdown was severe. She'd just had a baby. Her husband dropped her off at the hospital, in labor, and left, never returning to get her, though she fought with the hospital — that was Grace Hospital, in Detroit — not to put her and her baby out on the street."

I wanted to reach out to Dolly, who'd been that baby, but I didn't dare touch her. She sat so still. The look on her face was cold; her skin was pale.

"What was the police report about? She cause trouble at the hospital?"

The man read through the report then shook his head. "No, that wasn't it. It seemed she ended up at a Detroit motel, something arranged by Social Services. She was alone, except for her baby, of course.

He read on. "People in a room close to hers heard sobbing and screaming and called the motel manager. He called the police."

I wanted to say "Poor woman" but didn't dare, though I felt it deeply and wondered if there wasn't even a single dark corner of Dolly's mind that was melting just a little.

"When the police got there they had to break down the door."

He read on.

"Seems Audrey Delores was in the bathroom. She'd filled the bathtub to overflowing and was kneeling beside it. She had her baby's head under water, trying to drown the little girl."

Everything stopped in the room; there was only the drone of the man's voice, reading from a file, saying words that didn't affect him. Eventually Mr. Heilman sensed our alert stillness and looked up for a brief second, then down again as he continued to read and interpret.

"She was in a catatonic state when they brought her here after first being taken to Detroit Receiving. Her eventual diagnosis was schizoaffective disorder." He looked up. "Later, as diagnosis, treatments, descriptions, and clinical names became more precise, that diagnosis was combined with comorbid anxiety disorder."

We didn't make a sound. I couldn't. I imagined Dolly's

mind bumping to a halt.

The man sensed something more than official inquiry going on when he glanced at Dolly's face. She'd paled to a shade far beyond her usual pasty look. Her eyes were huge. She sat without saying a word, tight hands crossed in her lap.

After a while, Mr. Heilman cleared his throat and looked over at me. "This seems to be something of a shock, I'd say."

I nodded. "Awful thing."

"Some women break, especially after having a child. To be deserted, no money, no home, no family . . . add that to a fragile psyche to begin with, and postpartum depression, perhaps."

In a voice that came out small and suppressed, Dolly only asked, "What happened to the baby?"

He frowned over the report, then another official report attached to it. "I believe Social Services took the child. After that . . . it doesn't say."

"But where was Cate Thomas?" Dolly's voice was harsh. "Why wasn't she there for her? Why didn't Cate take the baby?"

"Maybe she never knew about the pregnancy. Families can be . . . well . . . If there was trouble over the marriage, perhaps. Who knows?"

The man looked disturbed, catching on that this was far more than a disinterested officer of the law he had in his office. All he said was, "She's not mentioned until later in the files."

He cleared his throat uncomfortably. "But . . . eh . . . those things we found in Audrey's room. It was a stack of letters from her mother. She'd hidden them in her mattress. One of our cleaning staff discovered the letters when she turned the mattress and found a bulge on one side. They'd been inserted through a slit. I don't know why she didn't take them with her."

"Many?" I asked, thinking thirty-three years of letters had to be hard to sleep on.

"A few. They seem of recent vintage."

"Can I have them?" Dolly said, not really asking a question.

The man shook his head. "I can show them to you but they remain Audrey's property. She might come back to claim them."

Dolly sat up straight. I knew the stance. She was about to argue with the man. I broke in, "We'd like to see them. There might be something that would help."

"I suppose so," he said and nodded. "Because of . . . I mean, Audrey's mother's manner of death. And this judge does say I'm to help in any way possible." He tapped the court order on the desk.

He pulled a small stack of letters, held with a large metal clip, from a file behind him and handed them to Dolly.

"You'll have to read the letters here in my office," he said.

Dolly gave them to me. I shuffled quickly through the envelopes. All were addressed to Audrey Thomas, followed by a ward number, and then the address of the hospital.

"I need to know where she went when she left here," Dolly said, turning back to the man. "You mentioned something like a halfway house."

"Well, yes." He nodded. "Because she'd been out of society for such a long time. There are places, paid for by the state, which provide a kind of reentry school for long-term patients."

"Teach them how to drive, do they?" Dolly asked.

He nodded. "Or reteach them. Help them get a license.

Show them changes since they first got sick, and help them adjust to things from drugstores to movies to TV programs to new foods and eating out in restaurants. Our culture changes fast these days. Changes that might seem small and easily managed to us can be huge to people catching up all at once."

"I'd like to talk to Audrey," Dolly said. "Could I have the address of this place she went to?"

The man's face changed. His eyes shut down. He drew in his chin and stared hard at his hands, laid flat on the table. "Well, after hearing from you I called over there, just to have them prepare Audrey for a visitor. But it seems there's a problem."

Dolly, as if not able to comprehend another shock to her system, said nothing, so I jumped in. "What kind of problem? Isn't she doing well?"

"No, it isn't that." He looked up and tried a smile. "You see, Audrey is as free as any other citizen. The court granted her freedom, having been adjudged mentally capable of fully functioning out of a hospital setting. And I'm afraid she's exercised that freedom. Audrey left the facility a few weeks ago."

"Where is she now?" I asked before Dolly could make a sound.

He shook his head. "That seems to be the problem. Nobody at the house knows where she went."

THIRTY-SEVEN

The next shock was in the letters from Cate to Audrey. Happy letters at first. Cate had found a good home up in northwest Michigan, I read to Dolly. And—joy of all joys—she was with a family member. Pretty little place called Leetsville. Nice people. Cate just knew Audrey would love it there, if she could ever visit. And more happy news to come, one letter said. But that was for later letters, Cate wrote. Something Audrey would be so pleased to hear.

At first there was no mention of Dolly. I opened two succeeding letters but the person who had to be Dolly was only mentioned as "family." As in: "So nice to have family," "I never thought I'd have family around me again," "You'd be so pleased to be with family like I am."

I opened another letter, written just that past January. How happy Audrey would be to know the "family member" Cate was staying with was about to have a baby. She went on to say how thrilled they all were, preparing, talking about painting the nursery. She described the nursery, and the changing table they found at a resale shop and painted white, and the darling little crib, and the pretty curtains.

When I opened the next envelope and drew out the letter a small, wallet-sized picture fell into my lap. Dolly reached over and picked up the photo. There was a slight intake of breath, then she held the picture out to me. It was one I knew well. Baby Jane's hospital picture: a little girl with a scrunched-up face and a striped knit hat on her head. Maybe not Jane's best photo to date, but precious since it was her first.

"Why'd she send this to Audrey?" Dolly demanded, nodding fiercely for me to read on.

"Er . . . uh . . ." I read but my brain wanted to censor what was on the page. There seemed to be something of treachery in Cate's words; or maybe these were the naïve words of a mother imagining a whole different future than the one that would be. "She says . . . uh . . . 'You'll be so happy to know the child in the picture is your granddaughter. What I haven't told you the truth about yet is that I'm living with Dolly, your own little girl. This is Dolly's baby. If you could only see her. A lot like you, I think. Everybody says she's a beautiful baby. Just like you were, my sweet little Delores, my own little Dolly. To celebrate her birth, I've sent you a present. You should get it in a couple of days . . .'"

She went on to describe going to the post office and taking the baby with her and how the ladies there made over Jane. And then she closed with a caution to please write her just one letter, let her know, this time, that she'd received the gift. "I know you'll like it. Same as always, only a lot more. And, baby girl, maybe I could bring our Jane to see you, if you let me. If you'd only answer one of my letters. I need that before you could ever come here. You know, I said you'd love it here. But first I need a sign from you, Audrey. Something. Just a sign."

The next letter implored Audrey to let her know if she'd received the jellybeans and to maybe let her know if it was okay to visit.

Dolly said nothing in the man's office, only thanked him for his help and hoped she could call with more questions, if she had any. He agreed and waved us out, saying he hoped we'd find Audrey and that she was still doing well.

I drove while Dolly sat like a knot beside me. At one point she covered her face with her hands. Another time she hit the dashboard with her fist. I jumped a good foot and worried about the trip home, after stopping at that halfway house, with this wound-up, angry Dolly Wakowski. Three hours of misery ahead and who knew what I'd be pressed into next—hunting for Audrey Thomas somewhere in Michigan, or maybe another state by now.

I practiced answers about work I had to get done, about stories for Bill, about turning the whole thing over to the Michigan State Police because I was already thinking that what was going on was beyond Dolly's capabilities, or maybe even beyond her emotional courage—looking for her mother.

"Maybe I'm just like her," Dolly said after a while. Her small face was morose. "Maybe I'm my mother all over again. I bring this stuff on myself and the people I love."

"Dolly." It was hard to see my odd little friend going through something so terrible. "Your mother is the tragedy. Not you," I said.

She was quiet awhile, thinking that over. "So, is she my enemy?" Dolly finally asked as I turned down a narrow Kalamazoo side street and parked in front of the address the director had given us. "What else can I think, Emily? Even the jellybeans. What else can it mean?"

I shrugged. Who knew if Audrey had any part in all of this? Jellybeans. Almost silly—to think they defined a murderer. Who knew if the poor woman wasn't simply gone again? This time not to France, and not into mental illness, but into the big wilderness that was the United States of America.

"Cate was proud of Jane. Didn't you get that from the

letter?" she asked after a long while.

I agreed wholeheartedly and happily. Cate was certainly proud of Jane.

"Me, too," she said. "Proud of my baby. But you know what else, Emily? I'm proud of me. I'm a good mother, don't you think? I mean, look what I came from."

I smiled as wide as I could smile. "You are the very best, Dolly. The absolute best in the world."

"I didn't have a man either. Like my mother. Not then. Did it all myself and held it together."

"You certainly have held it all together."

Her voice dropped when she spoke again. "Audrey didn't have nobody. Audrey didn't have hope. I can see how that could break a woman. I can see . . ."

"Me, too," I agreed gratefully. There was something new in Dolly's voice. Something I'd never heard there before. Pity. And in Dolly Wakowski's mouth pity sounded like a benediction, like a blessing in a church: forgiving, accepting, and . . . when I thought about it . . . knowing.

"Trying to drown me," she went on. "That could have been an act of love, you look at it one way."

I nodded, afraid to speak.

"Trying to save me from what was happening to her."

"And she paid with her life—all those years locked away in . . . that place."

Dolly sniffed hard a time or two. "Come on. Let's go on in here." She nodded to the house where we'd stopped. "Let's see if we can find out where she went to and then . . ."

"Yes?"

"Then we'll go get her."

"What happens after that, Dolly?"

She thought awhile. "When I see her I'm gonna tell her it's okay, what happened. It's okay and I'm glad she's my mother."

"But Dolly," I couldn't stop myself. "She still could be the one who killed Cate."

Dolly thought then shook her head. "She wouldn't have done that. Not her own mother. That black jellybean in the house had to be from some Cate kept for herself. Maybe stuck a handful in her pocket."

"And the car at the cemetery?"

She thought again and turned a terrible face to me. "I don't know, Emily. Stop asking questions. All I know is that my mother's out there somewhere and she needs me."

THIRTY-EIGHT

An overweight young woman answered the door of the ordinary house.

"Audrey?" she said when Dolly told her what we'd come about. "She wasn't here that long. Maybe a week. I think she left with Maisie Flanders from Grand Rapids. The two of them got to be friends pretty fast and Audrey was gone without a word right after Maisie left."

"Did Audrey have a car of her own?" I asked.

The young woman made a face at me, the kind of face that usually says "Duh." She didn't say it but still made it clear I had to be dense. "After as long as Audrey was in that hospital? I'd guess not."

"Did you help her relearn how to drive?"

"That's one thing they do here, among other things. But she didn't have a license yet. I mean, geez, she's old. Who wants her out on the streets?"

All I could think was fifty-three's not old but I didn't say anything. I just held it against the girl.

"Could I have the address in Grand Rapids?" Dolly asked, keeping her words nice and evenly spaced.

The young woman left us on the doorstep while she went back into the house. She came back with a torn sheet of paper in her hand. She gave the paper to Dolly. "To tell the truth, none of us here thought Audrey was ready to go off on her own like that. I mean, all those years kept away from people. Just trying to show her how to use a computer was like taking her into a whole different world. We went to one site where you have to put your information in before they'll let you on and she looked stunned, didn't want to do it. Like somebody was stealing something from her. Maisie was more patient than the rest of us with Audrey. They knew each other from the hospital. Maisie was good to her. Patient, you know. She was going through the same thing. Only not as bad. Sometimes the two of them would be there, in the living room, talking away about this and that and laughing their heads off. More like teenagers than grown women but that's how it goes sometimes. We all need to go back to who we were when we were well last. That's what my doctor says. Then we kind of catch up with the world we missed out on."

We thanked her and left, Dolly holding tight to the next piece of her puzzle.

I checked my watch. Three o'clock. "A shame to drive right through Grand Rapids and not stop at this Maisie Flanders's house." I hesitated. "I wouldn't blame you if you'd had about all you can take for one day. We could come back tomorrow. Go home. Get a good night's sleep . . ."

She looked over at me as if I was nuts.

"Yeah, we're going to go on by and Audrey could be at this woman's house right now."

"You want to meet her, don't you?"

She nodded. "She's . . . kind of real to me for the first time in my life. I understand a lot of things."

I pulled over to bring up directions on my iPhone then turned toward Rose Street as Dolly called Eugenia.

Maisie Flanders answered the door to a blue house on Rose Street. She was young. Maybe my age, thirty-four, and dressed in neatly ironed blue cotton blouse and slacks. She looked from me to Dolly, large-eyed and wary.

"Yes?" she said through the screen door.

Dolly explained that we were looking for Audrey Thomas. "We were told she left a facility in Kalamazoo with you."

The young woman frowned at Dolly then thought hard. "Well . . ." she began. "Actually she did come home with me but she was only here for a few days. She took off without a word. She's gone."

"Gone?" Dolly asked, her voice impatient. "Gone where?"

The woman shook her head. "I don't know. I thought she'd stay. You know, get on her feet. She was in Oakwood a long, long time. I was only there for a couple of months."

"She didn't tell you where she might be headed?"

"Nothing."

"Anybody pick her up?"

"Not that I know of. I just got up that morning—you know, and she wasn't anywhere."

"Did she ever mention other places in Michigan she'd like to get to?"

She shook her head again. "Not that I can remember. All she kept saying was that she had family somewhere up north. I never listened where exactly."

"Did she have access to a car? Did you lend her one?"

"I don't have a car to lend to anybody." She made an impatient gesture toward Dolly.

"What about money? Did you give her any?"

The woman lowered her head to look hard at her hands. "No. I don't have money just like I don't have a car."

"Did anyone in your house give her money at any time?" I

asked, hoping to catch her in a lie or whatever it was that was bothering her.

She shook her head fast then stopped and put an index finger to her bottom lip. "I don't like to say anything bad. Audrey was like a real friend to me at Oakwood. I mean, we shared a room."

"And?" Dolly prodded.

"Well, after she left, my mother said she was missing sixty dollars from her purse. Neither one of us liked to think Audrey would do us that way, but Mom just can't figure where the money got to. So, maybe she did steal from us. Maybe not. I just wish her good luck out there. If you find her, tell her that. Maisie sends her best."

On the long drive back to Leetsville all I could suggest was calling Audrey's doctor back at the hospital. Maybe the doctor knew more than we did. Something from therapy—but maybe there was a doctor-patient privilege that covered it. How did a woman disappear after being confined for thirty-three years?

I thought hard. If I were Audrey Thomas where would I go? Who would I want to see?

The only thing that came to me was a line from Cate's letter . . . *You'll be so happy to know the child in the picture is your granddaughter.*

THIRTY-NINE

We were barely north of Cadillac when Lucky called my cell.

"Emily?" he demanded in that deep "cop" voice he used when he was on official business. "Don't let Dolly know it's me, okay? You two have got to get back up here as fast as you can."

I cleared my throat and glanced over at Dolly, who had her head against the seat. Her eyes were closed.

"What's up?" I asked, keeping my voice light.

"There's been an . . . incident at Eugenia's house."

"Really?"

"A woman Eugenia'd never seen before came by a while ago."

"Okay." I drew out the word.

"She said Dolly called her and asked her to come help Eugenia with the baby." He hesitated. "Eugenia let her in but then she said things didn't smell right to her."

"So?"

"The woman played with the baby for a while then picked her up and headed for the door. The only thing that stopped her getting outside was Flora Coy coming in. Flora saw something was wrong and grabbed the baby right outta the woman's arms. Said she just pretended to make over Jane, hugging her and cooing at her. Well, you know how Cora can get. Flighty as those birds of hers. Eugenia started asking the woman how she knew Dolly and the woman stopped saying a single word. Eugenia said the woman stood there big-eyed for a little while then turned and ran out of the house. I came right over when she called, but I figure Dolly'd better get up here as soon as she can."

"Maybe an hour and a half yet," I said then looked over as Dolly stirred, opened her eyes, and turned toward me.

"What's going on?" she asked sleepily at first then snapped awake, sat up straight, chin out, demanding an answer.

"Tell her," Lucky said. "She's got to know what's happened here."

"You tell her," I said and thrust the phone at Dolly's face. News like this had to come directly from him.

Dolly listened, muttered a curse under her breath, hung up and said only, "Get us home, Emily. I'll handle any cops that stop us for speeding."

• • •

Eugenia's house, a ranch house on fifteen acres not far out of town, was buzzing with most of the waitresses from EATS as well as a lot of people from town, those with police scanners who'd heard the call come in and headed right over to protect Baby Jane.

Dolly grabbed a surprised and happy Jane into her arms and held on tight as Jane leaned back to take her mother's face in, then smiled a wide, gummy smile and wiggled from one end to the other. Dolly buried her face in Jane's shoulder. She made her way through the exclaiming women to where Lucky stood against one wall talking with Officer Omar Winston, whose face was as stricken as Dolly's.

Omar turned to Dolly and put a hand out. "Don't worry.

We're gonna get her. Thank God for that woman," he said as he nodded to where Flora Coy stood among the others. "She stopped her."

Dolly nodded. I was behind them, hoping to get information for a story I promised Bill I'd get to him as soon as we hit town.

"Anybody give you a description? Or see the car she left in?" Dolly asked everyone in general.

"Seems the women were too shocked," Omar put in. "Eugenia said she had straight hair, blue eyes, a red shirt. And one of the waitresses—Gloria, is that her name? She said she ran out on the porch and thought she saw the woman run off into the trees. She didn't hear a car."

Dolly nodded. "People patrolling the streets?" she asked Lucky.

"Everybody in town who's not here. Walking. Driving around. Using those lights they say they never use to shine deer."

"APB on that car stolen out in Norwood?"

He nodded. "Still in effect. Got the whole state covered. If she's on the road in that vehicle, we'll have her quick enough."

Omar reached out to take Dolly's hand. She brushed him aside.

"Dolly," he said. "I'm glad you didn't leave Jane with my mother. Just wanted you to know that. If this woman's following you, my mother would have been there alone with Jane. A lot safer here."

"Not safe enough. I've got to—"

"You and Jane come home with me tonight," I said quickly. "We can take turns staying up and keeping watch. This is all about Jane. We've got to protect her."

"She called your house once. Wouldn't trust your place."

"I'm not listed. All she got was a phone number—could have gotten that from the paper. But they never give out addresses. Honestly, Dolly, I think the best bet is for us to stick together from here on in."

Omar turned his unbendable body toward me and gave a curt nod. "I know Dolly won't go anywhere until we find this person, but it might be best if she and Jane came to Gaylord and stayed with us for a day or two. Nobody would find her there . . ."

Dolly reared back. "You two talk like I'm out of this. Like I'm supposed to lay low and sit in a corner shivering. Not on your life. I appreciate that you care about Jane, and even me, Omar. But nobody knows this country the way I do. I'm gonna be at the middle of everything until she's caught."

Omar sputtered but calmed down quickly as Dolly fixed him with one long, steady look.

She turned to me. "So it's your house and that big vicious dog of yours. I got my gun . . ." She patted her holster.

"I've got my computer. I can always throw it."

"Yeah. How about your neighbor, Harry? Think he'd bring over those hounds of his? They'd scare anybody away."

"What about asking Harry, himself, to come over?"

"That old codger? Geez." She cracked a smile. "I guess so. We could set him up in the window with a shotgun. You think Delia would mind? Him spending the night with two women?"

"Bet she'd bake us a cake. Harry off her hands for a little while!"

She had a short conference with Lucky, who promised to

call her all night long, if necessary, with anything that came in. I reached Bill at home, warning him I was sending the story from my iPhone and that there were photographs along with it. One picture of the heroine, Flora Coy, and one of Eugenia, who'd taken fifteen minutes brushing her hair into a remarkable up-do before she let me take it.

We packed Jane's stuff—yet one more time—thanked everybody for their support, and headed home to man the barricades and face whatever Sorrow had thought to present me with in the way of retribution for hours of confinement. I couldn't help but think maybe I should potty train my dog. I'd seen a TV show once that claimed it was easy to do.

FORTY

I ran up Harry's overgrown drive, brambles pulling at me like something out of *The Wizard of Oz*, but Harry's house was dark. I turned around, surrounded by a cacophony of mad dog bays and barks and the sound of wild bodies being thrown at a chain-link fence, while hurrying back out to the car.

I was spooked by everything. The outline of every tree seemed to have arms and legs attached. Every noise took my breath away. There was nothing like having a killer after you to heighten the senses and loosen the bladder.

I fell into the car, where Dolly was giving Jane a bottle. "He's not home so that means he's down at Delia's and I'm not going down there, or anywhere. I just want to get home and lock the door and climb in bed and pull a blanket over my head."

"Hmmp," she said, saving her comments on cowardice and the fine friend she'd picked for a standoff with a killer—and other things I knew she was thinking. She said nothing more.

At home, with Sorrow leaping in consternation at how perfidious I was and then running outside as if he just remembered something he had to do, I was shocked to find everything in perfect order, then figured Harry had been over to let him out.

Jane was put in an open drawer of my guest room bureau. Comfortable enough—the drawer stuffed with blankets—she fell right to sleep. Dolly and I sat in the living room—all curtains pulled closed, all doors locked and double-checked, all windows locked up tight—and drank wine (me) and coffee

254

(her).

And talked . . . and talked . . . and talked . . . half the night. Going over everything we knew and didn't know, all possibilities and then all probabilities.

Dolly pulled out the list of addresses the director at Oakwood had for Cate.

Dolly read them over—all in Michigan, from Detroit to Warren to Mt. Pleasant to Grayling, and many places in between. Nothing there.

I turned off the lamps, feeling safer in the dark and thinking maybe we could go to sleep, but we kept on talking, mostly about Audrey Delores and how she'd dropped her married name, went from Flynn to Thomas. "Like my cousin said, maybe she never was married," Dolly said. "Don't you think that's the most likely answer here?"

"Could have been the problem between Cate and her to begin with. So many families tear themselves apart about something as organic and ordinary as a kid having sex."

"So, he dropped her, literally, at the hospital door and kept on going."

"And that was that."

"Until she was alone at that Detroit motel and she couldn't see any way out for me or for her."

I nodded but she couldn't see me.

"You know what I don't get, Emily?" She didn't wait for an answer. I was moving in and out of sleep anyway. "I don't get why women are punished like she was. I mean, so she had a kid. Turned on by Cate, and all the organizations that should have helped her. Doesn't it seem like . . . I don't know . . . like this world doesn't much care for women?"

That woke me up. A little deep for me to get my mind around at that hour of the morning, still I tried to make sense of what she was saying. "I don't know. Religion did that, I think. Supposed to love each other but makes up ways to hate instead. Especially women, 'cause we're supposed to be weaker."

"You think that's true? That we're weaker?"

I stretched my neck, then rubbed hard at it and turned my body to lie down on the couch. "Sure we are," I said after a yawn. "In some ways. But smarter, intuitive. Smaller people have got to be smarter, watch people around them, be more alert. That's called self-preservation. So—weaker in one way, stronger in others."

"Yeah, that's what I think. Poor Audrey. Too bad she didn't have at least one person . . ."

"I think Cate was always sorry. You saw the letters."

"Yeah, and sending her jellybeans."

She was quiet a long time. "You think it was Audrey who killed Cate?"

The question was so loaded, from so many sides, I couldn't answer.

"I'm hoping not," she said when I was too quiet for too long. "I'm really hoping not. Just because I understand so much now . . ."

In the morning I made more coffee for her and tea for me while she heated Jane's bottle and bathed her in my sink. Sorrow was enthralled with such a tiny human being and had to be pushed away again and again from sniffing Jane and licking her bare legs.

Over toast and strawberry jam—all I had to offer—we laid

out how the day was going to go. First she wanted to call the doctor at Audrey's hospital, talk to her, and see if she had any clue as to where Audrey might have gone. Would she be in the Detroit area for any reason the doctor knew? Up north? Was there ever anything said about a desire to visit anyone from her past?

I went to listen in on my bedroom phone, making notes for my next article.

Dolly dialed the hospital, asked to speak to the director, and when she was connected, asked for the doctor's name and could she speak to her.

The director said it was Dr. Laura Cantwell she needed to speak to and dialed a single number. After a few rings a woman answered and the director asked if Dr. Cantwell was available. Another few minutes and a woman's voice came on.

"Dr. Cantwell," was all she said, a tired but pleasant voice.

The director spoke to her first, overriding Dolly's anxious "Hello. Hello." He explained what the call was about, that there'd been a court order to cooperate, and then hung up.

"How can I help you?" the doctor said. "You know Audrey was released from here close to a month ago?"

"Yes," Dolly spoke up. "But she's disappeared."

"From the halfway house?"

"Yes, ma'am."

"Where'd she go?"

"She left with another patient. Went to that patient's home in Grand Rapids."

"Have you tried her there?"

"Yes, ma'am. She only stayed a couple of days. She's gone. Nobody knows where."

"Well." The doctor took a deep breath and went on to ask Dolly why she was looking for Audrey. Dolly explained, coming as close to the truth as she evidently felt she could.

"What I wanted to know from you, Doctor, is if she ever mentioned any place she might go if she got out of there?"

"All I can imagine is that she would finally want to see her mother. I think the woman lives up in northwest Michigan now. Maybe start looking there."

"Her mother's dead."

"What! No. I've seen recent letters. Audrey showed them to me. She was so excited . . . something about a baby."

"Her mother was murdered last week."

There was an audible intake of breath.

"Then . . . eh . . . I don't know how I can help you. She never mentioned anyone else. Nor any other place. That baby—she was excited about that."

"I understand Audrey had a kind of . . . thing about babies."

"That was a long time back, Officer. Part of the schizophrenia. A delusion, of being pregnant. Not uncommon among women, especially those who once had a child."

"Director Heilman said Audrey would never let her mother visit. Never even wrote her a letter."

"Well, yes, that was true. But Audrey had changed recently."

"What'd she hold against her mother? She ever say?"

"I . . . don't like to . . ." The doctor paused. "Confidentiality, you understand. I know you've got a court order but there are some things I don't feel comfortable discussing."

"This is a murder case, Dr. Cantwell."

"Yes, I understand that but . . ." Again the doctor was silent.

After a long thirty seconds or more she said, "I'm going to tell you what I know but not because of your judge's order. I think I can safely discuss this with you because Audrey would often tell me things, when we met for a cup of coffee in the dining room, or even when I'd stopped by her room to bring her some of those black jellybeans she loves. These things were outside our official visits and, I feel certain, outside doctor-patient confidentiality."

More hesitation. "Audrey blamed her mother for losing her baby. The mother wasn't there at the time. I don't think she even knew about the baby before the court took her away permanently and placed her into foster care. But Audrey would only shake her head when I reminded her of that. She was sure her mother was behind the baby disappearing and that she still had her."

She sighed. "After the new medication there was one big breakthrough after another. She finally faced what happened in that motel room in Detroit. I'm assuming you know the records. Still, she did blame Cate Thomas. She thought she could have done something. There were even times she told me Cate stole the baby herself."

Another long pause and then an almost startled question. "Where did you say you were calling from, Officer Wakowski?"

"Leetsville, Michigan. Where Audrey's mother lived."

The doctor gasped. "I thought your name sounded familiar. Didn't you call me about my cottage in Norwood?"

Dolly said nothing.

"Officer? Are you there?" the doctor finally asked.

"That was your place?" Dolly asked. "Your house was broken into and your car stolen?"

"Right. I was coming up next weekend . . ."

"Did you ever talk about the place in Norwood with Audrey Thomas?"

"I . . . You have to understand, Audrey has been my patient since I first came to Oakwood. We became quite good friends toward the end of her stay. When I got back from vacation she always wanted to see photographs. It was as if she lived vicariously through me and I saw no harm in it."

"So she knew about the place up here?"

"Yes. We talked about her maybe visiting when she got out."

"Would she know how to find the house?"

"I have no idea. But she'd seen pictures of it and Norwood's a small village . . ."

"Audrey knows how to drive?"

"She drove before being admitted. She'd even had a half year of college before she got pregnant and her whole world crashed. But, stealing from me . . . I can't believe that."

Another pause.

"Where is she getting her medication, I wonder?" the doctor asked, almost musing. "She'll need her prescriptions . . ."

Dolly said she'd be in touch.

"Please keep me up to date," Dr. Cantwell said, her voice hesitant. "If I can help . . . I still consider Audrey my friend."

FORTY-ONE

Dolly hunched forward on the stool, her hands tight around a mug of coffee. "You know what this means, don't you?" she said.

Of course I knew. There was no question anymore. The woman who had smashed Dolly's car at the cemetery, the woman with three bags of black jellybeans in her car, the "Thou Shalt Not Steal" woman, the one who made the phone calls to me and Bill, who broke into that house in Norwood, who left the jellybean on the floor of Jane's nursery, who murdered Cate, who tried to kidnap Jane . . .

The sense of horror I felt was huge. I could only imagine what Dolly was feeling.

She went into the living room, looked hurriedly around her as if for a way out, then stood still, blinking at me.

"You've got to take care of Jane," she said to me. "You're the only one I've got."

I didn't understand.

She made a face. "I have to get back to that house in Norwood. We'll stake out the place. Think about it. Where else does she have to go but there?"

"Don't you think she'll be hanging around Leetsville, I mean, trying to get to you or Jane?"

"She saw the police cars last night. She sure isn't hanging around, waiting to be caught. If you keep Jane with you, she'll be safe." Her face crumpled, but only for a minute. "I trust you, Emily. I've got the feeling you'd die before you'd let her hurt Jane."

Well, yeah, I thought.

"I've got to get to Norwood. She may be there now and we can get her before anything else happens. I'll call Lucky on my way into town."

"You don't have a car."

"I'll take yours."

"Let me drive you. That makes more sense. I can't be out here without a vehicle."

She shook her head. "She knows that yellow Jeep. If she sees it, she'll come after me." She thought awhile. "Maybe that's good—her coming after me. Just me. Without Jane. But I don't want you that close to the middle of things."

"Okay," I agreed reluctantly, unable to think of anything else we could do. "But I'll be here alone and I don't have a gun. Not that I'd use one."

"You would. If you had to. You've got your phone. You see anything. Anybody. Call the state police right away. I'll call Omar, see if he can come stay with you."

"Not Omar. I swear, Dolly, if I'm spooked by anything, I'll call every cop I can reach."

We were in agreement, reluctantly on my part. I got a quick course in keeping a four-month-old fed and diapered and washed and napped. Things I thought I'd learned from my library book. Then Dolly was gone, promising to be back later that afternoon, as soon as they got other departments to help with the stakeout.

FORTY-TWO

We were in my living room. I sat in front of Jane, so we could stare at each other. She'd look at me for a while, get bored, check out the rest of the room, then back to me.

"So, are you doing all right?" I asked and smiled my best hostess smile.

Jane's eyes rolled toward the ceiling, then around to where Sorrow had jumped up to look at her. She was far more interested in him than in me so I left Sorrow in charge while I made myself a cup of microwave tea and sat back down, nerves jingling.

What a perfect time to go out and write in my studio. A whole day with nothing to do, but so nervous I had to keep my mind busy. I figured Jane could look at the ceiling in my studio as well as here in my kitchen so I packed her up and took her out through the trees to the little building where I wrote.

She liked the trip, listening to birds singing—tending to nests filled with eggs. She liked watching a single cloud shaped like a really long rabbit, twisting her head around to keep it in view. She liked Sorrow's jumping in the air near us and yipping and caterwauling after a fox. She bounced around in my arms to follow him behind the studio, almost falling as she threw her head back, trying to see behind her.

I held on tight and opened the studio door with my key. I set Jane up in a chair aimed straight at me, then sat at my desk and opened my MacBook.

There's something about total quiet. Sorrow worn out at my feet. Jane facing me but quickly sleeping. A single peaceful forty-five minutes before she began to stir. She made noises, every once in a while a tiny cry of protest. I'd just get into a new scene, with ideas forming, places to take the book deeper, and she'd coo, or burp, or had a few words to say in that unintelligible language of hers, and I was distracted, turning to smile at her, turning to talk to her, asking if she was hungry, as if I expected an answer. I figured she was probably soaked and would want her diaper changed. I told her I didn't blame her, I'd want mine changed, too, and not to feel bad about interrupting my — oh, so important — work.

As if sarcasm would get me anywhere with a baby.

By one o'clock we were back in the house and I'd said everything I could think to say to her and smiled all the smiles I could come up with and was totally bored.

At three o'clock I turned on my small TV, which rarely got turned on, and sat down with Jane in my arms to watch a talk show where the star gave out presents and all the women in the audience screamed.

I changed channels and found a mystery about people who'd married strangers and took much too long to find out their spouse had a terrible past — like cannibalism. Inane, but it held our interest so Jane and I sat watching until we both fell asleep and didn't wake up again until the phone rang.

Bill. He'd been in touch with Lucky, who told him I had Jane.

"Your last story really scares me, Emily," he said. "That woman's after Jane. Or maybe it's Dolly she's after. Anyway, Lucky said you're alone with the baby out there. I hear Dolly's gone to Norwood. You should have a cop with you. Somebody."

"Dolly'll be back as soon as she can."

"Why don't I come out?"

I was his employee. I was a reporter. Since when did reporters ask their editors to come and save them? I turned him down flat. "I'm working, writing, we're getting along fine. No strange phone calls. No strange cars in my drive. Nobody anywhere around. Sorrow lets me know if a squirrel runs across the deck so I think we're okay for right now."

He hesitated. "What if Dolly can't get back?"

"You mean before tonight?"

"Yes. I don't want to think of you alone in the dark."

I found the depth of his caring touching. But irritating.

I assured him again that I was fine and would get another story to him in the morning.

"I hope they catch her out there at Norwood. Put an end to this. She's got to be the one who killed Cate."

"I hope not. For Dolly's sake, I hope not. She's got enough hatred in her."

I hung up. The phone rang again. This time it was Omar Winston. He was going to Norwood but offered to drop his mother off to stay with me. I declined politely, swallowing what I thought of a few hours trapped with that particular woman, and hung up.

I fed Jane cereal. I gave her a bottle. I changed her then held her and sang a bunch of old Stevie Wonder songs to her and then K. D. Lang—especially my favorite about dreaming of springtime—then turned the TV back on just as the phone rang again.

Jackson Rinaldi, with a buoyant voice and a note of triumph. "You'll never guess, Emily," he said without as much as a "Hello" or "How are you?" or "You still alive?"

"A wonderful review. The *British Times*, of all places. They get it. They understand me. No academic carping. Oh, Emily, I can't tell you how good it feels to be accepted in Chaucer's own country, his own language, his own people of like humor."

Jane shot a raspberry I agreed with but I enthused over his news and congratulated him. When he'd gone through every superlative he could think of to describe the English press, he thought to ask me how I was doing and I told him.

"What?" he exclaimed again and again. "What? You're there with a baby? You? And a madwoman after you? Is this a joke? Something you thought up to top my story of success?"

I assured him that was it, letting sarcasm drip. Me getting even in my own passive-aggressive way.

"No," he said. "I can tell. You're serious. I'm coming up. I'll be there first thing in the morning. I have an evening class, you understand. Don't let anyone in that house. Do you still have that mangy animal of yours?"

I assured him I did.

"Then let him bark and howl to his heart's content until I get there."

"I don't need you, Jackson."

"I'm not falling for that, Emily. I just am not certain of the time. As early as possible."

We left it at that. I was too tired to argue. Too tired to point out to one more man the futility of riding to my rescue. And too tired, later, to do more than fry an egg for my dinner, and make toast to dip in it, all the while holding a bottle in Jane's mouth as she sat in her bouncing chair in front of me and watched with snapping brown eyes that seemed to be laughing.

I didn't hear from Dolly until almost eight o'clock.

"Nobody can spell me out here," she said. "I'm down the road, watching the house. Not many cars driving by, let alone any pulling up the doctor's drive. How's Jane?"

"She's fine," I said and kept the news from her of Jackson on his way to save me. "We're having a great time."

"Yeah, I bet. I know you. Not a baby person."

"I beg your pardon." I took umbrage at her judgment. "Me and Jane are fed and dry and about to engage in a conversation about modern philosophy."

"You are so full of it," she groused at me. "So, I don't know when I can get back there. Are you going to be okay? Omar was coming out here. I thought maybe I could get him to stay but he just called. There's been a shooting in a Gaylord bar so he's out of it for now."

"What about Lucky?"

"He's here with me. He made me leave your car at the station. Said it was like a big yellow lightbulb. Not the kind of thing you take on stakeouts. We're stuck here together."

"Told you I should've taken you back to town."

"Yeah, well, nothing like crowing over your shoulder."

"So when will you get back?"

"Could be the middle of the night. Who knows? You've got plenty of formula and lots of diapers. I didn't bring many clothes for her. Who knew she'd be staying? You could wash out that Onesie she was in today."

I assured Dolly we'd be fine but added, "Just get back, okay? Jane's getting bored with me."

"I will. I can't leave this place, Emily. It's all she's got to come to."

I put the phone down, looked over at Jane, whose eyes were half shut, and shrugged.

"It's just us," I told her, then glanced at my ratty dog that looked back at me with adoration in his eyes. I knew if anybody in the whole world would give his life for me, it was Sorrow. I reached down and patted his head, which made him drool on my foot.

I gave Jane a last bottle, washed her, changed her into her last pink Onesie, then held her until she drifted off just after ten o'clock. I set her carefully in the nest of blankets in the bureau drawer. Her lips shivered and sucked as she settled into a dream.

She reminded me of Sorrow, when he was deeply asleep and his paws were going, running in a field where he was happy and free.

FORTY-THREE

It was after eleven before it got truly dark, late spring dark that mirrored my face in windows. It was a dark that appeared thick but revealed moving shadows and lights where there shouldn't have been lights or shadows.

I went from window to window checking locks, then checking doors, then pulling the curtains aside quickly, certain I would catch a movement in the yard, or a face.

All the while I sidled from room to room, I told myself what an idiot I was. But that didn't make my heart stop racing.

A creak in a floorboard. The thump of Sorrow's tail. Any noise and I was up, out of my chair even before Sorrow stirred himself to give a weak "woof." I was aware of creaks from the crawl space. I jumped when the refrigerator came on. When I turned on the TV again, wanting to cover all aberrant noises in and outside of my house, I couldn't leave it on, always certain I'd heard a sound beneath the canned laughter, something at a window, a car in the drive, a footstep on the deck. Turning the TV off was worse. I put on music, then turned that down, too.

It was close to four a.m. when I'd tired myself out enough to get a pillow from my bedroom, look in at a soundly sleeping Jane, then lie down on the sofa, Sorrow on the floor next to me. I fell asleep for minutes at a time until finally falling into something like a cavern where I dreamed I was standing on the shore of Willow Lake watching a humpbacked monster swimming toward me.

Sorrow woke me with his barking and leaping in happy circles.

Someone at the door.

I checked my watch. Six thirty a.m.

Jackson. Maybe Dolly. I sat up, leaned forward, and dropped my head into my hands for just a minute. It was the ultimate disaster—Jackson here to add his needs and wants to an already intolerable situation. I was in one of those "Why me?" moments of self-pity as I got up from the sofa and hissed at Sorrow to shut up, for fear he would wake Jane.

I stumbled to the door, fiddled with the lock, and pulled it open while, at the same time, remembering I should be checking first.

Sorrow, my stalwart protector, distracted me, bounding out of the house and around toward the lake. I'd forgotten to let him out the night before. I blinked against the morning light, and was about to say something to Jackson about wishing he hadn't bothered . . .

The woman in red pushed me back and into the wall behind me. I think it was a red shirt. Maybe a jacket. There wasn't time to be afraid or think or notice much of anything as she came at me. I put my hands up expecting a knife and protecting my face—it was all I could think to do.

I looked out, between my spread fingers, at a ravaged face. At dark eyes, with black circles beneath—the kind of face you never want to see come at you in a nightmare. Dirty blond hair sprang out around her head.

First there was the seething face, and then a pair of hands up in the air, coming at me before I'd regained my balance. Fists hit me hard across the chest, then, after I fell, came down on my head.

I tried to fight back but it was like fighting a machine

running over me. There was pain. There was fear. My head was knocked back into the wall and I slid, closing my eyes.

Something else hit me or kicked me.

I was flat on the floor.

FORTY-FOUR

I wasn't completely knocked out, more dazed, confused, and not able to grasp what had happened until Jackson was bending over me, yelling at me, maybe more dazed and confused than I. Sorrow stuck his head between me and Jackson and licked my face until I pushed him away, saying something under my breath about a ne'er-do-well.

"I'm taking you to a hospital," Jackson yelled as if loudness was all it took to get through.

"The baby," was the first thing I croaked out, head in my hands, wincing at the pain when I tried to move. "Go get Baby Jane. Maybe you scared that woman away in time."

"I didn't see anybody coming in. Where?" he demanded. "Where's this supposed baby?" I heard him scramble to his feet and move away even as he asked.

Next his voice came from the living room. "Where is she? Did you mean the real Baby Jane? That movie thing? Maybe you're not coherent. I want to get you to the hospital right now."

He was a bit hysterical so I forced myself to be calm. I took deep breaths and ignored the pain. I held my head steady in both my hands. "Dolly's baby. She's in the guest bedroom. Go get her. Now!"

I struggled to rise from the floor, holding on to the hall bench, then pulling my shaking legs around under me. So many things to do. Call Lucky first—get all cars in the area looking for that Volkswagen from Norwood. Then Dolly . . .

Oh, no . . .

"Where is she, Emily? There's nobody on the bed," he called from back in the bedroom.

"Dresser drawer. She can't be sleeping through all of this."

"Dresser drawer?" I heard his bewildered voice as he moved to the other side of the room. "I'm standing in front of the bureau. One drawer is open. There's a blanket in it."

"Get the baby. Bring her out here." I put my hands against the wall and inched toward the back of the house.

"But Emily." He must have known what his words would do to me. His voice held back. I heard deep hesitation.

"Jackson—for God's sakes . . ." I'd reached the hall and groped my way toward the bedroom.

"Emily," he said again, then looked up as I stood in the doorway, holding on as my head lightened and the room moved in front of me.

"Emily. There is no baby."

He led me back into the living room and helped me sit down at the desk. I kept saying things: who we had to call, what had to be done, she couldn't have gone far, then in the middle I would simply dissolve and say nothing but, "Dolly, Dolly, Dolly," until he took the phone out of my hand and dialed the number I stammered out to him.

Lucky answered on the first ring. "Emily?" he said, recognizing my number. "Everything all right?"

"No. No." Jackson helped me keep the phone to my ear. "She got Baby Jane."

I was yelling. The words didn't sound right but Lucky got it.

"Calm down, Emily. Who took Jane? The woman who tried to kidnap her the other day?"

"Yes. Yes. She knocked me down. I don't know how long I was . . . out. The baby's gone."

"Oh no," he moaned at the other end of the line. "Okay. She's got to be around somewhere. If she's still driving that Volkswagen, we'll get her. Don't worry. You got a description?"

"Red shirt. Wild, dirty blond hair—medium length. Blue eyes like Dolly's. Big hands. Medium height. Medium build. Medium, medium, medium." I was getting hysterical.

Again he said, "Don't worry," as if to himself. "Dolly's on her way in from the stakeout. She'll want to be here, monitoring what's going on. I've got to get this right out. You want to call her?"

I knew why he was pushing this off on me. Something that went way back in a man's old brain stem: *Avoid a raging mother.*

"I'll do it," I said. "I hate to . . . with her driving."

"Don't worry about Dolly. She can handle anything. She won't be alone, Emily. Every man and woman up here will be looking. We'll get Jane back."

I shouldn't have, I suppose, but I did feel comforted by his reassurance.

I put the phone down and looked at Jackson, who'd gone to the kitchen to make me tea. I thanked him. A shot of caffeine might clear my head. Maybe I could recall that wild face better.

Jackson leaned over and smoothed my hair out of my face. He kissed my forehead as I dialed Dolly's cell number and reached out to take Jackson's hand, holding on tight.

"Officer Wakowski," Dolly came on, obviously not checking the caller ID.

"Dolly." I filled my voice with all the strength I had in me. "Dolly . . ."

My voice shook. But that wasn't going to help Jane. It wasn't going to help Dolly.

"Emily?" she yelled back at me, alarmed already. "What's the matter?"

"She got Jane," I spit out. "She came to the door. I thought it was Jackson and opened it. I was knocked down. Hit my head . . ."

There was no hesitation. She didn't take time to gasp or scream or wail as mothers did when they lost a child. "How long ago?"

"I don't know for sure. Maybe an hour."

"You see the car?"

"I was out for a while. I didn't see anything."

"You call Lucky?"

"Yes, he's bringing every department in on it. They'll be on the roads from Grayling to the bridge."

"Yeah. I'm heading into the station now. I'll see what's happening."

"What about the house in Norwood?"

"We've been watching it. Nothing going on there."

"Where else would she go?"

There was no answer.

"I'll meet you at the station," I said. "Jackson'll bring me in."

"Okay . . . Okay." Confusion hit her. "We'll get her. She wouldn't hurt Jane. What I've been thinking is, she thinks Jane's her baby. All that 'Thou Shalt Not Steal' stuff. She thinks Jane is me. While I sat out there in Norwood, I worked it out. She thinks Jane's me and she's getting her baby back."

"Oh, Dolly." My heart broke wide open for her.

"I can't think of that right now," she said. "What I've got to think about is finding Jane. That's all. I'll deal with my mother later."

She was gone.

I put Sorrow on the porch, a kind of punishment he seemed to understand and accept, and then had another argument with Jackson, who still wanted to take me to the hospital to get checked out. We headed off in his Porsche, into Leetsville and the police station.

FORTY-FIVE

By the time Jackson and I got into the police station the building was surrounded by cars and pickups, with more pulling in—a line of vehicles filling the parking lot, and along the street. People rushed past us. Not many talked or greeted each other. They were silent, heads down, getting there fast to help.

Inside, the station was in chaos. Everyone offered suggestions, huddled together to plot strategy, or circled Lucky at the front desk with a phone clamped to his ear.

He gestured toward me and shook his head.

"Do what you can do," he mouthed, then put his hand over the phone. "Help them, will you, Emily? Get 'em going on the back roads. She could be pulled into the woods, for all we know. Map's over there." He gestured to a large map of the northern counties, thumbtacked to the wall.

Then Dolly was there, mouth open and eyes wide at the sight of so many people.

I looked to Jackson, a head taller than everyone, bewildered by the noise and the crowd.

"Jackson—you do it," I called over to him. "Give people roads to cover. Clear them out of here. Write their names down —where they're going."

He nodded. At last a job he could handle—be in charge and making notes. "Ordering the disordered," he would call it as he applied his skills in research and alignment to the search for Jane's kidnapper.

I watched for a brief moment. A man who could still amaze

me, Jackson took a stance in front of the wall map, patted the air for order, then turned to punch at roadways calling out numbers, pointing to a man or woman to get out there and report back.

For just a second I wondered what if he'd been a different man in a different profession? Would our lives have been different? Maybe a cop—in crowd control. Or maybe with FEMA. Maybe a political organizer. Maybe a warden at a male correctional institution with no pliant women around.

Dolly and Lucky had their heads together. He was making notes and telling her which departments had cars out and where they were looking.

An amber alert had already gone out to TV and radio stations across the state.

This wasn't the time to ask questions or get my reporter's notebook out. I joined Dolly and Lucky, at first only listening as they exchanged information—Dolly had been busy coming in from Norwood.

"What can I do?" I asked, leaning into the tight space between them.

Dolly looked at me and frowned, as if she didn't know me. That struck me hard; maybe she blamed me for not taking good enough care of her baby.

I looked into her distracted eyes and sputtered, "It wasn't my fault . . ."

Dolly gave me a sad but impatient smile. She reached over and put an arm around my slumping shoulders. "'Course not. I'm just glad she didn't kill you, too. Don't worry, we'll get her," she promised.

Jackson got cars fanning out into the county and beyond, to

adjacent counties. Some were headed south, down toward Kalkaska—mostly on back roads since the state police had the main roads covered.

Others headed toward Grayling, to the I-75 corridor, which is what she'd have to take if she was headed downstate. That and US 127 toward Lansing. Instructions were to cover every freeway entrance. Maybe park on the ramps. Check out every white Passat.

After a briefing from Dolly, Jackson instructed the drivers that if they saw the car they were to call in immediately. "Follow only," he said. "At a safe distance and speed. Under no circumstance try to intercept the car. You could be putting the baby's life at risk."

At any other time, Jackson might have been funny, mouthing phrases from cop shows. Not now. He was effective. People ran out armed with a flyer Lucky'd printed with the description of the car and the woman.

The last of the searchers were soon on the roads, calls already coming in from those closer in, and from state and local departments all across northern Michigan. Lucky fielded most of them while Dolly stuck pins in the map.

"No sightings yet." She turned to me. We'd been at it for over an hour.

I thought I knew what she was saying. Someone should have spotted the car by now.

"She won't have food for Jane. No bottles. She's got to stop someplace. What do you think?" she asked me. "Where?"

I shrugged. "Depends which direction she's headed in."

"So, any grocery store."

"Even gas station convenience store. Every drugstore."

Dolly bit at her lip. "No help then."

"Why don't we get on the road? Maybe check out gas stations and stores along the main roads."

"Which direction?" she asked, her voice tired, even unsure.

I couldn't answer.

"What if she heads back to Norwood?" I asked.

"She wouldn't. Only one road out of that town. Well, one main road. It's a trap. She's got to know by now we're on to where she got the car."

"But we're not talking about an ordinary woman here, Dolly. She's obsessed. Maybe not thinking clearly. Probably off her meds. And, after all those years in the hospital, you think she's up to planning some big escape?"

Dolly looked at me hard. "Let's get out there. Wish I had a photograph."

"What about one from the album?"

She gave me an exasperated look. "Too old."

She turned to Lucky. "What do you think I should do?"

Lucky looked at her hard. "You can't do anything here. Head toward Norwood. Just in case. We'll hear if she's spotted along US 31 — going or leaving there. You'd be closer. You could check out stores on the way, not a bad idea to see if anybody remembers her buying baby food. Don't forget that red shirt."

Dolly nodded. I nodded. At least we were doing something other than waiting to hear.

FORTY-SIX

We didn't stop at stores. We knew that was a futile gesture. How many women might, after all, have forgotten to buy baby formula? Or stopped off for a pack of diapers? We only had a description, no photo to show.

We drove, always heading west, toward Traverse City, then down back roads. Each road we took seemed wrong the minute we turned so we turned around again and again, coming back to the same places, looking for a Volkswagen Passat until it seemed there were no such cars on the road. If we'd seen one we would have been in immediate hot pursuit—man or woman driving.

I stared into every car we passed. Any woman in a red shirt was suspect. Even if the driver didn't have on a red shirt and didn't drive a Volkswagen, if she had dirty blond hair I stared doubly hard, sometimes turning in my seat to take a second and third look.

There wasn't much to talk about except to reassure each other and make desultory comments about a road to take, a road not to take—and the artificial reasons we had for our choices.

"Audrey wouldn't hurt your baby," I said after a while. "You know that."

"She did once. Tried to drown me, remember?"

"Come on, Dolly. The woman was sick. She was desperate. She was alone."

"What do you think she's feeling now? This any different? And she's got a baby again."

Dolly's radio interrupted constantly: male voices, reports, cars and people stopped and checked.

Lucky came on from time to time to bring Dolly up to date. He told her newspapers from all over the country were calling for information. "Tell Emily her friend Bill is here. He's fielding the press and TV calls."

"What about Jackson Rinaldi? He still around?" Dolly asked.

"Still helping. He's coordinating information for us."

"Never expected it of him," she said, then pulled up close behind a white car.

A Ford.

Dolly looked over at me. "I can almost see why you married him."

"Me, too," I agreed.

"I said 'almost.'"

We turned down a road that dead-ended at the lake. I'd seen the Dead End sign but Dolly missed it. She backed up until she could turn around, then stopped.

"I can't stand it, Emily," she said.

I didn't look at her. "I know," was all I could come up with as she peeled back out onto US 31, heading north.

"Got any ideas?"

I shook my head.

"Want to go check Norwood again?"

"Sure." I shrugged; at least it gave us something to do. I sat back and watched as we passed greening fields and cherry orchards in full blossom. And then woods and more woods and vineyards and Lake Michigan off in the distance and it would have been so serene. My new world in bloom. Except that it looked like a painted backdrop to a horror movie right then.

We turned west at the Norwood sign and made our way up and over and around hills until we reached the corner church and turned.

The house looked as closed and abandoned as it had the last time we were out there. No car anywhere. Not a person in sight.

Dolly got out of the squad car and fumbled the house key from her chain. She put the key in the lock and then her shoulder to the door.

It was as chilly inside as it had been the last time, despite warming weather. We stood absolutely still in the living room, listening for the sound of a baby, even the creak of a floor.

She motioned toward the kitchen. Before we got to the room, I felt something different about the place. Dolly looked over at me. She sensed it too. Air stirring. As if someone had opened a door. Dolly reached for the gun at her side and motioned me behind her. One finger went to her lips.

The kitchen was untouched but the window that had been covered with cardboard the last time we were there was broken out.

Dolly pulled in a breath. We exchanged looks. Dolly moved her head toward the upper floor. There was only one staircase. We made our way slowly back the way we'd come and climbed the stairs, one at a time, though they creaked beneath out feet, making me cringe and bite down hard on my lower lip.

There was no one in the upper hall. We went to the first bedroom and pushed the door wide open. No one. Dolly motioned me to stay where I was as she entered the room, knelt to check under the bed, then opened the tall chifforobe. Only the same hanging jacket, jeans, and robe were in there.

We checked the next bedroom. Empty.

Then the bathroom.

Dolly stood in front of me, blocking the doorway. When she moved aside, I could see things had been moved. The bath mat was rumpled; a towel lay over the basin, another towel was thrown over the closed toilet bowl, and on the floor lay a pink Onesie, wet and dirty.

Dolly picked up the small garment. She closed her eyes as she gripped it in her hand.

"She's here," she whispered.

I nodded.

We'd been through the house. We checked again. Nothing. No sound. No baby cry.

"Maybe she had different clothes to put on Jane. That's all I can fig—" She looked at me and tears welled.

I shook my head at her. This wasn't the time to break down. Not yet.

"What about that barn?" I meant the large crumbling building out behind the house. "Maybe she saw us coming. You are driving a police car, after all."

"We gotta see," she said, heading for the door, punching the radio at her shoulder, then passing on to Lucky that Audrey'd been there and she was going to do a search of the property.

We ran down the steps then slowed and made our way deliberately around the house. We stopped, flattened against the wall, to look over the fields to the distant structure: low on the horizon, sloping roof half fallen in. There was no movement anywhere near the barn, or in the empty acreage around it.

We started out across the field; not a single tree to hide

behind. We were targets. Walking in the open. Neither of us said a word.

Dolly stopped a few yards into the blooming grass and pointed to tracks leading through the weeds, the weeds flattened and pushed aside. Two parallel tracks. A car had been through there recently.

We walked on, but faster now. Dolly didn't bother to take her gun from the holster. Whatever we were facing was beyond brute force. This was something between one woman and another. I couldn't imagine how it would end—Dolly facing Audrey Delores at last, but with this terrible weight of horror between them.

We drew near the decaying building. I took shallow breaths from time to time. Dolly ran to flatten herself against the front wall of the barn and stand there a minute, face set into something that didn't even resemble her. I stood beside her.

"What'll we do?" I asked. "Maybe wait for the others to get here . . ."

She shook her head. "I can't take the chance. I'm going in . . ."

Far off, as if from someplace beyond the barn, or even beyond the field, came a baby's choking cry, one of those cries I'd heard Jane make when she was overtired or had cried too much already.

Dolly heard it, too. "Come on," she whispered. "I need you with me. I'll get Audrey. You grab Jane."

I nodded and we edged along the wall and around to stand in one of the open doorways, adjusting our eyes to the darkness in the building.

There was a sudden roar of a car engine. And then the echo

of the roar reverberating from broken tin roof to decaying walls and falling hayloft, and then around us. An engine revved again. There was something like a screech, a streak of white, and the wall, where we'd been standing a moment before, cracked out as a Volkswagen Passat burst through the old timbers and bounced off across the field.

FORTY-SEVEN

Audrey Delores turned left at the road as we ran back toward where Dolly's car was parked in front of the house. Me, running as fast as I could run, but Dolly, heavy boots and all, out ahead.

"Watch her," Dolly screamed over her shoulder. "Make sure she doesn't turn around. We've got to know . . ."

I was panting by the time I got to the car. Dolly gunned the motor as I jumped into the passenger seat beside her. I slammed the door as she backed down the drive, punched the car into drive, and peeled left at the road.

There was no white Volkswagen ahead of us. Audrey'd had a head start but not much of one.

"This ends in a small park down at the lake," Dolly shouted as she stomped hard on the gas. "She's got no place to go. She's there. We'll get her. I'll pull straight in . . ."

Dolly took a hard right.

"I'll leave the car sidewise in the road. That'll block the only exit. She'll have to give up."

"Did you see her face?" I yelled at Dolly.

She nodded.

"Any sign of Jane?"

She didn't answer. Her look was fixed hard on the road. We sped between spindly stands of maple and birch, passed a swamp, then through gates that announced a county park: SPEED 15 MPH.

Dolly slammed on the brakes. I braced myself, both hands against the dash.

287

The white Volkswagen, both front doors flung wide open, was pulled into an empty parking area. Dolly turned her car to block the exit and we leaped out, running toward the vehicle.

Dolly had her gun out as we approached. Nothing. Nobody. The back was filled with trash. It looked as though Audrey had been living in the car. Dolly lifted a filthy blanket bundled on the front seat. All it hid was an empty car seat.

"She's got her," Dolly said, turning one way and then the other, looking to where a stream ran along one side of the park, then around to face Lake Michigan.

I didn't wait. I ran toward the lake. A set of wooden stairs led down to the beach. I leaped down the steps to the sand then stopped to search in both directions. The low gray sky outlined no shadows. Everything was flat and empty. In front of me, Lake Michigan was almost still, only the soft susurration of small, lapping waves. The woman couldn't have disappeared. People didn't. I ran to the very edge of the water, looking frantically south, then north.

I saw her. She was running along a low spit of land jutting out into the lake, a long finger of weedy ground ending in a virtual point at a place where the water turned from blue to green, where the lake deepened.

The woman ran awkwardly, her red back hunched over the bundle she carried.

I screamed at Dolly, who stood on the hill above the beach. I pointed as I ran, not looking behind me, not caring about anything but reaching Audrey and stopping her before she got out into the lake. There was no other way for her to go. If she turned, when the land ended, she'd have to come back through me.

288

Dolly wasn't far behind, yelling at Audrey, "Stop!" "Stop!" "Stop!"

I didn't hear the word after a few seconds, just the blood in my ears, and the thumping of my chest. My feet beat up and down as thoughts of falling streamed through my head and then thoughts of what I'd do when she stopped and turned to face me. And then thoughts of grabbing Jane from her. My hands clenched into fists, my nails dug into my palms. *I'll get you*, I told myself over and over. *I'll get you* . . .

"Stop!" Dolly called again as we ran across the muddy and stony bit of land. On both sides the lake licked softly. Water covered my feet.

I kept going because the woman ahead didn't stop. She ran, holding on to the bundle she clutched, elbows sticking out at either side of a broad back in a red jacket.

The ground ended. She should have stopped. She should have turned to face me but she kept going, struggling into the water, trying to run but having to slow, to plod, to lift one foot and then the other as water climbed her legs, soaking the black slacks she wore.

I ran faster, not asking myself if I could. Just doing it. Flying toward the woman who was in water up to her waist now, going slower and slower — as I was being forced to go.

It was a struggle, staying on my feet. Water climbed my legs — ankles to knees then up my thighs. My feet sucked downward into sand and pebbles.

Dolly gave a cry behind me, something from a wounded animal.

For the first time, Audrey Thomas hesitated. She looked over her shoulder at me; a benign look on a confused face, as if she wondered who I was and why I was chasing her.

"*Mama.*" Behind me, Dolly screamed.

Audrey, water lapping over her waist, turned, head bent to one side as if listening to something she couldn't quite understand. I slowed, but forced my way toward her, holding my breath.

I didn't want to startle her.

I had to reach Jane.

Water licked upward, darkening Audrey's jacket. Her face, a mask of indecision, was wet with spray. She turned her head slightly to one side as she fought against a wave. The wind rose, ruffling the lake to small whitecaps. Audrey stopped, listening to a sound I couldn't hear.

She turned. The bundle she carried moved in her arms. There was a single whimper. Audrey's eyes narrowed, first at me and then, behind me, at Dolly. She frowned hard.

Jane gave a full cry. Audrey looked down into the blanket she held. She blinked again and again as if startled by what was in her arms, then back at Dolly. She smiled and nodded.

She said a single word, a question, "Dolly?"

There was a deep intake of breath. I was close enough to touch her. I put out a hand, struggling against the deepening water, but she pulled away again, out of reach.

I heard Dolly stumble and splash down behind me, hampered by her uniform and the heavy boots she wore. When I glanced over my shoulder, she was fighting to get to her feet. At first she tried to swim then slid under the water again.

I forced myself to concentrate on Audrey. I swam full out, thinking I could pull ahead of her and herd her back toward Dolly. When I got close, I grabbed at her arm, trying for the fabric of her jacket. She flinched, pulling her arm and Jane out of reach. She turned a disturbed face to me. I prayed I hadn't scared her so badly she'd take Jane farther out.

My brain calculated how strong I was, what it would take to overpower Audrey, there in the water, and snatch Jane from her.

Behind me, Dolly sputtered and yelled and finally, after a shuttering cry, screamed, *"Mama. Please. I love you."*

Audrey's head snapped up. She turned fully toward where Dolly flailed behind us. Her mouth dropped open. Her face changed, from troubled and angry to pleased, almost pleasantly surprised—a woman getting a bouquet of flowers; a woman whose child had done something marvelous.

I was close enough to touch her. She looked down at me, where I awkwardly half swam, half walked, as if amused. She smiled. Confused, she shook her head, looked back at Dolly and said again, "Dolly?"

Her faced changed. Pleasure to horror. She looked at the baby she carried and then at me. As if caught in some terrible mirror, the woman's face went through one agonizing expression after another. Her head dipped. Her terrible eyes filled with panic.

I thought she was going to come back so I could help her. I put out my arms and tried to stand erect, the water rising, pushing me one way and then another. If I could just get my arms around her, hold on to Jane and her both, I thought. But when we were close enough to touch, she simply tipped the crying baby forward, sliding her out of her arms and into mine.

I grabbed Jane as hard and fast as I could grab and held on. I turned to Dolly, screaming, "I've got her. I've got her."

Dolly held one arm out to take her daughter. She stretched her other arm toward her mother, who'd turned back to the lake.

"I called. Rescue's coming," she yelled, voice echoing across the roughening water. "They'll get you out. We'll save you . . ."

Audrey Delores Thomas didn't turn again. She struggled away from us, arms disappearing, chin at water level. She slipped under a single, growing wave. At first there was a red glow in the water, where I could still see her jacket. Then there was an aureole of pale hair. And then there was nothing

"*Mama!*" Dolly screamed a last time.

Audrey Delores Thomas was gone.

EPILOGUE

Even Dolly urged Jackson to stay for Harry and Delia's wedding but he begged off. After the *British Times* had so praised his Chaucer book, he'd been asked by learned journals to write articles and needed to be back in Ann Arbor, he said. Preparations had to be made for his trip to Great Britain and yet another book.

I gave him a quick kiss on the cheek as he'd stowed his bag in the trunk of the Porsche and got in to drive away.

It was an odd leave-taking. Something had changed between us. Maybe it was his kindness, his worry about my safety, and the way he'd stepped up to help at the police station. Or maybe it was seeing something deeper in him, what I'd thought was there when I first met him. It felt like vindication for both of us. A sad good-bye.

Whatever the cause, a tie had been broken—finally.

The wedding had been postponed a week. The search for Audrey's body, and then the funeral afterward—when she was laid to rest as close to Cate and Grace Humbert as Dolly could get—had drained everyone in Leetsville. Now it seemed they were all coming to the wedding. Everyone wanted to be together, to celebrate life and joy and all those good things that brought people back from the brink of depression.

I was ready for a celebration, giving up my last self-upbraiding dictum: *You must be perfect in the eyes of the world*, and settling for doing the best I could. I cleaned and polished everything I could clean and polish. The rest of my stuff went into the closets so that I had to lean hard against the doors to get the latches to catch and then pray nobody needed anything from inside them.

Harry'd had the weeds between my house and lake mowed so there was plenty of space for the church people to set up tables and chairs. There was a bar with a keg set on top, and a big barbecue for the hot dogs. Coolers full of food came down my driveway like rocks in a landslide. Tables for the food were opened and set in a line from the barbecue to the bar. White tablecloths were spread. My scruffy lawn was turned into a sea of blinding white.

The day was beautiful. Fitting for a charming groom like Harry, all shaved and smelling of cologne, and a lovely bride like Delia, wearing her mother's creamy silk wedding gown circa 1925. The two of them, together, looked like an old-time couple on top of a wedding cake, maybe something out of Dickens: the ornament on Miss Havisham's ruined cake.

Bill called and begged off, disappointment in his voice as he said it was also the day of the newspaper's picnic. He couldn't be in two places at once, he explained. What I didn't tell him was how sorry I felt, missing the picnic, but even more, not going as his date. Though I did say, "I hope there's another time," and he did say, "Let's make it soon." Which was as close to a promise of a real date as I was going to get for a while.

Eugenia, hair done to a fantastic height and stuck through with a dozen rhinestone stars, arrived early to supervise the setup.

As two o'clock neared, the wooden bower was set up down at the lake, then twined with white ribbon and a few of my early roses.

Excitement grew. Harry and Delia, standing on my deck,

held hands, looking out at the lovely setting the people of Leetsville had created for them. After a minute, her steepled hands to her lips, Delia leaned into Harry and rested her head on his shoulder.

"You did us proud," Harry said as I passed behind the couple carrying catsup bottles for the food table.

Next the Reverend Runcival arrived and huddled with Harry and Delia, going over the ritual of marriage. Harry practiced his resounding "Yes" while Delia beamed up at him.

One by one the people, wrapped presents in their hands, arrived, the line of cars stretching up my drive and, I imagined, all along Willow Lake Road.

Omar Winston, in a blue suit that looked as close to a uniform as a man could get, walked down the hill in the midst of a clutch of other guests. He proudly carried a very dressed-up Jane in his arms and stopped for anyone who wanted to kiss the pretty little girl and express their joy that she was home, and safe.

I hurried to Omar from where I'd been taking salads from the coolers and setting them on the food table. "Where's Dolly?" I asked, surprised. It was the first time I'd seen him alone with his little girl. "She meeting that Realtor about getting her house on the market?"

He shook his head at me. "Don't you worry." He smiled wider than I'd seen that stiff, official face ever smile. "Got it done. She's selling the house. Then she had to go up to Kalkaska. Picking Ariadne up at the hospital. Got her released into her care for as long as she can swing it. Ariadne's going to watch Jane until the trial. It'll work out for both of them. Dolly said she'd be here fast as she can."

"Well." I was about to complain sarcastically that she'd sure turned out to be a lot of help, when I stopped myself and smiled at Omar. "That's good news," I said instead and went back to setting out bowls of salads and beans and baskets of rolls for the buffet lunch to follow the ceremony.

Dolly, with Jane back in her arms and Ariadne behind her, came looking for me in the house, opening my bedroom door without knocking and stomping in as I scrambled to get my blue dress down over my head.

"Geez," I complained, then zipped up the dress and hurried around the bed to hug Ariadne.

"She needs something to wear," Dolly said, herself in a freshly washed blue shirt and pressed pants. Ariadne was still in hospital blue. "I didn't know everybody was going to dress up like they was going to a ball or something."

She hurried out, to get a good seat, she said.

Easy fix, I assured Ariadne, her face still smudged with yellowed bruises from the beating she'd taken. She looked as if she wore the same size I did and, though my only other dress might have been slightly fashionable about six years before, she didn't mind and even seemed pleased with the summer print I handed her.

"I'm sorry we're late," Ariadne whispered as I zipped her up. "Dolly had to stop by the cemetery. Said she had a lot to tell her mothers."

She turned a shy smile on me. "Dolly says her mother's brain was broke. Said it's sad she never got to be the person she could've been. And so awful, Cate had to pay the price. Dolly loves Audrey, you know. Says she'll always love her. Oh, and you'll never guess what she told Audrey while we were kneeling down out there. Never guess in a million years."

I shook my head, impatient. The wedding march was booming down by the lake.

"She told her she's been waiting to decide who should be Jane's godmother. Until she had just the right person." She leaned in closer. "She's asking you."

Ariadne nodded and stepped back, pleased with her news. "Said you're like Jane's second mother now."

I don't know why I got tears in my eyes but I did, and they stayed there right through the shaky vows exchanged under the beautiful arbor.

Flora, seeing me cry, patted my back, thinking I was moved by the ceremony. She had to step over Sorrow, who hadn't left my side since the night Audrey Delores broke into my house and kidnapped Baby Jane.

Eugenia, still thinking I was worried about hosting such a grand "do," sidled up to say gruffly, "It's almost over, Emily. Don't you worry. Things are working out just fine."

Gloria put her arm around my shoulders. "I know this has been a lot on you, Emily." She leaned her head in to whisper, "But the whole town's grateful. Just look at the joy you're giving Harry and Delia, there. And I hear you're driving them up to the bridge for a honeymoon. Couldn't be a nicer gift."

I didn't even flinch. Of course I'd drive them up to the bridge. And back. All they wanted to do was take a look at the Mighty Mac and be home before dark.

Dolly stood on one side of me as the groom leaned over to kiss his new bride.

Jane peeked out of a way-too-big pink bonnet to give me a wobble-headed, toothless grin.

Ariadne stood on my other side. Three very different women, and a woman-in-training, all in a row.

I took Dolly's hand, then Ariadne's hand, and held them until the brittle kiss was exchanged, the happy groom gave a fist bump to the crowd, and one hungry, and impatient, Leetsvillian yelled out, "Let's eat!"

ABOUT THE AUTHOR

Elizabeth Kane Buzzelli moved to the shores of a little lake in northwest northern Michigan and never looked back. She lives, sometimes uncomfortably, with the crows and bears and turtles and finds her material in the villages and forests that surround her. With degrees from Macomb County Community College, Oakland University, and the University of Michigan, she now teaches creative writing at Northwestern Michigan College and at writers' conferences around the country.

 Her novels include: *Gift of Evil* (Bantam), *Dead Dancing Women, Dead Floating Lovers, Dead Sleeping Shaman,* and *Dead Dogs and Englishmen* (Midnight Ink).

Elizabeth is also fascinated with the craft of the short story and hers have appeared in *The Creative Woman, The Driftwood Review, Passages North, The MacGuffin, Quality Women's Fiction* (Great Britain), and elsewhere. With a grant from the State of Michigan she also created short stories that have been produced onstage as well as being read on NPR.

Her essays have appeared in magazines and books and newspapers, and she writes book reviews for *The Northern Express,* an alternative newspaper in Traverse City, Michigan.

For many years she taught in the International Women's Guild summer program at Skidmore College and appeared as a moderator and panelist at writing conferences. Her fascination with all things murderous began with a love for puzzles of all sorts, which was handed down to her by a mother who devoured mysteries. Sometimes playful, sometimes deadly serious, her books reflect a wide interest in women's lives and futures.

Made in the USA
Lexington, KY
24 August 2019